An undercover game . . .

Everly snaked out an arm and swept her onto his lap.

"What are you doing?" she whispered, shocked.

"You called this a game, didn't you?" His expression was pleasant, but his eyes blazed with a dangerous, angry light. "Play along."

His touch, though feather-light, thrilled her down to her toes. Awareness of his body flooded through her—his muscular thighs, his broad chest, the clean scent of his skin. A warm ache pooled low and deep within her. Such strange sensations—what was happening to her?

"Why are you doing this?" She squirmed and pulled back as far as his arms would allow.

He held her fast. "You demanded to come along, knowing full well what sort of party this was," he murmured. He nibbled at her earlobe. "It's time you learned that your rash actions have consequences."

Consequences? Amanda's eyes narrowed. He was doing this to punish her for defying him. Part of her wanted to slap him, but more disturbing was the part that wanted him to kiss her again.

The Traitor's Daughter

Elizabeth Powell

A SIGNET BOOK

SIGNET
Published by New American Library, a division of
Penguin Putnam Inc., 375 Hudson Street,
New York, New York 10014, U.S.A.
Penguin Books Ltd, 27 Wrights Lane,
London W8 5TZ, England
Penguin Books Australia Ltd, Ringwood,
Victoria, Australia
Penguin Books Canada Ltd, 10 Alcorn Avenue,
Toronto, Ontario, Canada M4V 3B2
Penguin Books (N.Z.) Ltd, 182–190 Wairau Road,
Auckland 10, New Zealand

Penguin Books Ltd, Registered Offices:
Harmondsworth, Middlesex, England

First published by Signet, an imprint of New American Library,
a division of Penguin Putnam Inc.

First Printing, September 2001
10 9 8 7 6 5 4 3 2 1

For Sue,
who showed me the way

AUTHOR'S NOTE

The actual commander at the Battle of Lissa (1811) was Captain Sir William Hoste, one of Nelson's favorite protégés and a brilliant commander in his own right.

Unlike Captain Everly, Hoste did not receive his well-deserved baronetcy until after the battle of Cattaro (modern Kotor) in 1814.

Chapter One

London
September, 1811

The rising wind carried with it the tolling of church bells. Every peal reverberated through Miss Amanda Tremayne like the dull thud of cannon fire. Half past ten—Harry was late.

The young woman stood on the shore of the Serpentine, oblivious to the curious stares of passersby, her eyes as glassy as the lake's surface. What if Harry had not gotten her note in time? What if his shipboard duties had delayed him? What if she had to do this without him?

The dank breeze lifted the hem of her cloak and chilled her; she wrapped her arms around herself and gazed up at the oppressive clouds scudding overhead. A storm was brewing, no doubt about that. Children pulled their toy boats from the water with obvious reluctance while their nannies hovered nearby. Equestrians turned their mounts for home. Coachmen pulled up the hoods of fashionable barouches to protect their occupants from the weather. Amanda grimaced and stamped her feet against the cold. Where was he? She couldn't wait much longer; she needed to get back. Heaven knew she was in enough trouble with her employer as it was.

Her eyes scanned the expanse of park around her with growing agitation, but nowhere did she spot Harry's tall, lanky form. Another gust knifed through her cloak and beneath her serviceable linsey-woolsey dress. Gooseflesh rose on her skin. She turned her back to the wind. If she were a ship, she would have lowered her sails and sought safe harbor long ago. Her face was cold, and so were her hands and feet. Enough was enough.

"Blast you, Henry Augustus Morgan," she muttered through chattering teeth. "You promised. I should keel-haul you."

"Amanda?" The wind bore words with it. "Amanda, that had better be you. By God, why did you want to met me out-of-doors in weather like this? Have you gone completely around the bend?"

Amanda whirled to meet the source of the voice.

Lieutenant Harry Morgan approached her with long-legged strides, his tall fore-and-aft bicorne worn low on his forehead, his heavy officer's cloak pulled closely around him. Months at sea had gilded his auburn hair and lined his face, but the most prominent lines this morning came from his downturned mouth and furrowed brow. Amanda would swear he was angry with her for meeting him out in inclement weather. Even after years at sea, Harry was still Harry—ever since childhood, he had blamed her for getting him into scrapes that were as much his fault as hers. Her own temper flared.

"If you'd been on time, I would not have stood here for the past half hour and risked getting pneumonia," she snapped. "And if I weren't freezing already, I vow I would box your ears. I told you the matter was urgent!"

The young officer seemed taken aback by her vehemence. "I'm sorry, Amanda—Captain Bennett was delayed at the Admiralty, and I couldn't just brush and lope without his permission." He squinted up at the roiling sky. "We're in for a good blow any minute. We should get under cover."

The church bells tolled the three-quarter hour. Amanda shook her head. "There's no time, Harry. I'm supposed to be on an errand, and I'm late as it is. Please, just hear me out." Her control slipped, and desperation tinged her words.

Harry's honest hazel eyes widened. "Your grandmother has not taken ill?"

"No, Grandmama is fine. Harry, when I saw you last

you promised you would do anything in your power to help me. Did you mean that?"

"Of course I did." Affronted pride warred with suspicion on Harry's tanned face. "What is it, Amanda? I know that look—you're up to something."

Amanda bit her lip. Harry knew her well enough that he might see through her fabrication. No time to worry about that now. She took a deep breath and plunged ahead. "I need you to take me to Admiral Locke's ball tomorrow night."

The young lieutenant's expression evolved from concern to confusion to consternation in quick succession. His brows arched skyward, and his eyes widened until the pupils were mere pinpricks in a sea of startled green and gold.

"You want me to what?" He drew away from her. "Is this a joke, Amanda? If it is, it's in very poor taste."

She glared at him, her jaw set at a stubborn angle. "This is no laughing matter. I need to get to that party, Harry. I will go alone if I must."

A gust of wind tried to unseat Harry's bicorne. He slapped it back onto his head, then steered Amanda beneath the sheltering branches of a nearby oak. "That's a little better. Now, care to tell me why is this party so important to you?"

"I need to speak with the First Lord." She cringed inwardly, hating herself for the lie.

Doubt creased Harry's forehead. "At a party? Why not just go to the Admiralty?"

"I've tried several times, but they won't let me into the building anymore. The guards at the door have standing orders to deny me entrance." This much was the truth. The memory resurfaced without warning, and tears of shame threatened the corners of Amanda's eyes. The red-coated marines had been apologetic but unrelenting when they escorted her out into the street. The hateful words of the sneering, self-important prig of a clerk who'd issued the command still echoed in her ears.

"I say," Harry protested. "They can't treat you like that—you're a lady."

Amanda made a little moue. "You forget that they don't consider me a lady. Since I can't get into the Admiralty, and I can't very well call on Lord Hardwicke at his home, this is my only option. The article in the *Morning Post* said the ball is to be a huge affair, and that many navy officers were invited. He is bound to be there. And I will certainly have more credibility if I'm with you."

"What about Admiral Locke? He was your father's commanding officer. Are you not worried that he might recognize you?"

She shook her head. "Admiral Locke has never met me. He won't know who I am, especially if I attend under an assumed name."

"To what end, Amanda?" Harry's tone was gentle. He took her gloved hand in his and squeezed it. "Your grandmother would never approve. This is foolish. Just let it go."

The young woman pulled away, her shoulders hunched. "I can't let it go—you know that. I will never accept what happened. And whether Grandmama approves or not, I am determined. I have to discover the truth."

Harry sighed. "What you're suggesting is dangerous, Amanda. Admiral Locke is one of London's most celebrated heroes; the cream of London society will be there. You can't think to accost the First Lord of the Admiralty at this party—you'll make a complete cake of yourself."

"I realize that, you nodcock." She frowned up at her friend. To hear Locke called a hero turned her stomach, but she could not reveal her purpose—not yet. "I promise to be discreet. I just want to ask him to reopen the investigation. Will you help me?"

Harry rolled his eyes with a hint of growing impatience. "Amanda, you have all the discretion of a first-rater firing a full broadside."

Amanda's cheeks grew hot. She took another deep breath and counted to five, unclenched her hands, and silently reminded herself that she needed Harry, no matter how much she wanted to slap him.

"You told me that you'd do anything to help Grandmama and me, especially now. Are you a man of your word?"

Harry started and drew himself up indignantly. "Of course."

"Then you know how much this means to me." Amanda spread her hands. "Please, Harry—I need you. If I don't succeed at the party, I will take Grandmama back to Dorset and put all of this behind us." She hated herself for spinning this web of lies, but she had to circumvent Harry's stalwart sense of honesty. He would never agree to help her if he knew the truth.

Harry wavered. He tugged at his black neckcloth. "What makes you think I can get an invitation?"

"Because you come from a family with a lengthy history of naval service, because your father is a viscount, because your captain is one of the most well-respected in the entire fleet, and because you're a promising young officer." She ticked off each item on a gloved finger.

Harry thought about that for several moments, then sighed. "This cork-brained scheme is one of your worst, Amanda," he groused. "Promise me at the very least that you won't cause a scandal."

Amanda rewarded him with her best, most dazzling smile. "I promise I won't do anything to hurt your career, Harry. I know how fond you are of that new lieutenant's uniform."

A telltale flush rose from the young man's collar. He threw up his hands. "All right, though I'm the biggest sapscull in the world for going along with this. I'll pick you up at your lodgings, then. What times does this folderol start?"

"Nine o'clock." Exhilaration cascaded through her. "But do not come to our rooms; I will meet you down at the street."

Confusion creased Harry's brow. "Eh? Why? Afraid of what your grandmother will say?"

Amanda dropped her guilty gaze. "Partially. She doesn't know about the party." Or about her granddaughter's plans . . .

"But what worries me most," she added, "is that Mrs. Jennings has the ears of an elephant, the tongue of an adder, and enough curiosity to kill a hundred cats. I mustn't give her any reason to start asking questions about Grandmama and me. The last time our landlord found out who we were, he barely gave us time to gather our belongings before he threw us into the street. I can't take any chances."

Harry cast her one last, probing glance, then nodded. "Deuced queer, if you ask me, but I gave you my word."

"Thank you, Harry!" Amanda threw decorum to the wind; she stood on tiptoes and placed a quick kiss on his weather-roughened cheek. "You are my very dearest friend."

"You said that just before we raided Squire Templeton's prized orchard," grumbled Harry, his face now quite red. "I couldn't sit down for a week after that. And you said it again before the incident at the mill, and the fracas with Throckmorton at the pond—"

Amanda sobered. "You have always been my dearest friend, Harry. I would never say such a thing lightly. And I would not ask you to do this unless it were of the utmost importance."

Harry muttered something under his breath that sounded suspiciously like, "Just don't make me regret this." He straightened and tugged at his jacket. "If we fail, it'll mean far worse than a tanned hide—we'll both be in the suds."

"We won't fail, Harry, I'm sure of it."

Amanda gave him another quick hug, then took her leave and hastened back toward Oxford Street. Dear, dear Harry! With his help, she would spike the enemy's guns and reveal him for what he truly was. She lowered her head against the first volley of raindrops that pelted down from the ominous bank of clouds overhead, and quickened her pace. She had to hurry; she had plans to make.

Captain Jack Everly did not need to look up at the leaden sky or smell the wet breeze to know that a storm was imminent. His right leg throbbed with a deep, teeth-gritting ache; the wound was mostly healed, but his refusal to remain sedentary and damp, chill conditions aggravated the pain. He knew when it would rain even before clouds appeared in the sky. A supreme stroke of irony, this. His own body was now more reliable than any ship's glass.

He descended gingerly from the carriage and stared at the flight of steps before him. If he had been thinking at all this morning, he would have ignored his pride and brought his cane with him. Like it or not, there were days when he needed its support. But he could not put off the admiral's summons, nor would he. He was recovered and ready for command, and this was his opportunity to prove it—if he had to spend any more time ashore, he would go mad. He straightened his jacket, placed one hand on the hilt of his sword and, his face grim, made his way up the stairs to the town house door.

Once inside, Everly realized that the front steps were only the beginning. He handed his heavy cloak to a footman, removed his braided bicorne, and tried to ignore the graceful sweep of mahogany stairs that arched above him to the first floor. More bloody stairs. He grimaced, but erased the gesture when the admiral's butler appeared.

Parkin greeted him with a stiff bow. "Good morning, Captain Everly. A pleasure to see you again, sir, if I may say so."

"Thank you, Parkin. I believe the admiral is expecting me." Everly resisted the sudden urge to smile. In all his many visits to this house, he had never seen the butler's expression deviate from wooden correctness. The admiral ran a tight ship, and expected the utmost discipline from his subordinates. Everly wondered if poor Parkin's face had frozen in place over the course of the years.

"Indeed, sir. If you will follow me." Parkin headed for the staircase. Everly gritted his teeth and followed.

By the time they reached the admiral's study, Everly was cursing himself for leaving his cane behind. His leg ached with merciless intent; he could feel the skin around his eyes and mouth draw tighter the more he tried to suppress the pain. He hoped his face was not as white as his waistcoat. Admiral Lord St. Vincent was no fool.

Parkin opened the paneled oak door and stepped aside. "Captain Sir Jonathan Everly," he announced in stentorian tones.

Hearing his name pronounced so formally made Everly hesitate on the threshold. He wasn't used to the title, even after six months. Every time he heard it, he wanted to look over his shoulder to see who "Sir Jonathan Everly" was, as if the name belonged to a complete stranger.

"Confound it, Parkin, stop shouting. I'm not half as deaf as you'd like to think me," came the irascible reply from the depths of the room. "Well, boy, don't stand there gawking like a green midshipman. Come in."

Despite his discomfort, Everly's mouth twitched into a half smile as he stepped into the admiral's study. His patron was the only man who could get away with calling him "boy." Everly's good humor, however, faded as he surveyed the room.

Admiral Lord St. Vincent, once known as Sir John Jervis, was an exacting man whom many credited with whipping His Majesty's Navy into fighting trim. At the age of seventy-six, "Old Jervie" still retained the fierce intelligence and acerbic wit that made him a legend in the British Navy. Although no longer in command of a ship, he maintained an orderly, regimented life, and his house reflected this sense of discipline. Today, though, Everly was astonished to see charts and papers strewn about the admiral's desk, weighted down by several books and a half-empty decanter of brandy. Despite the advanced hour of the morning, the heavy curtains remained closed. A low fire smoked in the hearth and did little to relieve the pervading gloom. The heavy, musty smells of old leather, books, and ashes formed an incipient sneeze at the back of Everly's throat.

The admiral himself, his gold-braided uniform jacket creased and rumpled, stood behind his desk and scowled at the documents in his hand. Weariness lined the elderly man's face and hunched his shoulders; veiled rage burned in his eyes.

Everly assumed a carefully neutral expression as he came to stand before the admiral's desk. He drew himself to attention. "Good morning, my lord," he ventured.

The older man harrumphed and tossed the stack of papers onto his desk. He clasped his hands behind his back and fixed Everly with a penetrating gaze. "I understand you've been to see the First Lord."

News traveled quickly. The captain started in spite of himself. "Yes, sir."

"Well?"

"The Earl of Hardwicke retains the opinion that I am not yet well enough for command." Everly's jaw flexed at the memory of that dismissive meeting.

"And I'll wager you would like me to convince him otherwise." St. Vincent paced to the window and peered out through the gap between the fringed velvet panels.

"I would, sir. I am recovered, and wish to reassume command of the *Hyperion,* or any other available ship, as soon as possible. I am anxious to be back at sea."

The admiral's narrowed eyes scanned the younger man up and down. "Out of the question," he pronounced.

A hot stab of anger lanced through Everly. He felt the tips of his ears begin to glow. "Might I inquire as to why not, sir?" Speaking became more difficult when he had to force his words through his teeth.

"Because any man with eyes in his head can see you're still in pain from that leg wound. You're pale as a ghost." St. Vincent seemed to relax; his expression eased. He sank into his cracked leather desk chair and waved a hand in his protégé's direction. "Sit down, Everly, sit down."

The captain lowered himself into an overstuffed wing chair, grateful to be off his feet but stung that the admiral had read him so easily. Neither the First Lord nor his own commanding officer believed him ready, and now his patron had added his voice to theirs. Admiral Lord St. Vincent was one of the most influential men in the Royal Navy; Everly *had* to convince his patron that he was fit for duty. Time to try another tack. "Sir, I ask you to reconsider. Other captains have sustained similar wounds or worse, and been returned to their ships."

"I know you feel out of place on land, Everly," St. Vincent replied with a slight, tired smile, "but the navy needs its captains—especially promising men like yourself—in one piece. You were damn fortunate, boy, that you did not die at Lissa."

Everly nodded once, loath to open that Pandora's box of remembrance. The battle of Lissa seemed so long ago, yet only six months had passed since he led a small squadron of frigates to fend off Commodore Dubordieu's superior forces. The battle had been a crucial victory for the Royal Navy; the French attempt to use Nelson's own tactics against the British resulted in the death or capture of over one thousand French sailors, and the ultimate loss of French naval power in the Adriatic Sea.

But that was not the first thing that came to Everly's mind. What he remembered most was chaos and agony and blazing heat and the screams of his men when the shell from a French 18-pounder plowed into the quarter-deck of the *Hyperion*. The explosion had sent him careening down to the deck below in a hail of shattered wood, breaking his right leg near the hip. A stray splinter had sliced his left cheek down to the bone. Given the horrific conditions at the hospital in Malta, Everly knew he had been fortunate to avoid gangrene, blood poisoning, and other potentially fatal complications. He had survived, but his senior lieutenant, one of his young midshipmen, and the ship's master had not. He would bear the mental and physical scars of that battle for the rest of his life.

"I didn't mean to bring up unpleasant memories, lad," Admiral St. Vincent said gruffly. "You know as well as I the bitter brew that is a captain's life."

Everly clenched his teeth, disturbed that these powerful emotions still held such sway over him, even after all these months, and even more disturbed that his face displayed them so openly. But he wasn't ready to strike his colors yet.

"I belong at sea, my lord, with my men," he insisted. "My duty lies with them."

The admiral's eyes glowed with renewed fury. He pounded the desktop with his fist and sent papers scattering. "Your duty is to England, sir, and the Admiralty decides how you will serve it best!"

Everly started to apologize, but St. Vincent waved him to silence.

"Never mind, boy, never mind," the earl muttered. "Damn dirty business has me out of temper." He rose from his seat and resumed his restless pacing. "You'll be returned to command soon enough, but there is something you must do first."

"My lord?" Perplexed by his patron's words, as well as by his uncharacteristic moodiness, Everly leaned forward in his seat. "Would this have anything to do with why you asked me to your house rather than your office at the Admiralty, and why you keep looking out the window as if expecting someone else to arrive?"

"Clever man." St. Vincent smiled and passed a weary hand over his brow. "Awake on all suits. That's just what we need."

The mantel clock had just wheezed the three-quarter hour when the door to the study creaked open on its massive hinges. Parkin reappeared and stood just over the threshold. "The Earl of Carlisle and the Honorable Grayson MacAllister," he announced.

Everly mused that Parkin would have made an excellent ship's master; his voice could be heard from the farthest reaches of the quarterdeck even in the worst gale. He pushed himself to his feet as the new arrivals entered the room. Parkin secured the door behind them.

"About bloody time, man," the admiral blustered. "You're late. Dawdling over your sherry, were you?"

The taller of the two gentlemen smiled slightly and inclined his head in greeting. "I thought it better if my driver took a more circuitous route and brought us in by your stables, out of sight. I apologize if my sense of discretion inconvenienced you, Admiral."

St. Vincent harrumphed, his pale cheeks tinged with

red. "Dirty business," he muttered again. "Well, let's get on with this. Carlisle, may I present Captain Sir Jonathan Everly, late of the frigate *Hyperion*. Everly, this is the Earl of Carlisle, one of Castlereagh's spymasters."

Lord Carlisle quirked an eyebrow. "You flatter me, Admiral," he drawled. He turned and extended a hand to Everly. "Captain. I've heard a great deal about you. You're quite a hero. London was all abuzz after your exploits in the Adriatic."

Everly shook the proffered hand and was surprised by the firm, calloused grip. He returned the earl's polite nod. "Not a hero, my lord. We all must do our duty in time of war."

Everly guessed the Earl of Carlisle's age to be within two or three years on either side of his own thirty. To the casual eye, Carlisle appeared every inch the Corinthian: tall and handsome in a rugged way, his sable hair cropped in the fashionable "Brutus" style, his clothes of such precise cut that Weston had to be responsible for their make, his well-made top boots with nary a scuff or scratch on their glossy surface. He gave every impression of being nothing more than a bored society blade. Everly wasn't fooled.

Much of Carlisle's demeanor reminded the captain of a hunting cat. He had walked into the room with the stealthy grace of a leopard—indolent, yet prepared to spring at a moment's notice. His body was that of an athlete, his slate gray eyes those of a predator—watchful, calculating, evaluating eyes that stripped Everly of all pretense and assessed his worth in the span of several heartbeats. Hairs rose on the back of Everly's neck, and he matched Carlisle's gaze with his best disciplinary stare.

"Do I meet your expectations, my lord?" he asked softly, in a tone that bordered on belligerent.

Some of the intensity left Carlisle's face, and he smiled. "You exceed them, Captain. May I introduce my associated, the Honorable Grayson MacAllister. He will be working with you on this assignment."

"Scotchmen," St. Vincent growled. "You would have to bring one of *them* into my home, Carlisle."

Everly ignored his patron's prejudice and shook the younger man's hand. Unlike his superior, MacAllister was slightly built, with a shock of pale blond hair. He regarded the captain with serious sea green eyes.

"This is an honor, sir." He spoke without a trace of an accent, and smiled enigmatically at Everly's surprise.

"Mr. MacAllister has worked for me for a number of years," Carlisle explained. "For all his apparent youth he is an experienced agent, and adept at assuming any role required of him."

"A Scotchman is a Scotchman," the admiral stated, scowling. "I don't approve, Carlisle."

Carlisle shot the older man a warning look. "I'm not interested in your approval, St. Vincent. We have a job to do, one which requires my most talented men. If you wish to challenge my authority, I suggest you take it up with Lord Castlereagh."

St. Vincent glared back. "No time for that. Sit down, all of you, and let us get on to business." He lowered himself into his seat.

Everly did the same. Carlisle and MacAllister pulled lyre-backed chairs close to the admiral's desk.

"I assume one of you will explain what all this is about," Everly said. The tension in the room almost made him forget the pain in his leg. He regarded each man in turn, his patron last of all. "To what 'assignment' do you refer, my lord?"

St. Vincent frowned and grumbled something unintelligible. He waved a hand in Carlisle's direction. "Tell him."

The earl nodded. "There is no delicate way to explain, Captain, so I will be blunt." He sat back in his chair and steepled his fingers. "There is a traitor in the Admiralty."

Everly's eyes went wide and he stared at Carlisle as if the man had suddenly produced a French flag and started singing "La Marseillaise."

"A traitor," he repeated. The very concept was unthinkable. Unconscionable.

"Important orders have gone astray or vanished. Supply ships have been ambushed and their cargos taken. Our fleet movements in the Mediterranean are anticipated with frightening accuracy. The clues point to the same source."

A red haze misted Everly's vision. "Who would dare—" he choked.

"We don't know, but whoever it is must be well-placed." St. Vincent's face was haggard. "Damned blackguard."

"Ordinarily this would be a matter for my agents," Carlisle continued. "But the navy is uncommonly close-knit; a stranger introduced into the Admiralty would be suspect. We cannot conduct an effective investigation. That is why we come to you, Captain."

St. Vincent shifted in his chair. "We want this traitor flushed out as quickly as possible, Everly."

"With all due respect, my lord, why did you select me for this mission? I am no spy." Everly's leg began to throb anew.

"True," Carlisle interjected, "but you are uncommonly resourceful. You are a decorated officer, well known to the Admiralty staff. I am certain the traitor would not suspect you."

A spy? Everly blinked. The word conjured up images of cloaked figures skulking in alleyways, exchanging illicit information. The very concept was foreign to him. He was a naval officer—what did he know of intelligence work?

"There is more, Captain." Carlisle exchanged a meaningful glance with his young associate. "The information we have gathered so far indicates that this traitor is not working alone."

"A conspiracy?" Everly demanded. "Outrageous. This muddle gets worse by the moment."

St. Vincent nodded. "Indeed it does. D'you know Rear Admiral William Locke?"

A yawning pit opened at the bottom of Everly's stomach. "I know of him, my lord. The papers call him 'The Lion of the Mediterranean.' "

The admiral snorted and reached for the brandy bottle. "You know I don't hold with such accolades, boy." He poured himself a glass of the amber liquid.

"Yes, my lord," Everly agreed. The press had a nauseating habit of awarding epithets to war heroes. His own was "Fair-Haired Jack," a title he loathed.

"Over the past eighteen months," continued the admiral, "Locke has not only paid off his creditors but he's grown wealthy as a Cit. Prize money might account for some of this, but it still smacks of hugger-muggery. Add that to the fact that until recently he was acting commander of the Mediterranean fleet, and our problems there occurred shortly after he took up his post—you can draw your own conclusions."

"Do we have any proof?" Everly asked.

Carlisle shook his head. "Nothing tangible, but then we haven't been able to investigate without arousing suspicion. That is where you fit into this puzzle."

Everly shifted in his seat. "Go on; I'm listening."

"Admiral Locke is hosting a ball at his town house tomorrow evening. We wish you to attend." Carlisle fixed Everly with piercing eyes. "Your goal is to find any evidence of Locke's involvement in this conspiracy."

Was the man mad? A muscle twitched at Everly's temple. He abhorred social gatherings, and now Carlisle wanted him not only to attend what was sure to be the biggest crush of the Little Season, but to play a role he wasn't sure he could handle. He struggled to form a reply. "What sort of evidence are you looking for?"

The earl shrugged. "At this point, we'd settle for anything. Follow him; see if he speaks to anyone suspicious. Eavesdrop on his conversations. If you have the chance, search his study. A wall safe or other hiding place would be the ideal place to conceal incriminating documents."

"If he keeps such documents," St. Vincent added over the rim of his glass.

Every aspect of this assignment went against Everly's principles. They expected him to eavesdrop, to spy, to rifle through a fellow officer's possessions? Worse yet, they wanted him to mingle with the *haut ton,* to exchange witticisms and *on-dits* with fashionable fribbles. He was a frigate captain, not a society fop who delighted in dancing and gossip.

St. Vincent must have sensed Everly's hesitation. He downed the rest of his brandy and set the glass down on the desk with a thud. "These are your orders. If you want another command, you'll accept them."

"With all due respect, my lord, that's blackmail," fumed Everly. He stared back at the three men who regarded him with expectant eyes.

The accusation did not deter St. Vincent. "So it is. Make your decision now, boy. Help us ferret out this traitor, or never hold another command."

His patron had never been one to mince words, but hearing his options stated so baldly raised Everly's hackles even further.

Carlisle spared a disgusted glance in St. Vincent's direction, then favored Everly with a persuasive smile. "The admiral has told us of your intelligence and resourcefulness, Captain. The mere fact that you hold the rank of post-captain at your age marks you as a man of exceptional talent. You're the only one who can help us. If we don't discover the identity of this traitor soon, it will mean more damaging information falling into French hands, and the loss of more English lives."

Everly balled his hands into fists and rested them on his knees. Was he up for such a monumental task, physically and mentally? He wasn't sure, but if this was what he needed to do to win back his command, he would make the attempt.

"I'll do it." His assent sounded strained.

Relief swept the room in an invisible tide. St. Vincent rose and poured Everly a snifter of brandy; as an afterthought, he filled glasses for Carlisle and MacAllister, as well.

"Good. It's settled, then. Confusion to our enemies," he said, raising his glass in a toast.

Everly took too large a swallow, and the heady liquor clawed its way down his throat. He stifled a cough.

Carlisle set his glass aside. "I will arrange for you to

receive an invitation to the ball, Captain. The rest is up to you."

"And what if I don't discover anything?" Everly stared into the amber depths of his drink.

The dark-haired earl assumed a pose of studied nonchalance. "If you find nothing tomorrow night, continue your surveillance. Attempt to gain Locke's confidence. After all, you are both well-respected officers who sailed adjacent waters. Do your utmost to find out how much he knows, and who else is involved."

"And then?"

"Then we go after the leader of this treasonous cabal."

Everly took another, more careful swallow of brandy. "How am I supposed to report what I find?"

"You may send word to me any time of the day or night by way of the admiral. Do not attempt to get in touch with me directly, for that might jeopardize the entire operation. I will also make Mr. MacAllister's services available to you. This is a dangerous business, Captain; consider him your secondary line of defense, someone to watch your back. Place him on your staff as a groom or footman—someone who can come and go without attracting too much attention. He will know where to find me, should you need to report anything urgent. He will follow your orders, but remember that he answers to me."

A "secondary line of defense" indeed, thought Everly with a wry twist of his lips. Well, at least Carlisle was diplomatic about it. He assessed the young Scotsman with a hard eye. True he might require assistance on this assignment. MacAllister also might have orders to keep watch on Everly, to make sure he did his job. Now Everly wasn't sure if he could trust his initial judgment of the man's character.

The others were waiting for his response. Everly cleared his throat. "I believe I could fit another groom into the stables. Are you any good with horses, MacAllister?"

MacAllister shook his head with a rueful grin. "Hopeless. My brother's the horseman of the family, Captain.

More than likely I'd get kicked or bitten on a regular basis. If you wish me to fit in, I daresay I'd be better off in the house."

Everly felt an answering smile tug at the corner of his mouth, though his suspicion was enough to quash it. "Very well, we'll see how you do in livery. Present yourself to Hobbes, my butler, first thing tomorrow morning."

"Of course, sir."

Carlisle nodded his approval and returned his attention to Everly. "Remember, Captain, anything you observe may be of value. I wish to be apprised of everything you see or hear."

It rankled to be given orders by a civilian, but Everly swallowed his indignation. "I shall not fail."

This seemed to satisfy the earl. "Excellent. I will make sure that you receive your invitation to the ball before nightfall."

"Hmph. Better have your man shine up the brass on your dress uniform," St. Vincent said. "Mustn't disgrace the Royal Navy."

Everly would have rather faced down a full French broadside than attend a society function, but instead he managed to quip, "Quite so, sir. It should prove to be a very interesting evening."

Chapter Two

If Amanda were the fainting type, she would have collapsed in a puddle of emerald silk right there on the grand staircase. All the assemblies in Dorset could not have prepared her for one evening amidst the *beau monde*. Not only was the crowd much larger than that found at a country house party, but Amanda had never seen such a profusion of titles as she had this evening. Earls brushed shoulders with commodores, admirals conversed with marchionesses. And this was just the receiving line. In her borrowed gown, with no jewelry or adornments, she felt very small, very out of place . . . and very afraid. What if someone recognized her?

She glanced up at Harry, resplendent in his dress uniform, but he appeared as discomfited by the august crowd as she was. Small wonder—Harry was more at ease in the wardroom than the drawing room. She gave his arm an awkward pat.

"I can't believe I let you talk me into this," he muttered. He tugged at his jacket. "Half of London society must be here."

"I'd say more than that," she replied. A shiver of revulsion seized her. All the wealthy and titled, come to see *him*. The source of her family's misery and shame.

Harry noticed her bleak expression and waxed sympathetic. "Steady on. It's not as bad as all that. You'll be fine."

"Of course." Amanda hid her grim thoughts behind a bright, forced smile. Oh, Harry—if only you knew why I really asked to come here . . .

As they neared the head of the line, Amanda began

to tremble; against all logic, her nerve-fired imagination convinced her that Admiral Locke would recognize her. Her hands grew clammy inside her long kid gloves. Her heart slid upward to lodge in her throat. She cast a furtive glance over her shoulder. There were too many people on the stairs, too great a crowd between her and the front doors; as much as her body screamed at her to flee, she had come too far to turn back now. She straightened her shoulders and tried to swallow around her dry tongue.

Rear Admiral William Locke stood at the head of the stairs, greeting his guests with gracious ease. His younger sister, Lady Desmond, stood next to him as his hostess, but Amanda scarcely noticed her; she fixed her entire attention on the man who had destroyed her family. He was nothing like what she had imagined. She gauged him to be near her father's age, and still well-favored despite years spent at the mercy of wind and sea. He was perhaps a head shorter than Harry, and stockier. Wavy, gray-streaked brown hair crowned his tanned face, a stark contrast to his pale blue eyes. The high planes of his cheekbones and the aquiline arch of his nose hinted at aristocratic lineage. In his heavily braided dress uniform, he radiated dignity and confidence. He didn't look like a monster at all.

As Amanda stared at him, she felt her anger rekindle and burn her fear away. She swallowed, hard-pressed to keep that fire under control; she mustn't give Locke any reason to suspect that she was anything other than a featherheaded female. She opened her sandalwood fan to cool her heated skin.

She barely heard Harry's voice as he introduced her. "Admiral Locke, may I present Mrs. . . . ah . . . Seagrave."

Admiral Locke did not seem to notice the lieutenant's hesitation; he smiled and bowed over Amanda's gloved hand.

"Welcome to my home, Mrs. Seagrave. I do hope you enjoy yourself this evening." His pale eyes flicked to her abundant *décolletage*, then back to her face.

"Admiral, this is such an honor. My late husband spoke so highly of you." Her greeting came out in a high, breathy rush. She batted her eyelashes and tried to appear pleased by his attentions, even as her stomach roiled and she resisted the urge to yank herself away from his touch.

"You flatter me, madam," Locke stated, his smile widening. "May I present my sister, the Viscountess Desmond? Letitia, this is Mrs. Seagrave and her escort, Lieutenant Henry Morgan."

Amanda curtsied to Lady Desmond, a sharp-faced, sharp-eyed matron dressed in a fashionable slip of gold net over a green crepe gown. She towered over Amanda like a ship's figurehead, distant and wooden, and eyed the younger woman up and down with patent disapproval.

"*Enchantée*," she intoned. Then she turned a dismissive shoulder to Amanda and graced Harry with a flirtatious smile. She tapped his arm playfully with her fan. "You must save at least one dance for me, Lieutenant. So rarely do I find a man whose stature complements my own. And I warn you—I don't take no for an answer."

Harry blushed and stammered a polite response. Amanda hoped he knew how to swim with barracudas.

Having exchanged the requisite pleasantries, Amanda and Harry moved past the receiving line and into the first of a series of chambers that formed the ballroom. Amanda exhaled in a slow, relieved sigh.

"What on earth possessed you to choose that name?" Harry growled at her. "Didn't sound strange until I introduced you. 'Mrs. Seagrave,' indeed. Rather transparent, don't you think?"

"You didn't think so earlier." She glared back. "I told you I'd been using the name since I came to London."

"Well, the name's only part of it," he declared. "You don't look like widow, not by half."

"Don't be such a half-wit," she snapped, but the reproach was hollow. Harry was right. At three and twenty, Amanda considered herself a spinster—old enough to play the part of a married woman. The dress she wore, however, might be considered too *outré,* even for a widow. She did not wish to think of that at the moment. "Besides, Locke didn't recognize me. I don't think you should be worried about me so much as you should worry about Lady Desmond."

"Why?" he inquired, suspicious. "I thought her very charming."

"Oh, never mind." Amanda lifted her eyes to Heaven and prayed for patience. For all his intelligence and naval acumen, Harry could be so obtuse when it came to the fairer sex. He would no doubt find himself well in over his head before the evening was over.

Amanda was astounded by the seething, suffocating mass of over- and under-scented humanity congregated in these rooms. The throng on the stairs had been nothing compared to this. The din was incredible, like the pounding of the surf against the shore in one long, unending wave. Dozens upon dozens of white beeswax tapers illumined the area; their light reflected off the inlaid wooden floor, and the sparkling jewelry on ladies' throats, wrists, and hair. The heat from the candles, added to that of bodies pressed in a confined space, turned the ballroom into a glittering furnace. Amanda felt a bead of sweat gather between her breasts, and she fanned herself briskly. This was society's idea of a party? Dressed, stuffed, and roasted—she felt more like a Christmas goose than a party guest.

Harry leaned down until his mouth was next to her ear. "Well, where do we begin?"

Amanda started, speechless. We? She hadn't counted on Harry's willingness to do anything beyond getting her to the ball. She stared up at him, measuring his anxious countenance. Harry was a loyal friend, but he would take exception to what she was actually here to do.

"Well," she began, "we can't really do anything until we see someone who can introduce me to Lord Hardwicke. I did promise you I'd be discreet, after all." She smiled at him, and was relieved to see some of the apprehension leave his face.

He squeezed her hand. "That's my girl. Shall we take a turn about the room and see who's here?"

Amanda nodded, her mind a mad whirl. She hadn't thought at all about what to do with Harry; she had hoped he would find an acquaintance or two and distract himself with conversation. So much for that. Her plan, though far from perfect, turned out to have some ship-sized holes in it. Then she seized upon an idea.

"We can cover more of the room if we split up," she said eagerly. "You go one way, and I'll go the other, and we'll meet back here."

The young lieutenant surveyed the sea of people and frowned. "I can't let you wander off unescorted. What if something happened to you?"

Amanda feigned nonchalance. She gestured to the room with her fan. "What could possibly happen to me with all these people around? Besides, this is not a social occasion; I do not wish to stay a moment longer than is necessary. I can take care of myself, Harry. I'm not a little girl anymore."

Harry scanned her up and down, as if seeing her for the first time. He blushed. "I can see that," he replied brusquely. "I wish you'd worn something else."

"It was the only gown I could borrow on such short notice." The vibrant green silk was one of Madame Molyneaux's most fashionable creations, but that didn't make Amanda any more comfortable with the low neckline and the drapey skirts. She felt positively undressed.

"Are you certain about this?" Harry sounded like he wanted her to change her mind.

"I'll be fine, Harry," she assured him.

He nodded, reluctant. "All right. I'll meet you back here."

They parted in opposite directions; Amanda guessed that she had between five and ten minutes to discover the location of Locke's study. If she found it now, she would waste less time later and lower the chances of getting caught. Since she couldn't descend the main staircase, she needed to find another way to get back to the first floor. This place was immense, as town houses went.

She would wager there was a servants' staircase toward the rear of the house.

Amanda battled through the assembled throng like a salmon swimming upstream. Guests seemed to occupy every inch of floorspace, and more than once Amanda bit back a cry of pain when someone trod on her toes or poked her with a bony elbow. She escaped through the last set of doors, and paused in the corridor to take a restorative breath. Heavens, what a crush. She brushed a damp tendril of hair from her cheek and proceeded down the hallway. A few guests spared her a curious glance as she passed, but she smiled and continued to walk with a sense of purpose, as if looking for someone. There was indeed a rear staircase, just as she had hoped.

Amanda spared a surreptitious glance over her shoulder. No one else had ventured this far back into the house. Her heart beat at a furious pace as she lifted the hem of her dress and crept down the narrow stairs.

The poor footman who was on his way up was as startled as she when they nearly collided on the landing.

"Excuse me!" the servant exclaimed. He leaned against the wall to steady himself; the champagne flutes on his tray clattered, but remained upright. He sighed with relief.

"Forgive me," Amanda replied, breathless. Her jangled nerves screamed at her. "I should have watched where I was going."

The footman appraised her with careful eyes. "Are you lost, madam?"

Amanda's heart plunged into the bottom of her stomach. What should she say? She giggled nervously and clutched her dress. "Oh—well, yes. I was looking for a way back to the cloakroom, and the main stairs were so congested—someone stepped on my hem, you see, and I simply must repair it before the dancing begins. Tonight is so important, and I must look my best!" She cringed to hear herself prattle so. Mrs. Siddons she was not, but she was desperate.

The servant gave her a knowing smile. "Of course, madam. Allow me to show you the way." He turned and descended to the bottom of the stairs, then waited for her to follow.

"Oh, thank you!" Amanda gushed. Her knees wobbled as she trailed the footman down the corridor. If she had waited a few moments more before going down the stairs, she could have explored the lower floor unhindered; she guessed that most of the servants were either in the kitchen or upstairs in the ballroom. It was her rotten luck to run into one at this very moment.

As the liveried footman led her down the main corridor, Amanda tried to guess which room was Locke's study. Two chamber doors had been left open; these led to the breakfast room and a formal reception room. No, she surmised, the study door would be closed. At least that narrowed down her choices, but trepidation nibbled at the edge of her resolve. What if the door was locked? What if someone caught her as she tried to open it?

The servant stopped at the cloakroom and bowed. "Here you are, madam. I trust your maid will be able to assist you."

Again Amanda assumed the air of a giddy miss, although the giddiness was genuine. "Oh, yes, thank you." She slipped into the cloakroom, made a show of smoothing her dress for the benefit of the other guests, took several deep, calming breaths, and reemerged. The footman was gone. A shudder coursed through her. That had been a narrow escape. Now she needed to get back up to the ballroom before Harry began to wonder where she was. Botheration—if only she had more time! Well, she would make another attempt later.

The main body of guests had gone through the receiving line, allowing Amanda to ascend the grand staircase unimpeded. Strains of music reached her ears. The dancing had started, which meant it might be easier for her to navigate through the crowd back to where Harry had left her, and be in place before he returned.

No such luck.

She wended her way through the people clustered at the edge of the dance floor. Harry stood where she was supposed to be, his face contorted in a scowl, his complexion flushed. Oh, dear—she had taken too long, and now Harry was going to fly into the boughs.

"Where the devil have you been?" Harry demanded as she approached.

She gave him a tremulous smile. "I'm terribly sorry, Harry. I didn't mean to worry you. But I saw someone—a friend of my father's. I thought he might recognize me, so I had to avoid him. I got caught up in the crowd." She hoped that God—and Harry—would forgive her all these lies.

Harry's glower lessened only slightly. "Well, did you see anyone?"

Amanda shook her head. "No, not right away. But there must be someone here." She surveyed the dance floor and felt a sudden longing. She hadn't danced in such a long time; surely one set wouldn't hurt. "Dance with me, Harry."

"Dance with you?" Harry's eyes widened. "What on earth for?"

She sighed. Harry had never been one for more refined pursuits. "Because we might see someone we know, and because I haven't danced in ages. Please, Harry, indulge me."

"Amanda, I'm not sure I—"

"Oh, come now, it's just a country dance. You do remember the figures, don't you?" she teased. She took his hand and led him toward the nearest set of couples. Harry was stiff as a wooden plank, but he managed to get through the figures well enough.

The dance ended far too soon for Amanda—she had enjoyed herself almost to the point of forgetting why she was here in the first place. The opposing lines bowed to each other at the final chord and began to disperse.

"There, that wasn't so bad, was it?" Amanda asked with a little laugh.

Harry didn't answer; his attention was focused across the room. "Ah . . . I think I see someone," he announced. "It's Captain Bennett. He said he might attend this evening. He would introduce you to Lord Hardwicke. Do you want me to get his attention?"

The butterflies in Amanda's stomach redoubled their fluttering. She needed a way to put Harry off the scent, and quickly. "Oh—well, I—oh, botheration!" she exclaimed, staring down at her hem.

"What is it? Did someone step on your dress?" Harry, bless him, did not disappoint her.

"I'm afraid so." She managed to disguise her panic. "I should go down to the cloakroom at once to repair it. If I don't return this dress in pristine condition, it will mean my head!"

Exasperation crossed Harry's face. "Oh, all right. But I should go speak with him. Dashed bad form not to thank him for getting us these invitations. I'll meet you over there."

More rotten luck; Harry was too determined for his own good. "Of—of course," she stammered. "I shan't be long."

At least this meant that Harry would be occupied for a time. Eager to make her escape, Amanda turned away, but with such haste that she collided with another body. She stared at the broad chest before her. Her gaze rose along the line of waistcoat buttons, up the elegant white waterfall of the cravat, and finally reached the man's dark, sardonic face. Heavens! Amanda retreated.

"Oh! I didn't see you." She fumbled for the words. "My apologies. Do excuse me." She started to move around him, but the stranger reached out and snagged her hand.

"No apologies are necessary," he said with a smooth smile. "I can only consider it a stroke of luck. You find yourself without a escort, and I find myself without a partner for the next set. Perhaps this is Fate."

Amanda recognized the gentleman from the country dance set. With his athletic figure, raven hair, and deep brown eyes, she supposed him very handsome. His predatory gaze, though, disturbed her; he regarded her as if she were a sweetmeat ready to be devoured.

"I beg your pardon," she replied with more confidence than she felt, "but we have not been introduced."

The man's expression turned calculating. "A mere for-

mality, easily remedied. I am the Marquess of Bainbridge, at your service." He raised her fingers to his lips.

"G—good evening, my lord," she stammered, non-
plused. "I am Mrs. Seagrave. But if you will excuse me,
I really must—"

"How unchivalrous of your husband, ma'am, to leave
you alone in the middle of this crush." Lord Brainbridge
kept hold of her hand, ignoring her protests. His gaze
caressed her body with almost physical force.

Amanda wished that Harry hadn't left her alone, after
all. A warning, a sense of imminent danger, raised the
small hairs on the back of her neck. "That was not my
husband, my lord, merely a friend. I—I am a widow."
Again she tried to pull her hand away.

Lord Bainbridge did not release her. He arched a dark
eyebrow. "Indeed," he murmured. A devilish smile lit
his handsome features. He turned her hand over and
drew his thumb across the palm. "Do you miss your husband very much?"

"Miss him?" Amanda blinked. Really, he was standing
far too near for comfort; her brain had turned to treacle.
She tried to assume an air of frosty detachment. "You
are impertinent, my lord. Let me go."

The marquess drew closer, so close that Amanda could
smell his musky citrus cologne and the faint scent of
cheroot smoke. His eyes were dark, potent pools of per-
suasion. "Forgive me if I seem too bold. I had the impression that you need someone to lift your spirits. If
that is the case, I will gladly volunteer." He pressed his
lips to her palm. His touch seemed to burn through her
glove and scorch her skin.

Alarmed beyond the boundaries of reason, Amanda
snatched her hand away. "My—my spirits have no need
of lifting. Pray excuse me." She lurched backward and
nearly tripped over her own hem.

He reached out for her again—to steady her? She
thought not! Amanda skittered away and dodged into
the crowd.

Lord Bainbridge's resonant chuckle rippled like water

over velvet. "Oh, you are a treat! I must have you," she heard him declare. "Come back, little nymph."

Was he following her? Feeling very much like prey, Amanda darted through the crowd. Her breath came in frightened gasps, her face was flushed, and her skin tingled where Lord Bainbridge had touched her. What on earth was she doing here? She didn't know how to swim with barracudas, either. She spotted an alcove shielded by a broad-leafed potted palm and dashed into it. There, in the semi-darkness, she gulped for air and tried to calm herself. Without Harry she was free to continue her search, but she was also in danger from rakes like Lord Bainbridge. This wasn't her world; she didn't belong here. She shivered. The evening was getting more dangerous by the moment—and given what she had yet to do, it was bound to get worse.

Captain Jack Everly had but one thought as he sipped his lukewarm champagne: he was a sorry excuse for a spy. In the hour since his arrival he had followed Admiral Locke from one end of the room to the other, listening to the man's conversations, but he had heard nothing even remotely suspicious. He was beginning to wonder if he was on some sort of wild-goose chase. Everly didn't know the admiral, but Locke was reputed to be a competent officer. The thought of this man in the middle of a traitorous conspiracy was mind-boggling. To look at him—in the prime of life, replete with honors and decorations—Everly would have considered the suggestion absurd had it not come from St. Vincent himself.

At the moment, Locke was occupied in an animated exchange with a small cluster of naval officers. Some of them Everly knew, but none of them seemed suspicious. Neither was their conversation. At present they were arguing the merits of another captain's promotion.

Everly stood just behind this little group, eavesdropping with one ear while engaged in conversation himself. He realized early in the evening that he would need to blend into the crowd to cover his activities; to do so, he needed to socialize, something he dreaded. At one time he had felt at ease in the ballroom, for his handsome face and charming manner had attracted women to him by the score. Well, he was still handsome, he supposed, despite the thin scar that graced his cheek—but he could not disguise his shuffling, syncopated gait, no matter how hard he tried. Bad enough that his infirmity made him stand out in a society that celebrated physical perfection. He wished more people were discreet about their stares and whispered speculations.

Even so, Everly had to admit that he was not the social pariah he had expected to be. He was no longer the hero of the moment as when he first returned from the Adriatic, but society still remembered that he had been granted a hereditary baronetcy for his victory at Lissa. His lips quirked in a sardonic smile. The *beau monde* was a fickle lot. Even if some had forgotten the circumstances of his elevation, they hadn't forgotten his fortune. Prize money had made Everly a very wealthy man.

Unfortunately, plump pockets and a title had also turned him into a target. This evening he had had to sidestep more than one overzealous matron who wished to introduce him to her daughter. Or daughters. Everly shuddered. Just now the Honorable Mrs. Denton Claremore had attached herself to him like a remora and proceeded to expound upon her progeny's virtues. If Admiral Locke didn't move soon, Everly would have to find another method of escape. At present, all he could do was nod politely as Mrs. Claremore rattled on, all while stretching his senses to catch fragments of the admiral's conversation.

After another minute Locke excused himself—at last!—and headed toward the doors at the far side of the room. Relief surged through Everly.

"Forgive me, Mrs. Claremore," he said, interrupting the lady's monologue, "but I am promised for this dance. Perhaps I could meet you daughter some other time."

"Oh, a moment, Captain!" The feathers on Mrs. Claremore's turban quivered with excitement. "Here is Georgianna now—allow me to introduce you."

Everly pretended not to hear her. Locke traveled quickly through the crowd, and Everly had to be discreet in his pursuit. To his dismay, the woman's brassy voice made discretion impossible.

"Captain! Yoohoo, Captain Everly! Just a moment, if you please. My daughter is most eager to make your acquaintance!"

Heads turned in their direction, but Mrs. Claremore was undaunted. She scudded after Everly like a ship of the line under full sail, her voluminous tangerine satin skirts billowing out behind her, one plump hand firmly clutching the wrist of her equally plump daughter as she towed the mortified girl in her wake.

If he didn't keep moving, she'd get close enough to loose her boarding hooks.

Ahead of him, Locke detected the commotion and turned, a slight frown on his face. Everly's heart plummeted into his polished evening pumps. Now this was a pickle. He couldn't trail Locke without the man's notice, but if he stayed where he was the redoubtable Mrs. Claremore would overtake him. A strategic retreat was in order. Everly ducked around a large cluster of guests, sidestepped behind a Grecian column, and slipped into an alcove that was half hidden by a potted palm. He watched the women approach and prayed that they had not seen him decamp.

Whatever deities heard his impassioned plea took pity on him; the woman surged past, skirts flapping like unchecked sails as she dragged her protesting progeny behind her.

"But I don't *want* to meet him, Mama!" the girl wailed. "He's only a baronet, and that dreadful limp—I cannot bear to look upon him. I—I vow I shall faint!"

Mrs. Claremore shushed her daughter and stared into the crowd. "This is no time for the vapors, girl. He's rich as Croesus, and don't you forget it. A fortune makes up for a host of defects, even such as his. You must marry a wealthy man, you know that, and beggars cannot be choosers."

In the alcove, Everly's broad shoulders drew tight, his

jaw clenched, utterly appalled to hear these sentiments spoken aloud. He had hoped never to hear such terrible words again. Felicia's rejection had thrust like a dagger through his heart. To his dismay, the blade was still there, and now it wounded him afresh.

Mrs. Claremore, determined in her pursuit, scudded with her daughter into the nearby refreshment room. To guard against discovery, Everly faded further back into the shadows of the alcove. He was completely surprised when he shouldered into another warm body.

The stranger, equally startled, uttered a little gasp, teetered, and fell against him. Everly found himself with an armful of jasmine-scented silk—and a nicely rounded armful it was, too. In the dim light, he was aware of disarrayed dark curls, immense eyes, and one of the finest bosoms he had ever seen in his life. He couldn't resist staring.

"I beg your pardon!" the young woman exclaimed. She quickly extricated herself from his embrace and backed away from him, her eyes wary.

Everly shook himself, and remembered his manners enough to bow.

"No, it is I who should beg forgiveness, for I am entirely at fault," he replied with a jaunty smile. Poor girl—she looked like she expected him to eat her. "I didn't mean to alarm you. I had no idea someone had laid prior claim to this alcove."

His gambit worked; she hid her face with her fan, but not before Everly spied the deep dimples in her cheeks. Egad, dimples!

"You—you startled me, that's all. Are you a fugitive, as well?" Her soft voice grazed his senses like the brush of a feather.

"A fugitive? Well, not exactly—" Everly broke off as the impatient Mrs. Claremore reappeared a short distance beyond the alcove, her hands planted on her ample hips, her head thrust forward, her narrowed eyes scanning the assembled throng of guests. The plump matron's chins quivered in testament to her agitation.

"By God," he muttered, "give that woman a commission and she'll have Boney at bay in no time."

With a smothered laugh, Everly's companion put a gloved finger to her lips, cautioning him not to speak further. Everly needed no second warning and fell silent.

"Drat the man!" exclaimed the garrulous woman. Her words carried well above the general din of the room to grate on Everly's ears. "Wealthy or no, he is exceedingly rag-mannered. A sign of ill breeding. Hero he may be, but I have half a mind to box his ears." Taking her daughter once more by the wrist, the large woman barreled back toward the ballroom floor.

"So you are indeed a fugitive," Everly's companion declared, her face alight with merriment. "You were wise, Captain, to avoid being broadsided by such a warship. I vow she boasted ninety guns, at least. She would have blown you from the water."

Everly found himself grinning at this description of the imposing matron. "An interesting turn of phrase, coming from a young lady," he commented.

She ducked her head, embarrassed, and a few ebon curls swayed loose from their moorings to dangle tantalizingly over her shoulder. Everly resisted the urge to reach out and twine his fingers in them.

"My late husband was a lieutenant on the *Nereide*," she replied at length. "He fell at Grand Port last year. I'm afraid I picked up more than my share of nautical vocabulary from him. I do hope I haven't shocked you."

"Not at all." Everly's smile lost some of its luster. An officer's widow, here among the fribbles? Perhaps she felt as out of place as he, perhaps that was why she sought respite in a darkened alcove. "Forgive me. I did not mean to cause you pain."

"You didn't," she said quickly. Everly didn't believe her.

A long silence spanned the gap between them. More than anything, he wanted to restore the lady's good humor. "Truth be told, ma'am, I must say I found your analogy remarkably apt. Ninety guns, eh?"

She nodded, and rewarded Everly's efforts with a tiny

smile. "Certainly large enough for a second-rate ship of the line. Although perhaps she has aspirations of being first-rate." She glanced at him from under lowered lashes, a mischievous twinkle in her dark eyes.

Everly grinned again. "But I have reached safe harbor, for the moment."

"For the moment. Let us hope she does not signal the rest of the fleet for assistance."

Who was this lovely young woman? Her sense of humor was delightful, her artlessness refreshing. If he discovered nothing else tonight but her name, he would consider himself fortunate. He cleared his throat. "I don't believe I've made your acquaintance. I would certainly have remembered that remarkable smile."

The remarkable smile faded. She hesitated a moment, then curtsied. "I am Mrs. Seagrave, sir."

Seagrave? He had never heard of a Lieutenant Seagrave on the *Nereide,* but that didn't matter. "I am delighted to make your acquaintance, ma'am. Captain Sir Jonathan Everly, at your service." This was the first time Everly had ever introduced himself with his title, but now he rather liked the way it sounded. He took her gloved hand and raised her fingers to his lips.

The lady uttered a sharp gasp, and Everly looked up, startled. Surprise and shock were written on her elfin face; he could see that clearly even in the shadows of the alcove. Her eyes widened to saucerlike proportions; her body stiffened.

"Captain . . . Everly," she echoed. She pulled away from him.

Her sudden change of mood baffled the captain. "I hope you give no credence to the newspapers, madam," he said with an attempted laugh. "The press is prone to exaggeration."

"Exaggeration. Of course." Her face had become deathly pale, so pale that he feared she might faint.

"Are you unwell, Mrs. Seagrave? May I fetch you something to drink?" His desire to please her took him by surprise. The lady made charming company, and the few minutes that he had spent with her had been the most enjoyable in months.

"No—no, that won't be necessary. I just need some air. Excuse me." Before he could stop her, she gathered her skirts and was gone, slipping quickly from the alcove and out into the ballroom.

After a moment of stunned disbelief Everly gave chase, but saw no sign of her. She had disappeared into the crowd. A faint trace of jasmine lingered in the air, but it faded quickly and gave him no clue to her direction. Everly stood next to the marble column, frowning, oblivious to the curious stares of the other guests.

Something had clearly frightened the young woman out of her wits. He rubbed his chin, perplexed. Was it his name? It had to be; she had not seemed to notice his ungainly limp. No, the lady had not shown him any disfavor until he'd introduced himself. Strange. Another puzzle for him to put together. Perhaps he would encounter the elusive Mrs. Seagrave again this evening, and have the chance to do just that.

Chapter Three

Amanda stumbled into the empty drawing room and clutched the back of a chair for support. The world seemed to spin around her. Blood thrummed in her ears. Her breath came in sharp, painful gasps. Tears overflowed her eyes and streamed down her cheeks in long wet trails. She pressed her fingers to her temples, trying to banish the hateful name that reverberated through her head.

Everly. Captain Sir Jonathan Everly.

One of the tribunal that had found her father guilty of treason.

Amanda choked back a sob. She could recite the entire membership of that captains' tribunal like a litany: Everly, Davenport, Hamilton, Fitzgerald, Collins. She had seen their names on the poster publicizing Captain Alexander Tremayne's supposed crimes; their wrongful judgment had meant her father's death.

And she had just met one of his executioners. Oh, God! She dragged herself before the low fire in the hearth. Her entire body was so cold. She wrapped her arms around herself and shivered. She had imagined confronting each member of the tribunal one day, armed with the truth and full of righteous rage—not shaking and crying and more than half hysterical. Amanda bit her lip and fought back fresh tears. As much as she yearned to avenge her father, she was proving to be less than useless.

Her hands shook as she fumbled for her kerchief. She pressed the perfumed linen square to her face, fighting to restore her shattered poise. Guilt spiked her misery.

Before she realized who he was, Amanda had thought the fugitive captain one of the most attractive men she had ever met. She bit her lip. Well, he was still handsome, but beneath that comeliness lay a heart black as pitch. Never mind his broad shoulders or his vivid blue eyes. Never mind his golden hair or his stirring presence. Amanda shuddered, repulsed by her own feelings. Rational—she must be rational about this.

Urgent footsteps sounded in the hall; before Amanda could recover herself, Harry burst into the drawing room.

"Amanda! I say, are you all right? What happened? I saw you run from the ballroom." In his haste to reach her, Harry collided with an overstuffed chair, which tumbled to the floor. Scarlet-faced, he set it upright once more. "Amanda? You've been crying. What's wrong?"

Amanda squeezed her eyes shut and turned away. The tender concern on Harry's face was enough to induce another round of tears. Her conscience gave a painful twist. Perhaps she had been wrong to withhold her mission from him. He had been her friend for so many years, and right now she desperately needed to confide in someone.

"Harry," she said in a small voice, "I need to tell you something. Please close the door."

Harry, somber, did as she asked.

Amanda stared at the dull, cracked surface of the oil painting above the fireplace, her thoughts as jumbled as the still-life fruit portrayed on the canvas. She toyed with the crocheted edge of her handkerchief and wondered where to begin.

"I knew something was troubling you," Harry said quietly. "More than you were willing to tell me in the park."

She avoided his forthright gaze. "You know why I wanted to come here tonight."

He cocked his head to one side. "To speak with the First Lord, or so you told me."

Amanda pressed her lips together. "That's not entirely true."

Harry clasped his hands behind his back and waited.

"I see you may have guessed that already." Amanda

tried to smile, but couldn't. Better to just come out with it. "I came here to try to find evidence that Admiral Locke framed my father for treason."

"What?" Harry rocked back on his heels. "Confound it, Amanda, you *have* gone mad. This is as queer as Dick's hatband."

"No! This is not a flight of fancy," she insisted. "My father was innocent—you know that as much as I do. He was a loyal officer who would never, ever betray his country."

"So what makes you think that Locke was responsible?" A tic began in Harry's jaw.

"Because Locke was my father's commanding officer; my father's orders had to come through him. Locke would have been the one to send my father to the coast of France with those men and supplies, and orders for such a secretive mission would have originated from the Admiralty."

"Amanda . . ." Harry hesitated, as if grasping for the proper words. "Amanda, what you're suggesting is outrageous. Are you sure you are not imagining this? Locke publicly denied any knowledge of those orders. The Admiralty had no record of them. I know your father's death came as a shock—"

"His execution, you mean," Amanda countered. She clenched her hands into fists. "He was hanged like a common criminal."

Harry ran a hand through his hair, visibly uncomfortable. "I admit that the circumstances surrounding your father's arrest were a little queer. But that doesn't mean that Admiral Locke was to blame."

Amanda set her jaw at a pugnacious angle. "My father would never have agreed to that mission without specific orders. Since the Admiralty had no record of his mission, I suspect those orders were counterfeit."

Harry shook his head. "Counterfeit? Amanda, be reasonable. Why would Locke go to such great lengths to destroy your father's career? What would he have to gain?"

Amanda could read the doubt in Harry's expression,

hear it in his voice. She gritted her teeth and plunged ahead. "My father suspected that Locke was involved in something illegal, perhaps even traitorous but he had no proof."

She glanced toward the door; her next words came out in a bare whisper. "You remember what an insomniac Papa was. In good weather, he would spend part of the evening watch on deck, and one night he noticed Locke rowing from his ship into port. After a few such occurrences, my father realized that each of Locke's nocturnal excursions was followed within a few days by misfortune—supply routes plundered, ships ambushed. He began to document each of Locke's few visits to shore, and the calamities that ensued. Papa became suspicious—these series of events were too convenient for circumstance—so one night he followed Locke into port.

"Locke went to a dockside inn, and there he met with a cloaked figure. Papa could never see them clearly enough to recognize the second man, nor could he hear their conversation, but it was enough to warrant further investigation. He started asking questions—of the innkeeper, and of the crew of Locke's gig at the dock. Apparently, everyone thought Locke was indulging in a clandestine affair. If only that were the case.

"The next day, Commodore Locke summoned Papa to his cabin and ordered him to cease his impertinent questions, that Locke's activities were of an official nature, and none of his business. Papa had no choice but to obey, but Locke's vehement reaction made him all the more mistrustful. So he sent inquiries to the Admiralty. Three weeks later, Locke ordered my father on that terrible mission. You know what happened after that. The army's disastrous defeat, the arrest, the trial—all of it meant to transfer suspicion and guilt away from Locke, and to get my father out of the way."

Harry's brows drew together in a severe line. "This is only conjecture, Amanda," he admonished. "You have no proof."

Amanda felt like an erring midshipman taken to task.

Stubborn, she stood firm. "I have letters my father sent to me."

Harry shook his head. "Those won't stand up in court. Look here, I'll admit that the circumstances seem suspicious, but—"

Amanda rounded on her friend. "Suspicious? The man's a traitor, Harry. Who knows how far this treasonous influence extends? Why else would he have invited members of my father's tribunal to this party?"

"He . . . what?" Harry's jaw dropped.

"When you saw me dash from the ballroom, I had just encountered Captain Sir Jonathan Everly. I didn't know who he was until he introduced himself. I—I just had to get away from him."

"Captain Everly? What is he doing in London?"

"That's what I would like to know." Amanda suppressed another shudder, and willed her thoughts away from Captain Everly's stunning smile and back to the task at hand. "Although I suspect the two of them are in league. It fits together like a bizarre puzzle. My father suspects Locke of illicit activity. To get him out of the way, Locke implicates my father for his own treasonous actions. Then he bribes Everly—and others, perhaps—to insure that the trial is quick and decisive. Have you never wondered why my father was convicted and executed with such speed?"

"Well, yes, but as I said we need proof, some concrete evidence of wrongdoing."

Amanda smiled triumphantly. "I intend to remedy that tonight."

Harry's eyes widened. He wagged a finger at her. "Oh, no. No, you don't. You're not actually considering—"

She lifted her chin. "I am, Harry. I'm going to search Locke's study for incriminating evidence. He must keep some sort of documents in the house, and I intend to find them."

The young lieutenant seized her shoulders and shook her. "Amanda, stop this madness. Do you have any idea what would happen if you were caught? You'd be arrested, deported . . . God knows what!"

"It's worth the risk." Amanda batted his hands away. "He's taken everything from my family—our house, our lands, our honor. I have nothing left to lose!"

"What about your grandmother?" Harry loomed over her. "What would happen to her if you were thrown in prison?"

Amanda paced away from the fire and back again as indecision reared its ugly head. Her grandmother was her weak spot, and Harry knew it. She glared at him. "I know what you're trying to do, Harry. I won't be caught."

"How can you be so certain?" Harry demanded, hands on his hips.

She wouldn't let Harry talk her out of this; she must resume the offensive. "I know I won't be caught," she said softly. "Not if you help me."

Her salvo had immediate effect. Harry stared at her, robbed of speech, his mouth gaping open and closed like a fish caught out of water. After a few moments he stepped back and pinched the bridge of his nose as if to ease a headache. "This is sheer lunacy. Devil take it, Amanda, I'm not going to help you commit a crime."

"I'm not asking you to," Amanda said. "All I need you to do is leave the house about ten minutes from now, and have the carriage waiting around the corner. I'll join you when I'm finished."

"I can't believe I'm listening to this," he exploded, his face suffused with angry color. "This is your craziest scheme yet. It could mean my career!"

"Lower your voice, before someone hers us!" she hissed. "I am grateful for everything you've done for me. This is the last favor I will ever ask of you."

He grasped the hilt of his dress sword with whitened knuckles. "You always say that, but it's never the end. Good old Harry, he's sure to come through," he mocked. "No more, Amanda. If you don't find anything tonight, as God is my witness I'm going to pack you off to Dorset myself."

"This is my last chance to redeem my father," she

pleaded. "I have to prove his innocence. I can't let Locke get away with this."

"You've always been a willful creature." Harry leveled his grim gaze at her. "Nothing I say will make the least bit of difference, will it?"

She drew herself up. "No."

He grimaced. "I thought not. Very well, I'll wait for you in the carriage." He started for the door, then turned and glared over his shoulder. "I won't wait forever, mind you. If you take too long, you can walk home."

Amanda's relief made her light-headed. "Thank you, Harry," she breathed. "You're a godsend."

Harry scowled. "No—I'm a complete idiot." He opened the door and flung himself into the hall.

Weariness washed over Amanda; arguing with Harry had left her drained. She wanted to sit down, to rest, to collect herself, but she had no time. She needed to get into Locke's study while she had the chance. Her year-long quest was almost over, her goal just down the hall.

But if she was discovered . . .

As much as she didn't want to think about it, Harry was right; the penalties for burglary and theft were steep. A tremor of fear began at the base of her spine and radiated in gooseflesh over her body. She must not dwell on what might happen. She needed to do this to clear her father's name. She had no choice.

Amanda went to the doorway and peered into the corridor. Music mixed with the drone of conversation drifted down from the balcony. Then the sharper, more immediate sound of a laugh caught Amanda's attention. She looked up to see a couple descend the stairs with languorous ease; the woman's edged voice floated ahead of them. Amanda ducked behind the door and waited until they passed. When she emerged several heartbeats later, the first-floor hallway was deserted. The coast was clear.

She crept down the passage in a whisper of silk, her ears straining to hear anything beyond the low ambient hum of the crowd upstairs. Approaching the first of the closed doors, she reached out her shaking hand and grasped the knob. It turned easily. Amanda peered around the edge of the door. Disappointment formed a leaden lump within her as she surveyed the rows upon rows of leather-bound volumes on the shelves. The library. Botheration. She must keep looking.

Amanda ghosted to each room in succession until she came to the last closed door. No light shone from beneath the doorsill. The hinges gave a low wail as she pushed it open, setting her teeth on edge. She slipped inside and closed the door behind her, her pulse beating a frantic tattoo in her breast. Oh, how she wished she hadn't had any champagne—nerves had twisted her stomach into a large, unhappy knot. She hoped she wouldn't cast up her accounts all over the floor. She was not cut out to be a spy. Amanda forced herself to take several deep, calming breaths before she looked around the room.

A low fire burned in the grate. The red embers provided the only source of light, but their glow did not extend beyond the hearth rug. Amanda stood with her back to the door and waited for her eyes to adjust to the gloom. At length she could make out shapes of furniture—chairs, a sofa, a few assorted tables, and a large desk by the French doors. Relief surged through her. Locke's study!

Light—she'd need more light. Amanda found a lone candle in a pewter holder and lit it. The glimmering flame revealed more of the room. Amanda noted in particular the fine Aubusson carpet, the marble bust of Pallas Athena in one corner, and the portrait above the fireplace. She lifted the candle and stared at the painting. The antique style and dramatic flair marked it as one of Lawrence's works, a woman just past the blush of youth. She was beautiful; Amanda envied the woman's glorious red hair, pale skin, and luminous gray eyes. Those eyes smiled out at her, as though the lady enjoyed some secret amusement. Who was she? Locke wasn't married, to Amanda's knowledge. She shrugged. The portrait wasn't what she was here to see.

Locke's desk was covered with books, papers, and documents of various sorts. Amanda sighed; she didn't have time to go through every single sheet. She scanned the topmost layer, but found nothing out of the ordinary. Of course, Locke would be a fool to leave any incriminating evidence in plain sight. Amanda moved behind the desk and set the candle down, then began to search the drawers.

A few moments later she stood up in frustration and blew a stray curl away from her eyes. Nothing! There had to be something here, there just had to be. Had she gone through the drawers too quickly? Had she missed something?

Amanda reopened the first drawer with an impatient yank—and gasped. Although the drawer appeared to be filled with nothing more than blank stationery and envelopes, she heard a clunk from the back. Something hard had hit the wood. She took off one glove, then reached in and felt the back wall. It felt solid enough. Then she moved the vellum and envelopes and examined the bottom. It, too, seemed ordinary. No, wait. Toward the back, her fingers brushed against what felt like a tiny metal spring. A false bottom? This had to be what she was looking for. . . .

So absorbed was she in her examination that she didn't hear the doorknob turn. The hinges groaned a warning. Amanda looked up in horror. Her skin turned to ice.

Heavens! She stared wildly around the room, but nowhere could she find a place to hide. Wait—there was something. With terror racing through her veins, Amanda darted behind the damask curtains that covered the French doors. She huddled in the narrow recess, shivering. She heard the door scrape slowly open, then shut again. Soft footsteps crossed the room. Amanda heard a clink, followed by a dull thump. More footsteps, then the rustle of papers. A tall silhouette appeared on the curtains, distorted by their folds. A bead of sweat trickled with agonizing slowness down Amanda's spine. She stood utterly still, not daring to move or even breathe, her senses strained to the breaking point.

Silence claimed the room. The silhouette turned and seemed to hesitate.

The curtains exploded apart, and a strong hand gripped Amanda's arm and hauled her away from the window.

Amanda shrieked.

She glimpsed golden hair and a captain's uniform, enough to recognize Captain Sir Jonathan Everly. The instinct to flee overwhelmed her, and she reacted without thinking. She cocked back her fist and threw her hip into the blow.

Captain Everly caught her hand just before it connected with his jaw.

"None of that," he growled. He yanked her forward, off balance, and she tumbled against his chest.

Amanda's mouth went dry. Everly held both her hands, and she was pressed most indecorously against him. She resisted, but couldn't get away. She stared up at the captain's stern, resolute jaw, at the thin scar on one high-planed cheekbone, then met his blazing blue eyes. If he was at all discomfited by this situation, he gave no sign.

"Now, little hellcat, tell me what you're doing here." His tone brooked no opposition.

Amanda pulled back as far as his grip would let her. Despite her compromised position, she remained defiant. "I might ask you the same question, Captain. How did you know I was here?"

Something she couldn't identify flitted over Everly's face. "Your perfume," he replied. "I remembered it from our encounter earlier this evening."

Amanda flushed. She wore the jasmine scent because her father had brought it for her from Egypt, and because she adored the fragrance. Apparently it had made an impression on Captain Everly, as well.

He tightened his grip on her wrists. "Now—tell me why you were rifling through Admiral Locke's desk. What were you looking for?"

"Let me go," she said coldly. "You're hurting me."

"My apologies." If Amanda didn't know any better, she would swear he was embarrassed. He relinquished his hold on her right arm.

Amanda shook out her hand, but not to alleviate any pain. Her skin tingled where he had touched her. She gave herself a mental slap. This man was the enemy. He had helped murder her father. She shouldn't want anything to do with him.

"Who are you working for?" Everly demanded, his face thunderous. "I warn you, Mrs. Seagrave—if that is your real name—I do not countenance women who lie."

Amanda glanced around Everly to the disarrayed desk. Oh, heavens—not only had she forgotten to close the drawer, but she'd neglected the candle as well; it sat atop the desk like a beacon. Everly was bound to tell Locke she'd been snooping. Well, her father had told her that the best defense was a good offense.

"And what about you, Captain?" She tilted her chin at a mulish angle. "Were you looking for information to try to blackmail your compatriot? You seem very interested in the contents of his desk."

Her acrid retort seemed to blindside the captain, but not in the way she'd imagined.

"Compatriot?" He stumbled over the word. "What are you talking about?"

"Oh, come now, Captain. I know you." Derision dripped from her words. "What other reason would bring you to Locke's study? No honor among thieves, I see."

Everly searched her face, his eyes bright and hard. He turned her ungloved palm upward and examined her work-roughened skin. "Who are you?" he demanded. "Why did you run away from me earlier?"

"I am no one of consequence," she replied through clenched teeth. She closed her fingers over her palm and tried to tug her hand from his grasp, but the captain kept hold of her.

"I won't let you go until you tell me who you are." He leaned closer. "Or until you tell me what you found."

He was too close for Amanda's comfort. "I didn't find anything," she whispered. His lips were inches from her own.

He quirked a gilded eyebrow at her. "Really?" he said softly. "Now, why don't I believe you?"

Amanda's reply was cut off by the sound of voices from the hallway. Both her head and Everly's jerked toward the door, a pair of puppets on the same string.

"Someone's coming," she breathed. She took advantage of the momentary distraction to free herself. She pulled away and stepped back to the recess, picking up her fallen glove.

The captain snapped to action. "Quickly—out onto the balcony," he ordered in a low voice. He met her questioning expression with a scowl. "I think you'll agree that the curtains are an imperfect hiding place."

Amanda felt her face go scarlet. She nodded.

Everly opened the French doors to reveal a tiny balcony with a wrought-iron railing. Below the balcony, glistening in the veiled moonlight, lay the gardens.

Amanda leaned over the railing and swallowed hard. "It's at least twelve feet down."

Everly turned and surveyed the wall. "I'd say more like fifteen. There's a trellis here. Can you climb down?"

Amanda had not climbed anything since she was twelve, but she nodded. "Of course."

Everly climbed over the rail and tested the trellis. It wobbled. "If it doesn't hold, I can withstand the fall better than you."

The voices came nearer. "Just hurry!" Amanda urged. She thrust her gloves into her reticule. Climbing was best done with bare hands.

Everly descended the trellis with the agility of a young midshipman; Amanda could readily imagine him among a web of ship's rigging. He reached the ground and gestured up to her.

"Now—your turn."

Amanda hitched up her skirts and clambered over the railing, then scowled down at Everly. "Look up my skirts and I'll plant you a facer you'll never forget," she warned.

Everly grinned, and the gesture once more transformed his face from handsome to devastating. Amanda's breath caught in her throat. She swiveled back to the trellis, then took hold of the wet wood and cold, slippery vines. She had to concentrate on what she was doing, not on the captain. One step, then the next. The trellis shuddered beneath her.

The study door squawked on its hinges. Terror shot through Amanda, and she gasped; her foot slipped off the trellis. She reached out wildly for the next rung, but encountered only air. Well, she'd jumped from greater heights than this. She let go. The world skewed at a wild angle, she collided with something solid, then crashed into a flower bed. Beneath her, Captain Everly gave a grunt of pain.

Amanda stared down at him, realizing that she was lying on the captain's broad chest. The double row of brass buttons on his jacket pressed painfully into her tender skin.

His eyes strayed to her generous expanse of neckline, presented to him as it was. "As much as I am enjoying this little escapade," he wheezed with a weak smile, "we need to get out of here."

Indignant, Amanda scrambled to her feet. Captain Everly had a more difficult time. His right leg didn't want to support him. Reluctantly, Amanda offered him her hand. He accepted it, and she helped brace him as he struggled upright.

Raised voices sounded from the study. More lights flared to life in the room.

"This way!" Everly said. He limped along the paved path toward the back of the garden. Amanda followed him.

They came to the expanse of stone wall, with no exit in sight. "Some navigator you are," Amanda groused. "You'll have us aground and at the mercy of the enemy in no time." She shot an apprehensive glance over her shoulder. They were out of sight of the balcony, but she heard urgent voices in the garden.

"There has to be a gate somewhere," muttered Everly.

Amanda scanned the ivy-shrouded wall and caught a glint in the moonlight, metal dusted with heavy dew. "This way!"

The gate hinges were even less well oiled than the

study door had been. Amanda winced at the raw rasp of metal against metal. Halfway open, the door stuck.

"That's as good as we're going to get. Hurry!" Everly grabbed Amanda's shoulder and pushed her toward the door; she slid through with room to spare. Everly followed, but had trouble squeezing his large frame through the opening. They hurried through the mews, then down the alleyway toward the street.

"We can take my carriage," Everly gasped.

Amanda hesitated. Why had the captain helped her escape? Why hadn't he turned her in? There was no time to guess his motives now. Sounds of pursuit came from behind them.

"Forgive me, Captain, but I've made other plans," she stated, and before Everly could reply, she lifted her skirts and dashed down the street. Behind her she heard Everly utter a sharp oath, but she did not stop.

Harry's carriage was waiting where he promised it would be. He must have seen her coming; he opened the door for her and extended a hand.

"Good God, Amanda!" he exclaimed. "What is going on?"

Amanda all but threw herself onto the seat next to him. "No time to explain. Drive!"

The carriage gave a lurch and started away down the street, and Amanda leaned back against the squabs, breathing hard. Yet for all her exhaustion, her narrow escape thrilled her. Heavens, was she turning into an adventuress? A tiny smile lifted the corners of her mouth. Then her thoughts returned to Captain Everly, and how she had sprawled so wantonly across his body in the garden, and the smile vanished. Yes, Captain Everly was a very attractive man. He was also the enemy. Or at least he seemed to be. She shivered, and it wasn't entirely due to the cold night air.

Harry took off his jacket and draped it around her shoulders. "There, that should keep you warm. Now, will you please tell me what went on at the house? Why were you running down the street like the Furies were after you?"

Amanda huddled into the warm wool. The high excitement started to fade, leaving her drained and cold. "You needn't make such a face at me, Harry. I'm all right, and I didn't get caught."

Harry heaved an exasperated sigh. "Yes, yes—but what happened?"

Running right over Harry's blustering attempts to get a word in edgewise, Amanda related the events in Locke's study—that she found Locke's secret hiding place, but hadn't been able to discover what it held before she was forced to flee. She thought it best not to mention Captain Everly, the part he had played in the evening's events, and especially not her attraction to him. She was loath to admit that much even to herself.

"It may not be much, but it's still progress," she was quick to point out in response to Harry's deepening frown.

"Confound it," the young lieutenant muttered. "You think that Locke is hiding something, but you don't know what it is? And you call that progress?"

Amanda's fingers tightened around the thick fabric of Harry's jacket. "Yes, I do."

Harry rolled his eyes. "So what will you do now, hmm? Go back to the house in the morning and ask the admiral if you might continue where you left off?"

"You needn't be so cross at me," Amanda reproached him.

He glared at her. "Why not? You take this appalling risk, get me to help you, and in the end have nothing to show for it."

"Cut line, Harry. No one saw me, and I did not get caught. And I know now that Admiral Locke *does* have something to hide."

"Again, I ask you: what are you going to do about it?"

Amanda answered his challenging gaze with defiance. "I don't know yet," she stated, "but I will think of something. I do know that I cannot go back to Dorset—not until I have discovered Locke's secret."

Chapter Four

A manda trudged up the tenement stairs as though weights hobbled her ankles. She was tired, very tired. After Harry brought her home, she stayed up for hours trying to restore her dress; she had used all the ingenuity at her command to remove the water and mud from the skirt. In fact, she had not gone to sleep at all. She needed to return the dress before Madame Molyneux discovered it missing, which meant getting to the shop before Madame—and Madame was always early. Three days later, she was still exhausted.

Amanda paused on the landing to rub her aching shoulder. She had nearly fallen asleep over her work this afternoon, and Madame had rapped her across the back with a cane. There was sure to be a bruise, but at least the pain had helped keep her awake. She must not be so careless again; Madame was a harsh taskmistress. At least she was still employed; she was fortunate that the mantua-maker had not noticed anything amiss with the green silk.

Amanda's eyes lost focus as she stared up into the dim stairwell. Had all that effort been worth the results? She thought about the feel of silk against her skin, about the delight she took in dancing, about the discovering of the drawer in Locke's desk, about her narrow escape from the house . . . and about Captain Sir Jonathan Everly.

She shook her head. Although these vivid memories still tantalized her, the little cinder girl had gone back to the ashes. Amanda sighed and resumed her upward journey. Somewhere nearby a baby wailed; its cries pierced the thin walls like grapeshot through paper. The Browns' youngest was teething, and would likely keep everyone on the second floor up all night. And Mrs. Kennedy had cooked cabbage for supper again. Amanda wrinkled her nose. Her stomach was pinched as a miser's purse, but one whiff of cabbage was enough to spoil her appetite.

She could not help but contrast the drab lodging house, with its pungent smells and dusty halls, to her family's bright, airy home in Dorset. Her father had been a gentleman, and her mother a knight's daughter. They had lived a comfortable life at Bridford House. Comfortable and happy, that is, until their world fell apart over a year ago. Had it been so long since they received word of her father's arrest, trial, and execution, since agents of the Crown seized their house and lands? The nightmarish memories made Amanda shudder. She, her mother, and her grandmother had been forced to rent rooms in a neighboring town; no one of their acquaintance, even distant relations, would take them in.

Even as they had tried to cope, the Charybdis-like whirlpool of circumstance kept pulling them under. Amanda's mother, who had never been strong, died of shame and grief six months after her husband. The *coup de grace* came when the townsfolk found out who they were—traitor's kin—and nearly stoned them in the streets, forcing them to flee. At least London afforded them anonymity, and a way to support themselves. And an opportunity for vengeance.

In her dreams—real dreams, not nightmares—she stood on the cliffs at Lyme Regis, looking out over the rocky coastline, the smell of the sea all around her. But she hadn't seen the sea in months, and had to make do with the brackish water of the Thames. Amanda's spirits were as leaden as her feet by the time she arrived at their rooms.

"There you are, dearest," said her grandmother. The small, elderly woman bustled to greet her granddaughter. "I was worried about you. You are seldom home this late."

"Hello, Grandmama," Amanda replied with a weary smile. She returned her grandmother's embrace. "I almost fell asleep at the worktable today, so Madame Molyneux kept me late as punishment."

"As if that will make you any more alert," the older woman grumbled. "Makes no sense at all, but she's French, so what else can you expect? Here, dearest, let me hang that up for you. You're burnt to the socket."

Amanda's bruised shoulder protested as she shrugged out of her heavy wool cloak. "Madame is no more French than you or I. When she gets angry her accent slips, and you can hear a definite Yorkshire brogue underneath. She has a head for fashion, though, and none of the ladies of the *beau monde* can tell the difference between a real Frenchwoman and a false one."

"Well, she may know what is *au courant*, but she doesn't know how to treat her employees. Look at you— you're exhausted, your fingers are nearly raw, and I'll wager you haven't had anything to eat since breakfast. Go and wash up, and I will dish up some supper for you."

"But, Grandmama—" Amanda began.

The older woman waved her granddaughter's protests aside. "You have made such a point of caring for me, Amanda, but I am not in my dotage. At least, not yet. I am certainly not so infirm that I can't manage supper. Go on with you now."

Amanda nodded wearily and shuffled toward the bedroom she shared with her grandmother. She pulled the hated muslin cap from her hair and tossed it on the dresser, then poured cold water into the basin. How much of this affair could she hide from her grandmother? At three-and-seventy years, Mrs. Albert Tremayne was as spry and as sharp-eyed as ever. Amanda had gone to great lengths to conceal her quest for justice for fear it would upset her grandmother, but now matters had gotten even more complicated. Amanda sighed into the towel as she blotted her damp skin. Just now Grandmama had regarded her with questions in her dark eyes, but she had said nothing. Perhaps she knew already.

Her grandmother was ladling soup into dishes when Amanda emerged. The bread and cheese were already on the table. Amanda's stomach growled, her appetite renewed.

"Sit down, dearest, and eat. I can all but see through you." Mrs. Tremayne poured her granddaughter a cup of hot tea. Steam curled from its surface.

Amanda settled herself at the table and wrapped her chilled fingers around the chipped porcelain cup. "You should have eaten already, and not waited for me."

"Rubbish," declared the older lady. She sat down across from Amanda and laid her napkin across her lap. "We are not so uncivilized as all that. Besides, this is quite the proper hour for supper."

"Thank you, Grandmama." Amanda sipped her bohea, and tried to swallow her tears along with it. Throughout their entire ordeal, her grandmother had never complained about their circumstances, about the hardships, about economizing.

Mrs. Tremayne lifted her spoon and stirred her soup. She glanced up at Amanda. "I've never seen you so exhausted, dearest."

Amanda stared into the dark depths of her tea and didn't answer.

At length her grandmother set down the spoon. "Does it have anything to do with why you went out with Harry Morgan three nights ago?"

Amanda's cup nearly slipped from her fingers. A few drops of tea splashed onto her dress; she dabbed them with her napkin. Anything to avoid her grandmother's eyes, eyes so like Amanda's own.

"Ah, I see it does." Mrs. Tremayne nodded. "If you would like to talk about it, I would be willing to listen." She picked up her spoon and resumed her meal.

The tea turned to ditch water on Amanda's tongue. She had underestimated her grandmother, and she despised herself for it.

"I didn't know you were awake . . ." she faltered.

"So it seems." Mrs. Tremayne did not accuse or reproach. She merely waited.

Amanda took a deep, steadying breath, and set down her cup. She wondered if she looked as miserable as she felt. "I didn't tell you because I feared this business would upset you."

"Perhaps you should let me be the judge of that." Mrs. Tremayne fixed her with a direct, even gaze.

Well, this was it. Despite her best intentions, everything was coming out. "It all began when I received Papa's letters, shortly before his . . . his death."

"Letters? What letters?" Mrs. Tremayne leaned forward, attentive.

"He wrote me several letters, detailing his suspicions about his commanding officer, Admiral William Locke. He thought that Locke was involved in treasonous activity, but he couldn't prove it. He wanted to make sure there was a record of his doubts, should anything happen to him."

Now her grandmother frowned. "But why did he send these letters to you, dearest? What could he have expected you to do with this information?"

"I'm certain that he didn't tell Mama for fear she would worry, and that her health would suffer. Papa said he trusted me to do what was right."

"And what did you take that to mean?" Mrs. Tremayne asked in a gentle tone.

Amanda did not bother to hide her feelings. "Avenge him," she replied heatedly. "Avenge him and right the wrongs done to our family."

Mrs. Tremayne's dark eyes went wide. "Amanda, you can't . . . This is a job for our family solicitor, or for the Admiralty, not for a young girl!"

"I wrote to our solicitor, Grandmama. Mr. Cosgrove said there wasn't enough evidence, that the letters were nothing more than hearsay. Then I wrote to the Admiralty, but they did not even respond."

"This is why you wanted to come to London, dearest, isn't it?" Mrs. Tremayne reached out a hand and covered Amanda's. "You wanted to exonerate your father."

Amanda gave her grandmother's fingers a gentle squeeze. "We had to leave Dorset. After the posters proclaiming Papa's sentence went up, too many people knew who we were. We needed to move to a large city, to hide ourselves from prying eyes. With the Admiralty in London, it seemed the logical choice. I hope . . . I hope you don't think less of me for bringing you here."

"Oh, my dearest child." Tears shone in Mrs. Tremayne's eyes. "I would never think that. Do not reproach yourself. Indeed, we are very comfortable here."

Amanda made a moue of distaste as she surveyed the threadbare carpets and battered furniture that graced their dim, cramped quarters. "You have a talent for exaggeration, Grandmama."

The elderly woman smiled slightly. "Perhaps. But you must finish your story. Where does Harry Morgan fit into all this?"

Amanda sighed. Yes, Harry. Harry, who had quarreled with her in the carriage all the way home. He had not been flattered when she told him he'd make a better fishwife than a lieutenant. "I went to the Admiralty several months ago, to make an appointment to see the First Lord, or any member of the Navy Board. Once they knew who I was the clerks wouldn't let me in, and one of them ordered the marines at the door to escort me from the building, and never permit me to enter it again."

"Never!" exclaimed Mrs. Tremayne. "What infamous treatment!"

Amanda's jaw tightened, and for a moment all she could do was nod. "And that is when I dragged Harry into this mess. Do you remember when he called on us, and said that he would do anything in his power to help us?"

Mrs. Tremayne's concerned demeanor evolved into guardedness. "Yes. Harry has always been a dear boy, if a trifle . . . ah, shall we say, obvious about his affection for you."

"For me?" Amanda's vision blurred at the edges. "What are you talking about, Grandmama? Harry and I have been friends forever, but affection? We grew up together, rough and tumble like two puppies. He thinks of me as nothing more than an incorrigible younger sister."

"Mmm." Mrs. Tremayne measured Amanda with in-scrutable eyes. "I might be mistaken. Go on, dearest."

"Well, I learned that Admiral Locke had arrived in Town—to a hero's welcome. To think, that blackguard receiving a hero's welcome, after what he did to us! It is beyond imagining." Amanda reined in her mounting fury. "Then, a few days later, the *Morning Post* said that the admiral would host a grand ball at his town house."

"A ball? Dearest, why should that concern you?"

"I thought that if I could see Locke in person, I could find out if Papa's suspicions were true. And if they were"—she swallowed around her guilt—"I hoped to find some evidence of his crimes."

Mrs. Tremayne closed her eyes and shook her head; the lappets on her cap swayed to and fro with the move-ment. "You are as headstrong as your father ever was. Or worse. What happened?"

"I borrowed a dress from Madame Molyneux and went as Mrs. Seagrave." She pretended not to notice her grandmother's disapproval and continued. "When I got to the house, I went to Locke's study and found a secret compartment in his desk. Before I could find what was in it, I heard someone coming and had to leave." She didn't want to tell her grandmother about Captain Ev-erly, and the part he played that evening. She didn't want to think about it too much herself.

A sigh of relief escaped her grandmother's lips. "Thank goodness you were not discovered. And was Harry involved in this plan of yours?"

"No," Amanda answered. "Not really. I asked him to get me in to the party, and to see me safely home after-ward. I had to tell him everything, though."

"Oh, dearest, do you realize the risk you took? This is not a childish lark, Amanda. If you had been caught, the penalties would have been severe. And if Madame Molyneux, *faux* Frenchwoman that she is, had discovered your ruse, it would have cost you your position."

"I know, Grandmama, but I thought it worth the chance. Papa was innocent, and Locke is to blame. He is neck-deep in treason, I know it."

"You cannot be certain, dearest."

"Someone has to have a record of those orders," insisted Amanda. "Everything points back to Admiral Locke."

Confusion hovered in Mrs. Tremayne's eyes. "If Locke is a traitor, dearest, why would he keep a record of his crimes? Wouldn't that incriminate him if he were caught?"

Amanda paused. "I don't know. But there was something in that secret drawer, something Locke doesn't want anyone to see."

"Well, whatever it is, dearest, you will never know now." Mrs. Tremayne picked up her spoon and stirred her cooling soup.

Amanda contemplated her own dish. Her grandmother was right. There was no way she could return to Locke's house.

"So what will you do now?" Mrs. Tremayne's voice echoed the one in Amanda's head.

Misery closed in a tight fist around Amanda's throat. "I don't know," she whispered. "To have come so far, only to fall short . . ."

Mrs. Tremayne cut a slice of bread, added a meager slice of cheese, and handed it to Amanda. "Early in your father's naval career, his letters home were rife with tales of derring-do, of battles fought and prizes won. I suspected at the time that he wanted to impress the young lady he wanted to marry—your mother." She smiled knowingly at Amanda. "Of course, he also mentioned a number of his commanders, men who impressed your father with their skills and intelligence and dedication to duty. Men like Nelson, Adam Duncan, and Sir John Jervis, who later became Admiral Lord St. Vincent. As a matter of fact, I believe Lord St. Vincent is here in town, to be close to the Admiralty."

Amanda stared back at her grandmother. "He is in London?"

Mrs. Tremayne brushed a few crumbs from her fingers. "Eat your soup, dearest, before it gets cold. Yes, I recall reading that he has a house in the West End. Your father admired St. Vincent for his stalwart sense of duty, and his passion for justice."

"Justice is what we need, Grandmama. Oh, I pray he can help us. I must get a note to Harry at once." She leaped from her chair and hurried to the writing desk. She pulled out paper and ink and began to scratch a hasty message.

"Do be careful, dearest," advised Mrs. Tremayne. "Harry may be fond of you, but you must not take advantage of him."

"I am going to ask that he accompany me, nothing more. Harry is a friend, Grandmama. Besides, even if he did feel some sort of romantic attachment to me, which is utterly ridiculous in the first place, he knows he could never marry me—I'm a traitor's daughter. An alliance with our family would sink his career." Amanda did not glance up from her writing; only an increased zeal in the scratch of pen against paper marked her agitation.

"You must do what you think is best," Mrs. Tremayne murmured. She straightened in her chair, clasping her hands in her lap. "But I want you to promise me one thing."

Amanda folded the letter and placed it in the envelope. "What is it, Grandmama?"

"Look at me, child." The older woman's words rang like a captain's command.

Amanda lifted her head, surprised. Rarely did her grandmother raise her voice.

Mrs. Tremayne cleared her throat. "I know you would go to great lengths to clear your father's name, Amanda, but I do not wish you to put yourself in any further danger. You are the only family I have left. If nothing comes of your visit to Admiral Lord St. Vincent, I want you to promise that you'll agree to return with me to Dorset. I miss the sea. I know you miss it, too."

Amanda's face crumpled. "But, Grandmama, we can't go back. The last time—"

"That was over a year ago, dearest, and we can settle in a different portion of the county."

"What about money? 'Tis a vulgar topic, but one we

must consider. Without my income from the dressmaker, we will be hard-pressed to find a suitable living arrangement."

"We shall have money," professed Mrs. Tremayne. "I will sell my jewelry. I have been reluctant to part with it, for it will be your inheritance, but I will do it for your sake. The rubies in particular should fetch a good price. There is enough for a small cottage, perhaps, with a garden."

"Your jewelry! Grandmama, you mustn't."

The older woman drew herself up further. "I can, Amanda, and I will, if it means seeing you safely settled. You must think about the future; I will not live much longer."

Amanda fell silent. Her grandmother was willing to sacrifice her most prized possessions to insure their comfort. Amanda's comfort. Guilt tugged at her. To return to Dorset without revealing her father's innocence was to admit utter defeat.

"Promise me, dearest."

Amanda hesitated. She must consider her grandmother's needs as well as her own. The young woman lowered her head and sighed. "Very well. I promise."

"Your father would be proud of you, Amanda," Mrs. Tremayne said softly. "You have accomplished far more than any other young lady would ever dream of doing. You did what you could."

"I am not finished yet, Grandmama. We must hope that Admiral Lord St. Vincent will listen, and that he can aid us." Amanda brandished the sealed letter. "This battle is not over yet."

She should have known better than to pin all her hopes on one man. Amanda tried to reason with herself, but logic was a cold comfort. A tear slid down her cheek, followed by another. She tried to hold them back, at least until she and Harry had attained the privacy of the coach, but to no avail. The floodgates opened; she laid her head in her hands and sobbed.

"There now, Amanda . . . it's all right." Harry reached

into his jacket and handed her his handkerchief. "You'll feel better after you've had a good cry."

Amanda stared at him through the mist of her tears, incredulous. Was Harry trying to comfort her, or was he just being dense? "Better? St. Vincent had his staff throw us from the house, Harry! He wouldn't even see me. How much worse can it get?"

"Well . . ." Harry scratched his jaw. "At least he didn't call the watch."

Amanda blew her nose. Passersby stared at them as she and Harry stood on the sidewalk outside St. Vincent's town house, but she was beyond caring. "I thought he could help me, Harry. I really did. He was my last hope."

Harry lifted his shoulders in a gesture of helplessness. "I'm sorry, Amanda."

"So am I." A black gulf of despair and guilt yawned within her; she began to shake. She stared up at the house with loathing. " 'Get that traitor's brat out of my house.' The whole street must have heard him."

"You had no idea he would react that way," Harry was quick to point out.

Her laughter cut like a razor's edge. "No idea he would humiliate me? Trample all my hopes underfoot because he refused to listen?"

Harry set his hands on her shoulders and turned her to face him. "Amanda, go home—go back to Dorset. You have done all you can here."

Amanda stamped her booted foot. "I'm tired of being treated like a stray dog. 'Go home, Amanda, go home.' I need someone to listen to me, Harry, someone who can help me find the evidence I know exists."

The young lieutenant shook his head; the first traces of anger lined his face. "What you're asking is impossible. I have done all I can for you, Amanda, really! And what I've accomplished already has probably harmed my career. You must accept the fact that you've lost. You cannot do anything more."

Amanda jerked away from him. "But what about my

father's letters? They all but prove his innocence. There must be something I can do."

Harry raked a hand through his coppery hair. "Well, perhaps I can make some inquiries. But don't get your hopes up," he warned. "Go back to Dorset with your grandmother and leave this to me. I'll do what I can."

"But—"

He cut her off with an impatient wave. "No more 'buts,' Amanda. This is not something you should be doing. I told you that from the start. In case you've forgotten, you're a woman. No one wants to deal with a woman who acts like a man."

"I do not act like a man!" She stamped her foot again. Oh, if he continued this pontificating, she would slap him! Never had Harry sounded so pompous, so arrogant.

"Your behavior hasn't exactly been ladylike. Spying, telling lies, running down alleyways in the middle of the night, stealing property from your employer—"

"I *borrowed* that dress."

Harry rolled his eyes. "Stop trying to mince words. Ever since you began this crusade you've become a veritable hoyden. It's not proper, not by half."

"If my determination intimidates you, Harry, then just come out and say it." Her anger acted like a tonic; the hot flames of fury held her despair at bay. "Are you telling me that a woman cannot concern herself with her family's honor? Balderdash! I refuse to sit by and allow Locke to get away with murder."

"There you go again," Harry said tightly. "Now who sounds like a fishwife?"

Amanda gasped. "Is that what this is about? You're still angry with me from the other night, aren't you?" She would have turned her back and walked away in a fit of pique had Harry not seized her hands in an iron grip.

"That's not the point. Damn it all, Amanda, look at me! I just want you to be safe. You promised your grandmother that you'd go back to Dorset if this gambit failed. And as much as you don't want to admit it, you *have* failed. You asked me once if I was a man of my word. Are you a lady of yours?"

Amanda's reply died before it reached her lips. Her anger ebbed away; the tide of sorrow rolled in. She thought of her grandmother. "Yes," she whispered. "I cannot prate about family honor and disregard my own. Of course I will honor my promise."

"You'll be happier in the country. And I'll come to visit you when I can."

Amanda read the relief on Harry's face. She pulled her hands from his. "Happiness doesn't matter for me, Harry, no matter where I live. My father is dead, my mother is dead, my family name is reviled, and there is nothing I can do about it."

"Things will be better when the war is over," Harry stated. "Everyone will forget what happened, and life will return to normal."

"Harry," Amanda whispered, "you are ever the idealist."

Chapter Five

"Have you reported all of this to Carlisle?" St. Vincent demanded, his snow white brows drawn together in a line.

"Of course, my lord," Everly replied. "Although I am rather at a loss as to how I must proceed. To gain access to Locke's house again, I must be an invited guest, and I hardly know the man as it is."

St. Vincent sat back in his chair. "There are ways, my boy, there are ways. Carlisle will come up with something. The man is as devious as the devil himself."

This description did little to encourage Everly. He endeavored to keep the doubt from his expression. "As you say, my lord. I am to meet him this afternoon to discuss our options."

"You did well, boy, for your first assignment," said St. Vincent with a slight smile. "This whole affair is foreign ground, but you've upheld my faith in you."

The admiral was never fulsome in his compliments. In fact, praise was rare and hard-won. Everly sat up straighter in his chair. "Thank you, my lord."

"I have made some inquiries at the Admiralty as to—yes, Finch, what is it?" St. Vincent looked to the doorway, irritated.

"Pardon the interruption, my lord," said the footman, "but there are persons below asking to see you. They claim the matter is urgent." He crossed to the desk and offered a salver to the admiral. St. Vincent took the letter from the tray and waved Finch aside.

The admiral broke the seal and scanned the contents. His eyes grew dark with anger. "What the devil!" he roared. "Of all the effrontery! And you let this creature into my house?" His piercing gaze skewered Finch where he stood.

The footman cringed. "Y—yes, my lord."

"Well, I'll not stand for it." The admiral lurched to his feet and strode past the astonished footman to the fireplace; he threw the missive into the flames. "I want her out of here now!"

The footman edged to the doorway. "She was most insistent, my lord—I do not think she will leave without making a scene."

"Then get Parkin to help you! Get Adams, get Royce! Just get that traitor's brat out of my house!" St. Vincent's bellow reverberated through the halls.

Alarmed, Everly rose to his feet. He had never seen his patron so incensed. "My lord," he began.

St. Vincent glared at him. The old man's quivering cheeks were mottled red and purple with the force of his rage. "This does not concern you, boy. Wait here." Shouting to his staff, he followed Finch out into the hall.

What had come over the admiral? Something in that letter had sent him off like an overloaded 32-pounder. Everly moved toward the fire. Part of the letter had fallen to the hearth, its edges blackened. He bent to pick it up, ignoring the twinge in his leg. Although the message seemed written in haste, the hand was distinctly feminine. Who was this woman, and why did her presence have such a profound effect on St. Vincent? Curiosity got the better of Everly. With the fire tongs, he rescued another scrap from fiery death.

He blew out the flames before they consumed the paper, but not in time to save much of the text. All that remained was part of the signature, enough to read the last name: "Tremayne." Everly stood, stunned, as though a thunderbolt had struck him. Tremayne. A name steeped in infamy.

No wonder St. Vincent had exploded. Captain Tremayne's treason had rocked the Royal Navy to its very foundations; to have a distinguished, well-respected post captain turn his coat was unthinkable. Everly stared at the charred scrap in his hands. Tremayne's daughter must have written this. What did she hope to accomplish by coming here? Apparently she had not realized that of all the officers in the navy, St. Vincent had the least sympathy for anyone connected with convicted traitors.

Everly tossed the paper back into the fire and watched the flames devour it, shriveling it to a thin sheet of ash before a draft sucked it up the chimney. A door slammed somewhere downstairs. Everly cocked an ear toward the corridor; the shouting had been replaced by muted mutterings. Driven by a sentiment he couldn't explain, he walked over to the window and looked down toward the street. A small figure in a drab cloak and bonnet stood on the sidewalk, her head in her hands, comforted by a young navy lieutenant. Everly frowned and turned away. He went to the sideboard and poured himself a glass of brandy to wash away the bitter taste of self-recrimination. He was partially responsible for the lady's grief, for he had not been able to save her father.

He had been duty-bound to sit on the tribunal that judged Captain Tremayne. A court martial required the participation of at least five post captains, and in time of war this was no small feat. The *Hyperion* had been in Malta for refitting when Everly received word of the trial; four other captains were in port, he made the fifth. With his ship temporarily out of service, he had had no choice.

Captain Alexander Tremayne was charged with the most grievous crime of treason, of violating Articles of War numbers three, four, and six. Namely, he stood accused of transporting men, guns, and ammunition to the French republicans. Captain Tremayne denied all the charges, and claimed that his commanding officer, Admiral Locke, had ordered him on this mission. He further stated that Locke told him the men were French royalists, men who sought to start a counterrevolution that would spread to Paris. Tremayne had been stunned to learn from the tribunal that the very men he had transported to the French coast, men he claimed had worn the fleur-de-lis of the Bourbon monarchy while aboard his ship, had in actuality marched to reinforce a failing republican garrison. This garrison had later repulsed and driven back Wellington's forces, inflicting heavy losses and preventing the English from securing a much-needed strategic advantage in the region.

Shaken, Captain Tremayne insisted that Admiral Locke had given him those orders. The mission was so secretive that Locke commanded Tremayne to destroy the orders after he had read them. He did so, even kept the details from his own crew, but he had duly recorded the mission in his ship's log. To his shock and dismay, he discovered later that this particular page of the log had been cut out. The Admiralty had no record of this mission, and Locke denied giving Tremayne those orders. Everly scowled at the memory. Tremayne had not impressed him as a man capable of treason, and the circumstances surrounding the missing orders seemed suspicious at best. Everly had wanted to begin an investigation to uncover more details, but unfortunately his fellow captains were not inclined to be so generous. After much debate, Everly had to concede the likelihood of Tremayne's guilt; the evidence against him was overwhelming, and the man had nothing tangible to offer in his defense. The tribunal found him guilty of treason, and he was hanged the next morning. Naval justice was nothing if not swift.

Everly rubbed his jaw. Locke had been involved in that incident, and was now suspected of treason himself. The "Lion of the Mediterranean" might well have framed Captain Tremayne for his own crimes, but why? Had the captain discovered something shady about Locke, forcing Locke to resort to drastic measures? That had all happened over a year ago—had Locke's treasonous activities gone unchecked for so long? If so, Captain Tremayne was not the only victim of Locke's despicable doings. Everly's thoughts returned to the poor woman in the street.

Everly glanced toward the open door of the study. Why hadn't St. Vincent made the connection between Tremayne and Locke, and realized the link between their investigation and this girl's appearance? He stared into the amber depths of his brandy as if to divine the answer. St. Vincent had never approved of Captain Tremayne's liberal politics and reformist tendencies; would he let that prejudice blind him to the truth? It seemed so. Perhaps Locke had counted on that reaction.

Heavy footsteps heralded St. Vincent's return. "My apologies, Everly," he grumbled. "Poor form to fly off the handle like that."

"No apologies are necessary, my lord," Everly replied. He swallowed the last of his brandy and set his glass aside.

St. Vincent stood before the hearth, breathing heavily. He mopped his forehead with his kerchief. "Captain Tremayne's chit thought I would help her exonerate her father. Of all the cheek! You sat on the man's tribunal, didn't you, Everly?"

"Yes, my lord." A muscle twitched at Everly's temple.

"Shameful. Utterly shameful. But I sent her packing." St. Vincent wandered to the sideboard and uncorked the decanter of brandy for himself.

Everly felt another pang of sympathy for Miss Tremayne. It was one thing for a hardened sailor to withstand the force of St. Vincent's anger, quite another for a member of the fairer sex to do the same. "Your pardon, my lord, but I must take my leave. I must attend to a few other matters before my meeting with Lord Carlisle."

"Eh, just so. I won't delay you any longer." The old admiral set the decanter aside, unopened. "I wanted you to know that I am making inquiries at the Admiralty about another command for you. Don't get your hopes up, Everly. I am an old man, and my influence is not what it once was."

Everly smiled. "Thank you, my lord. I appreciate your efforts on my behalf."

St. Vincent harrumphed. "Mind you, you won't be seeing another ship at all if you don't bring me that traitor's head on a platter. Keep me apprised, my boy."

"Yes, my lord." Everly drew himself to attention, then

departed. In the foyer, he recovered his cloak and hat from Parkin, whose frazzled expression took Everly by surprise. Something had penetrated the servant's reserve at last, but it had taken an embarrassing fracas to do it. Everly murmured a polite farewell before he stepped out into the brisk autumn air.

The young woman and her escort still stood by the curb, embroiled in a heated argument. Everly could hear their raised voices quite clearly. So could everyone else who passed by; the pair were garnering more than their share of curious and disapproving attention, but neither appeared to notice. Everly could not help but overhear as he descended the steps.

"Happiness doesn't matter for me, Harry," the woman claimed, "no matter where I live. My father is dead, my mother is dead, my family name is reviled, and there is nothing I can do about it."

The lieutenant said something else, but Everly paid no attention. He stopped dead in the water. That voice—he knew that woman's voice. It belonged to Mrs. Seagrave, his mysterious and alluring widow from Locke's ball.

As he approached the pair, the young lady looked up. Shocked recognition crossed her delicate features, and she didn't bother to hide it. All traces of color fled her cheeks. Small wonder. In all likelihood she had thought she'd never see him again. Everly allowed himself a thin smile of satisfaction. She may have taken pains to disguise her name, but she could not disguise her appearance. Dowdy clothes and drab colors could not conceal those lush curves, nor could that ridiculously oversized bonnet hide her delicate features and delectable full lips. His groin tightened.

She stared at him as though he were a ghost, her eyes huge pools of velvety brown. "C-captain Everly!" she sputtered.

The young lieutenant turned, spied Everly's gold epaulets, and immediately stiffened to attention. He touched the brim of his bicorne in salute. "Sir."

"Lieutenant," Everly acknowledged. His eyes swiveled

like gun sights back to the lady's pale face. "Miss Tremayne."

He did not think it possible, but she turned paler still. Everly tamped down his urge to interrogate the girl then and there. He could not start barking questions here on the street as if he were on his own quarterdeck. Even he had learned discretion over the years.

"It is a pleasure to see you again, Miss Tremayne," he said quietly.

The lieutenant scowled at Everly and stepped in front of his companion. "With all due respect, sir, I do not think it proper that you have any contact with Miss Tremayne. You've done enough to her and her family as it is."

Everly raised an eyebrow at the youth. "Are you a friend of the family, Lieutenant?" His own officers knew to tread lightly when he used that particular soft, dangerous tone, but the lieutenant plowed on, oblivious.

The young man's chin came up. "I am, sir."

Irritation grated against Everly's patience; he did not have time to mince words with this overprotective stripling. He knew from experience that the lady could take care of herself. "Tell me then, Lieutenant—were you friend enough to escort Miss Tremayne to Admiral Locke's ball last week?"

Miss Tremayne shot Everly a guarded glance.

"I was, sir," the lieutenant replied with undisguised hostility.

"Indeed." Everly ignored the young man's belligerent stare, focusing instead on Miss Tremayne's ashen countenance. Questions ricocheted through his mind. This youth was a newly minted officer; the white facings on his jacket showed not a smudge of smoke, tar, or gunpowder. Had Miss Tremayne recruited him into her little plot? Everly thought not. The youth's misguided chivalry and outraged bluster suggested that he was too honest and forthright for spying.

Which brought him back to his primary focus: what the devil was this chit doing in Locke's study? She had every right to loathe Locke as much as she loathed Everly himself; he knew now why she had run away from him at the ball. Yet he had to consider that she might have a part in this treasonous conspiracy. His instincts told him she did not, but he wanted to hear the truth from her own lips. Her own very luscious, rosy, kissable lips.

Everly shook himself. Miss Tremayne had lied to him, run from him, and nearly planted him a facer worthy of Gentleman Jackson. And now all he wanted to do was kiss her. Their collision in the garden must have addled his wits.

A carriage drew up to the curb, to the lieutenant's obvious relief. "If you will excuse us, Captain, I must see Miss Tremayne home."

"A moment," Everly interjected. "Miss Tremayne and I have some unfinished business."

"I have nothing to say to you, Captain," the lady said in clipped tones. She wrapped herself in her mousy brown cloak as if the drab garment provided protection against his presence.

He smiled, and tried his best to make the gesture reach his eyes. "I would like to continue our discussion of the other evening. Admiral Lord St. Vincent is my patron, and has employed me on a matter of great importance. I believe you might be able to help me."

"Help you?" Her reply carried a wealth of disbelief. "Why should I help you, after what you've done to my family?"

Everly leaned closer to her, an almost conspiratorial pose. "Because we both seem to want to know what is in Locke's study."

She started. The tip of her tongue darted out to moisten her lips. "Very well," she agreed.

Everly wrenched his attention away from that lovely mouth. He straightened up and motioned to his own carriage, which had just pulled up ahead of the first. "I will be very happy to see Miss Tremayne home, Lieutenant. Surely you have other duties which require your attention." This time he made sure his tone was that of a captain who expected his orders to be obeyed.

The lieutenant hesitated.

Miss Tremayne laid a reassuring hand on her companion's arm. "It's all right, Harry. I'm sure that Captain Everly will see that no harm comes to me. I will see you later."

"Are you certain of this, Amanda?" The lieutenant hovered by her side, glaring daggers at Everly.

She gave a tiny nod. "I'll be fine."

The younger man made a strangled sound of disagreement.

"I would hate to make your departure an order, Lieutenant," said Everly quietly.

"Sir." The lieutenant snapped to attention, sullenness exuding from every inch of his lanky form. He shot one last worried look at Miss Tremayne, then climbed into his own carriage.

Everly watched him depart. How was that young officer involved in all of this? Such protectiveness was usually found in brothers, fathers—or lovers. A hot spurt of something that felt suspiciously like jealousy shot down Everly's spine. He scowled. Why should he concern himself with Miss Tremayne's amours? Bad enough that he could barely keep his eyes from her. Angry with himself, he set a tight clamp on his emotions and hoped it would endure at least for the duration of their conversation.

He bowed stiffly and gestured to the open carriage door. "After you, Miss Tremayne. We have a great deal to discuss."

Amanda ignored the hand Captain Everly offered her, avoided looking at him as she climbed into the coach. As much as she tried, she couldn't fathom his mood. One moment he seemed perfectly agreeable, the next hard and wooden, almost angry. She peeked at him from beneath her lashes. At the moment, sitting across from her in his uniformed splendor, he was unreadable. Impassive. She sighed.

The soft sound caught his attention; Amanda found herself the focus of the captain's intense blue eyes. She fought the urge to squirm in her seat. Suddenly the view from the carriage window was very appealing.

"I realize now why you were so shocked to learn my name, Miss Tremayne," he said, breaking the awkward silence. His rich baritone sent tiny shivers across her skin. "And why you ran away from me."

She spared him a curt nod, disturbed by his nearness in these close confines. She was reminded too much of the alcove.

"Although what puzzles me most," continued Everly, "is what you were doing at Locke's ball in the first place, and under an assumed name."

Amanda wrapped her arms close to her body and clamped her mouth shut. This man helped convict her father on false charges. She did not owe him an answer or an explanation.

He persisted. "Did it have anything to do with your father?"

Amanda could not help herself; her head twitched in Everly's direction. The captain noted her reaction and relaxed back into the padded squabs.

"It does, doesn't it?" he asked.

"Even if your guess is correct, Captain, my affairs are none of your concern." Amanda concentrated on the scenery passing outside the windows, for the look in Captain Everly's eyes, blue as the Aegean Sea, made thinking difficult. Botheration. She was mooning over this man like a lovestruck widgeon. He was the enemy. He was dangerous. She must remember that.

"Your affairs do concern me," Everly countered, "especially where traitors are involved."

That got Amanda's full attention. "Are you accusing me of treason, sirrah? The apple does not fall far from the tree, is that it?"

The captain smiled a small, infuriating smile. Amanda uttered a little gasp of indignation, then shut her mouth with an audible snap. The man seemed to know just how to provoke her.

"I admire your pluck, Miss Tremayne," he chuckled. "Your outrage rings true."

Amanda forced her reply through clenched teeth. "From what I know of you, Captain, you do not know truth when you see it." The captain took her meaning exactly as she'd intended; she was gratified to see his amusement evaporate.

His eyes narrowed. "I can understand our reluctance to confide in me, but I was sincere when I told you that you might be able to help me."

She slid a sidelong glance at him. Once more, his face was unreadable. "And how is that, Captain? Why would you need help from a traitor's daughter?"

"There is treason afoot in the Admiralty, and I have been commanded to expose the traitor."

Amanda sat in stunned silence for a moment. "You work for the Crown?"

"Just so. And Admiral Locke may be the key, and I suspect he is connected to your father's conviction, as well. Now you know why I am so interested in your presence at his party." Everly leaned forward and propped his hands on his knees. "What were you doing there, Miss Tremayne? Why were you in Locke's study?"

She bit her lip, consumed by silent speculation. A traitor in the Admiralty. So Locke wasn't working alone. That would explain why there was no record of her father's mission. Whoever the traitor was, he and Locke had conspired to eliminate her father. What confused her most was that Captain Everly was working against Locke, not for him. Had she been mistaken in her estimate of his character?

"Miss Tremayne!" Everly snapped.

Amanda jumped. "I—I was not attending."

Everly sighed and shook his head. "I sincerely hope you are not involved with Admiral Locke or his fellows," he said. "I would hate to have you arrested."

"Arrested?" she squeaked. Alarm constricted her throat. "But I have done nothing. Locke is a blackguard, and I intend to prove it. He framed my father, who took the blame for Locke's crimes. My father was a loyal officer—he was innocent!"

The stern lines of Everly's face softened. "I respect

your regard for your father. For your sake, however, I hope that something more than fervent conviction drove you to rifle through Locke's personal belongings. You put yourself in great peril, Miss Tremayne."

"I have letters from my father, letters detailing his suspicions about Admiral Locke, but no one would listen. No one at the Admiralty, no one on the Navy Board. I had to take matters into my own hands."

"Letters?" Everly's golden brows arched toward his hairline. "What do these letters contain?"

"Documentation of my father's suspicions about Admiral Locke. Activities, dates, apparent consequences."

"Why did he send this information to you, and not to the Admiralty, or even to his solicitor?"

"He tried to warn the Admiralty, but he also feared that Locke was not working alone, so he sent home a copy of the information. He trusted me to do what was best."

"I don't think he meant for you to go off half-cocked like this," Everly muttered. "You should have given the information to you family solicitor and let him deal with it."

Amanda twisted her hands together in her lap. "After we received word of the trial, our solicitor respectfully declined to represent us in any further legal matters." Try as she might, she could not keep the bitterness from her voice.

"Then he was a fool," Everly said. He stared straight into her eyes; his azure gaze captivated her. "Listen to me, Miss Tremayne. This is not a matter for a woman of your sensibilities. Give me your father's letters, they may aid me in my investigation. I assure you that I will do my utmost to find out what Locke is hiding. If I find evidence to exonerate your father, I promise you that I will."

"You want me to trust you with my father's letters? Do you take me for a gudgeon, Captain?" Her scorn sliced through the air between them. Surely he did not think her so naïve! She was not convinced that he wouldn't destroy the letters; she vowed not to let them leave her care.

Everly let out an exasperated sigh. "No, Miss Tremayne. You are many things, but I do not think you are a fool."

Amanda wasn't sure whether to be flattered or piqued. "Don't you?" she accused.

"No," he insisted. "What have I done—lately—to earn your disfavor?"

"You never asked my direction. We have been driving around in circles for the past quarter hour."

She had embarrassed him; a slow wave of color washed over his face from jaw to brow. "You're quite right, Miss Tremayne. I can be very single-minded at times. If you would be so kind?"

Amanda gave him her address, and Captain Everly opened a window and relayed it to his coachmen. The steady clop-clop of the horses' hooves combined with noises from the street to dull the silence between them.

"Allow me to apologize," Everly offered with a small, self-deprecating smile. "Too much time ashore has compromised what manners I have left."

Amanda smiled back in spite of herself. He was charming, wickedly so. "About the letters, Captain . . ."

Everly sat up, intent.

"It's not that I do not wish to aid your investigation," she continued, "but I have come too far to be shunted aside now. I will let you read my father's letters, but they must remain in my possession."

He scanned her face as if searching for duplicity. He must have found none, for he nodded. "Very well, Miss Tremayne. I agree to your terms."

Relief bloomed within her; she sighed. "Meet me tomorrow afternoon by the gates to Green Park at half-past three. I will bring the letters."

Everly's expressive mouth broadened into a pleased smile. Laugh lines appeared around his eyes. Amanda's heart staggered sideways in her breast, and she looked quickly away. Oh, heaven help her if she became too fond of that smile; Everly had yet to redeem himself. She could not trust him until he had.

The carriage pulled to a halt in front of the lodging house. Everly squinted out the window, his good humor faded.

"You live here?" he asked, incredulous.

Pride stiffened Amanda's spine. " 'Tis the only place my grandmother and I could afford."

Everly seized one of her bare hands in his and stared at her work-worn fingers. The touch of his warm, calloused skin made her dizzy. She jerked her hand away.

"You work to support your family?" His eyes were hooded, his expression inscrutable.

Amanda's neck went hot with shame. "I had no choice, Captain. The Crown seized our lands and what money we had. Faced with the choice of work or starvation, I chose the former. If you must know, I am employed as a seamstress. Now, if you have no more rude or impertinent questions, I must ask you to excuse me."

Amanda would have bolted from the carriage the minute the footman opened the door, but Everly placed a restraining hand on her arm.

"I'm sorry," he said simply. "You did what you must."

This was too much. "I do not want your pity, Captain," she snapped. "Only your assistance. Green Park, tomorrow. Do not keep me waiting."

She caught only a glimpse of Everly's surprised expression before she darted into the lodging house. She uttered an unladylike oath under her breath. Did he expect her to be indebted to him? No doubt he thought himself very magnanimous for helping a poor woman in distress. Of all the arrogant, condescending . . . Amanda paused on the landing, wrestling to cork the genie bottle of her temper. Yes, the captain was arrogant. And condescending. But no matter her opinion of him, right now he was the only one who could help her achieve her father's redemption.

Amanda resumed her ascent at a more dignified pace, and wondered how she was going to tell her grandmother that they were not going back to Dorset.

Chapter Six

Instinct alone prompted Everly to brace himself with his cane as his carriage turned a sharp corner, for his mind was preoccupied. The memory of Miss Amanda Tremayne's lovely face lingered in his imagination, no matter how hard he tried to exorcise it. Egad, she was a fetching thing, even with shadows of distrust in her dark eyes. Fetching, yet prickly as a sea urchin.

The more he thought about the girl, the more she mystified him. She was a walking contradiction. Lovely, but grim. Young, but hard-edged. A pocket Venus who could throw a punch as well as any man. How could she be so idealistic and confident of her ability, yet so reckless, determined, and completely blind to the peril in which she had put herself, let alone the potential consequences of her actions?

Everly found it hard to believe that a slip of a girl had undertaken such a monumental task, or come as far as she had. When he met her in the park, he would have to do his best to convince her that she had done enough, she should allow him to continue the battle. This was no longer her fight. If Locke or any of his ilk found out about her letters, Miss Tremayne would be in considerable danger. He had to protect her, for her own good.

His carriage came to a halt, and Everly stared out at the formal façade that was Boodle's gentleman's club. He hadn't been here in months, ever since . . . well. He'd rather not remember the last time he was here. He pulled the message from his pocket; Grayson MacAllister had slipped it to him earlier in the day. *Meet me at No. 28*

St. James's Street, 4 o'clock. The message was unsigned, but obviously from Carlisle. Secrecy again.

Everly alighted from the carriage. He felt a muscle spasm in his jaw as he made his way up the stairs. Of all the potential meeting places in London, why did Carlisle have to choose this one? No matter. Everly handed his hat and cloak to the porter, but kept his mother-of-pearl inlaid cane by his side. More rain in the air, more pain in his leg. He was growing weary of this.

"Thomas will show you the way, Captain," said the porter, before Everly could say anything.

So, he was expected. In unfamiliar waters, a captain did not *like* to be expected. Alert, Everly followed the footman up the stairs to a private parlor near the back of the building. The room was empty. The footman bowed and departed, closing the door behind him. Everly settled down in a chair by the hearth.

He had never been in this particular room. It was much smaller than any of the other parlors, but close surroundings did not bother him. After all, a frigate's wardroom was hardly larger than this, with a much lower ceiling and worse smell. No, the problem was not the room, but the furnishings. The mahogany furniture with dark leather upholstery, the black marble mantelpiece, and the heavy bottle green velvet curtains which framed the single window all contributed to a rather Stygian atmosphere. Some might feel cozy in a room like this, but Everly felt downright claustrophobic. He shifted in his chair, feeling a sudden longing for the bright, open sea and the feel of wind against his face.

Minutes trickled past like treacle from a spoon, and the longer Everly waited, the more annoyed he became. Where the deuce was Carlisle? He checked his timepiece yet again. A full quarter hour had passed. Stiff and awkward, he rose from his seat and yanked on the bellpull, determined to get to the bottom of this.

An elderly servant, stooped with age but still spry, answered Everly's call. "Yes, sir?"

Everly frowned. "I've never seen you here before."

"I've been employed here for over forty years, sir," said the man with great dignity.

"Hmmm. No matter." Everly paced before the mantel. "I was supposed to meet a certain gentleman here, but he has not arrived. Is there any message for me?"

The footman shut the door. "Patience is a virtue, Captain, especially in my business." Before Everly's eyes the man straightened up, his hunched shoulders disappeared, and he seemed to grow a foot taller. He approached Everly with a confident stride.

Everly gripped the head of his cane, stunned. "Carlisle?"

The earl made Everly an elegant, self-mocking bow, then put a finger to his lips. "Softly, Captain, if you please. I regret the deception, but I had to be certain you were not followed, and that we were insured complete privacy."

Everly examined Carlisle up and down, from his powdered wig to his rusty black livery, lingering with incredulity on the complex makeup that had transformed the earl into an old man, complete with wrinkles and liver spots. "Forty years' service, indeed. You have a flair for the dramatic, my lord."

Carlisle grinned, displaying yellowed teeth. "I ran off to join a traveling theater company when I was fifteen, and actually managed to learn a few things before my father found me and dragged me home."

Everly's eyes narrowed. "Why were you so certain I'd wait for you?"

"You don't strike me as the type of man to leave in a fit of pique," answered the earl. "This mission is too important to you, and to England. I meant to join you sooner, but several gentlemen in the gaming room have been quite demanding, and kept me busy."

Carlisle must have noted Everly's surprise, for he continued. "Part of my disguise is fitting in to my surroundings. With a recent influx of members, the club management has had to hire more staff, so a new face—even an older one—isn't unusual. No one would recognize me, dressed like this."

"Quite so," Everly agreed. "Now that you're here—how should I proceed on this rather delicate matter?"

Carlisle's eyes shone with cunning. "As it happens, Admiral Locke is also a member of Boodle's. His presence has all but eliminated the club's reputation for dullness."

Everly raised an eyebrow. "Does that have anything to do with why you asked me here?"

"It does, Captain. Locke is one of the demanding gentlemen in the gaming room. Gambling is one of his favorite pursuits, and he has a taste for deep play. He believes that many gentlemen of the *beau monde* think themselves above his touch, so Locke prefers the company of navy officers. They have as much blunt as the nobs, but with fewer pretensions."

Everly responded with a humorless smile. "For the most part."

"I have also learned that the admiral's ball was not as successful as he would have liked. It seems that most of the *ton* were not impressed by his hospitality, and Locke did not make many favorable connections. Seems that most of the high sticklers consider him a mushroom, a parvenu."

"So much for the Lion's aspirations," Everly muttered.

Carlisle nodded. "Exactly. To proclaim him a hero is one thing, but to socialize with him, or even have him court one's daughter is quite another. This situation works to our advantage. As a result of last week's disappointment, Locke plans to give a smaller, more intimate card party on Saturday for a circle of friends who share his tastes. This will be the perfect opportunity for you to get back into the house."

"Card party?" Everly waited for Carlisle to elaborate.

"If you wish to call it that. From what I've been able to uncover, Locke has engaged a notorious hostess, Mrs. Danvers, to turn his house into a gaming hell for the evening. Cards, dice, and ladies of questionable repute will be the bill of fare."

Everly met the earl's eyes. He did not need to guess

what Carlisle expected of him. "How am I supposed to get an invitation to these . . . festivities?"

"Simple, Captain. All you need to do is join Locke at the table downstairs. How are you at vingt-et-un?"

"Tolerable, I suppose," Everly mused.

"Splendid. You should also know that Locke tends to socialize with men of rather shady reputation. Play the role of disgruntled captain as well as you do the cards, and I am confident that your virtues will prompt Locke to give you an invitation." Carlisle smiled.

Everly repressed a guffaw. "If I didn't know better, my lord, I'd swear you just insulted me."

"Good luck then, Captain. I shall hope for results." Then, as Everly watched, Carlisle bent his spine, stooped his shoulders, and transformed himself in the span of a few heartbeats into the aged footman who had first entered the room. The result was like watching a butterfly climb back into its cocoon.

Everly straightened his cravat and hoped he had not overestimated his skills at the green baize. "So shall I." He turned to say something more to Carlisle, but the earl had vanished. The door to the hallway stood open.

"Like a bloody ghost," the captain grumbled. "He probably walks through walls."

Everly had no difficulty locating Locke's game of vingt-et-un; the din carried to the top of the stairs. The captain observed the group carefully as he approached the table, peering through the thick fog of cheroot smoke that hovered around them. He recognized several individuals, and the company did not please him.

Facing Everly sat Captain Peyton, a rotund man turned prematurely gray; he had a reputation as a brute who flogged his crew for the slightest infractions. Next to him sat Captain Lambert, the fourth son of an earl, a pretentious fop who had risen through the ranks on influence alone. Across from Lambert was Lieutenant Edward Hale, one of Locke's protégés, a young man with a dangerous temper and a taste for high-stakes gambling. A sterling trio, Everly mused. And at the center of everyone's attention was Admiral Locke, who considered his cards and raised the wager.

"Too rich for my blood," snorted one gentleman, shaking his head.

"Why, you old pirate!" exclaimed Lambert. "I'll match that wager. I'll get the better of you yet."

"That's enough for me," grumbled a middle-aged lieutenant. He flung down his cards in disgust and left the table.

Everly moved in to get a better view.

"Apparently Neville doesn't have the stomach for high stakes," said Lieutenant Hale with a thin, malicious smile. "Perhaps he should stick to playing Pope Joan with his mama on Sundays."

A low roll of laughter greeted this remark.

Captain Lambert stifled a yawn. "Shut up and play, Hale. If you were half as good at the cards as you were at flapping your jaw, you wouldn't find yourself down by five hundred pounds."

Hale bristled. "Watch yourself, Lambert," he growled. "I don't care what rank you hold, or who your father is—one of these days you'll regret baiting me."

"Gentlemen, gentlemen. This is just a friendly game, remember?" Locke revealed his cards with a slight smile. "Twenty-one. I believe this hand goes to me, and the double stakes, as well."

"Locke, you have the devil's own luck," blustered Peyton. The corpulent captain's face flushed an unhealthy claret color. "You must give me a chance to recoup my losses. One more round."

"Not for me—I'm out," announced a rather dandified youth. He scribbled his vowels and added them to the pile of winnings on the table. "As entertaining as this has been, Admiral, I must get ready for the Duke of Atherton's masquerade. How unfortunate that you will not be able to attend; it is sure to be the social event of the Season."

Locke's expression clouded, and Everly realized that the dandy had stung the admiral right where it hurt most.

No doubt Locke had hoped for an invitation from the duke, but hope had eluded him.

"On the contrary, Walbridge," the admiral drawled. "You might enjoy capering about the dance floor in some ridiculous costume, but I prefer more masculine pursuits. Good afternoon." Locke turned his attention back to the table, and began gathering cards back into the deck.

Young Walbridge flushed and stormed out from the room, head held high.

The last civilian at the table, a man with red hair and a sharp face, watched him depart. "Pay no heed to Walbridge and his airs, Admiral," he advised, stubbing out his cheroot. "His father has declared that he must marry this Season—and catch himself a wealthy chit to help him out of dun territory. I hear tell he's even considering a match with a Cit's daughter, because no one else will have him."

"Poor Walbridge. How very . . . uncomfortable for him," Locke commented, much to the merriment of the others. He snapped his fingers at two nearby footmen. "You there—more wine. Dammit, man, do you expect me to get it myself? Look lively!"

"Bring the brandy while you're are it," chimed in Lambert.

The footmen hurried to do as they were bid. Everly noticed that Carlisle was not among them; he expected that the earl had long since departed. He was on his own. He cut through the ring of onlookers and approached a vacant chair. "Your company has thinned somewhat, Admiral," he said. "May I join you?"

Locke glanced up. Everly thought he detected a trace of scorn cross the admiral's face. Then Locke recognized Everly's uniform, and any hint of disdain vanished.

"Ah, another of our distinguished officers. Of course you are welcome to join us, Captain Everly." He waved to a vacant seat.

Everly nodded and accepted the chair next to Captain Lambert.

"This is an unexpected pleasure, Captain," continued

the admiral. "I have not seen you since the party last week. You did not stay long, if I recall."

Everly slouched into his chair. "Forgive me, Admiral, if I seemed a rude guest, but I couldn't stomach any more condescension from the fashionables. They may call me a hero, but they can't bear to look at my battle scars. They don't seem to realize the price we pay for victory."

"Here, here," Peyton agreed, lifting his glass in salute.

Locke considered this remark as he shuffled the cards. "Exactly so, Captain. Little does society know the sacrifices we make on its behalf."

Everly gestured for the footman to pour him a glass of brandy. "And yet they seem to think us beneath them. If it weren't for our efforts, the French tricolor could be flying over Whitehall."

Locke uttered a bark of laughter. "Then you find yourself in good company, Captain. You know everyone here, I think, except Lord Sillsby."

The red-haired lord examined Everly with patent interest, like a fox eyeing a plump pullet. Malice glinted in his dark eyes. "You are rather severe upon the members of the upper ten thousand, Captain."

Everly nodded. "Not without reason, I assure you."

"Oh, I do not doubt it. Your name seems familiar, Captain. Have we met?"

Everly met the man's gaze, unruffled. If Sillsby thought to prompt him into losing his temper, the man was sadly mistaken. "I do not believe so, my lord."

Locke dealt one card facedown to each player, followed by another card faceup. Everly found himself with the ten of diamonds faceup; an auspicious beginning. He looked at his other card. Hmmm. Perhaps not so auspicious, after all.

"No, I am certain I know your name," continued Sillsby. A sly smile stole over his lips.

"Your wager, Everly," prompted Locke.

Everly considered his cards and ignored Sillsby's needling. "I am feeling lucky today, gentlemen," he declared. "One hundred guineas."

A fire kindled in Locke's ice blue eyes. "We shall see how long your luck holds," he replied with a calculated smile.

"I'm in," said Peyton.

"And I," added Lambert. Hale also followed suit.

"Now I have it," Sillsby said, brightening. He gave Locke a vague nod to indicate he would wager the same amount, but kept his spiteful gaze fixed on Everly. "About five months ago, wasn't it, Everly, when your little fiancée jilted you for that pink of the *ton,* Viscount Radbourne? I have it on good authority that she got one look at your limp and ran screaming for her mama. Not surprising that she ended up with Radbourne. Fellow's got two good legs, a handsome face, and a handsome pocketbook to match."

Everly clenched his teeth and signaled for another card. He felt the other men's eyes on him, watching, evaluating. Tension gathered between his shoulder blades. He wouldn't let Sillsby unnerve him, though he longed to draw the man's cork. Too much was at stake here, much more than money. "Miss Felicia Harding was a scatterbrained little hussy, and I am well rid of her," he said in a bored tone.

"Still, it was rather galling, wasn't it?" Sillsby smirked. "I heard that you came here afterward and got yourself so cup-shot that you challenged everyone in the place to a duel before someone took pity on you and dragged you home."

Unpleasant memories danced at the edge of Everly's vision and added their mocking whispers to Sillsby's. He fought them off, concentrating instead on his cards. He would think about Felicia's betrayal later. This was battle, and he was not an unlicked cub to be distracted by such crude means. The ten of diamonds, along with the trey of spades and the seven of hearts, made as good as score as he could get with this hand. His eyes flicked to the cards lying faceup before the other players. Only Hale and Locke had hands likely to rival his own.

Sillsby rattled on. "Worse yet, Radbourne is besotted with her. Makes sheep's eyes at her wherever they go.

Better that she married him than you, Everly, else society might have coined you 'Beauty and the Beast.' "

A strange calm settled over Everly. Sillsby was the sort of bully who enjoyed the pain of others, given either with words or with blows. "No doubt," he agreed affably.

"It really is too bad about that leg, Captain. But I'll wager there are Cyprians aplenty who are willing to overlook it, if you pay them enough."

"If you say so." Everly indicated that he stood firm on his hand.

Across the table, Hale sniggered, but kept his eyes on his cards. He was too devoted to gambling to be diverted from the prospect of winning. Sillsby, however, played like an automaton, paying little attention to the stakes and barely glancing at his cards, so intent was he on getting a rise from Everly. Everly kept a lock on his neutral expression and upped the wager again. Let the bastard sink himself.

"Eighteen," said Locke, turning his cards up.

"Damn!" exclaimed Peyton, throwing down his hand.

"I also have eighteen," said Lambert silkily. "It seems we have a draw."

"Not so fast," said Hale with a sneer. "Nineteen." He reached for the pile of winnings.

"A moment, Lieutenant," Everly interjected. He flipped over his cards. "Twenty."

Hale's face fell. Locke chuckled.

Everly turned to Lord Sillsby. "Unless you have a better hand, my lord."

Sillsby consulted his cards. His eyes flew to his stack of vowels on the table, and all color fled his face. "No," he said flatly. He turned his cards facedown. "The hand is yours."

In ordinary circumstances Everly would have let the man walk away with his pride intact, but today he played a different role. "Oh, come now, Sillsby. We have all revealed our cards. The least you can do is show us the same courtesy."

He reached for Sillsby's cards; the man tried to keep them from Everly, but wasn't quick enough. Everly displayed the cards and tut-tutted. "You really must learn your mathematics, Sillsby. A six, a seven, a deuce, and a knave make twenty-five."

Peyton threw back his head and gave a hearty guffaw. Lambert snickered. Hale smiled the nasty smile of a bully who has just seen a rival get his comeuppance.

"Next time, my lord, perhaps you should pay more attention to your cards." Everly grinned and pocketed his winnings, not bothering to count them.

Sillsby glared at each officer at the table, Everly last of all. His nostrils flared, his lips pressed together in a grim line. "This round goes to you, Captain. Enjoy your winnings. I'm certain you can now purchase any feminine affection you desire." With this last barb, Lord Sillsby rose and stalked from the room.

Locke sipped his brandy and regarded Everly with amusement. "Well done, Captain. Sillsby's a rotten little snipe."

"A snipe with very plump pockets," added Lambert. "I may not like him, but I'll gamble with him."

"He actually thought he could get the better of me with gossip. Men like that don't understand us," Everly said, punctuating this pronouncement with a pompous smile. "We're responsible for ships of the line, while all he cares about is the fall of his cravat. 'Tis no wonder he came out the worse for the encounter. I find that most society bucks have more hair than wit."

A few of the onlookers took umbrage with this pronouncement; Everly noted how they scowled before departing. He cringed inwardly and hoped his reputation survived this mission.

"It seems that a few of our fellow members disagree with your estimate of their character," Locke observed.

Everly shrugged. "In all honesty, Admiral, I don't give a fig for what they think. I've had enough of high society to last me a lifetime. I may have come into a title, but were it not for my damned leg I'd be back at sea by now, and I wouldn't have to worry about keeping up appearances."

Locke's gaze slid to Everly's cane, which rested against the edge of the table. "Yes, a pity about your wound."

"How long until you get another ship?" Lambert inquired.

"Not soon enough," Everly grumbled. "The bureaucrats at the Admiralty aren't convinced of my recovery. They'll keep me ashore long enough to drive me mad."

"Then you must find something to occupy your time. Eh, Locke?" Peyton nudged the admiral's elbow, then leaned close and whispered something in Locke's ear.

Everly caught the knowing glance that passed between the two men. Anticipation sharpened his senses.

"I believe I might have just the diversion for you, Captain." Locke inclined his head in Everly's direction.

"I hope it's something more appealing than dancing with featherbrained young chits," Everly drawled. He indicated his cane. "As you can see, I don't dance."

"Oh, this is infinitely more appealing." Lambert's knowing smile melded with the curved rim of his glass as he took another sip.

"I'm having a little soiree at my house on Saturday," Locke explained. "For navy officers only."

"Well, at least the company sounds exceptional," Everly replied, cautious.

Locke chuckled. "No insipid lemonade or chicken-stakes cards, I promise you. You seem the sort of man to appreciate more adventurous pursuits, Captain. What would you say if I told you that I had arranged for high-stakes gaming, and the company of lovely, willing women?"

Just as Carlisle had explained. Not exactly Everly's idea of a pleasant evening, but he had to play along. He forced a smile to his lips. "I'd say it sounded intriguing."

"Not quite the word I'd use," Hale said. He licked his lips. "Sybaritic is more like it."

"Amen," Lambert replied.

"I merely wish to provide my fellow officers with enjoyable entertainment," Locke stated. "We begin the evening at ten o'clock. You know the address, of course."

Everly's smile broadened. "Of course."

*   *   *

Everly woke early the next afternoon with cannon fire pounding through his head. He tried to sit up.

"Who the devil ordered that broadside?" he croaked. The pounding continued, but it wasn't cannon fire. He groaned and pinched the bridge of his nose. His head hurt. His eyes hurt. Dammit, even his *hair* hurt. His mouth felt like it had been stuffed with a dirty cannon swab. That might explain the state of his stomach. Ugh. He grimaced and rang for Stubbs.

His servant was not sympathetic. "Got yerself good and foxed, didn't ye? Stayin' out till all hours, comin' home reekin' o' brandy and tobacco smoke—it's not like ye."

"Enough, Stubbs," Everly muttered. "This was all in the line of duty."

Stubbs shook his grizzled head and poured hot water into the basin. "In all the years I've served ye, Captain, I've never see ye in such a state. Except . . ."

Everly winced. "Except after Felicia jilted me. How thoughtful of you to bring that up on a morning like this, Stubbs."

Stubbs's face fell. "Beggin' yer pardon, Captain."

Everly waved the man's protests away. Felicia. Damn Sillsby for bringing back those painful memories. She had been his golden angel, and he had loved her, yearned to be with her all those years he was at sea. And when they had been reunited, she hadn't been able to accept a flawed Adonis as her husband. Everly ran a hand through his tousled hair. Odd . . . when he tied to remember Felicia's face, her pale golden locks were replaced by ebon curls, her blue eyes by deep brown ones. It wasn't Felicia, but Miss Amanda Tremayne who stared back at him. Everly shook his head; lancing pains shot through his temples. At least it was enough to get Miss Tremayne out of his mind. Felicia had hurt him, and he didn't want to give another female the chance to do the same thing.

Stubbs picked up Everly's jacket from the back of a chair and tsk-tsked at its sadly wrinkled condition. As he brushed it off, several scraps of paper fell from the pocket. "Eh? What's all this?"

Everly bent and retrieved the papers from the floor. Despite his aching head and smarting eyes he recognized them as vowels he'd won the night before. He made a quick tally. Egad, he had over five thousand pounds here—a small fortune. He didn't remember winning that much. Then again, he had imbibed a great quantity of brandy after Locke and the others had left, an attempt to rid himself of Felicia's taint. He supposed that he had been temporarily successful.

He gave the papers to Stubbs. "Put these in my desk," he ordered. He squinted at the clock. "And get me as presentable as you can. I must meet someone at half-past three."

Stubbs grinned crookedly and brandished the razor. "You 'aven't given me much to work with, Captain."

Everly answered his servant's smile with a tired one of his own. "Do what you can. You've seen worse."

With Stubbs's help, Everly arrived at the gates to Green Park just as the bells tolled half-past three. Drizzle shimmered down in a gray curtain. Here in the park, the rich smells of wet grass and moist earth overcame the odor of smoke and sewage. Everly spied the small, drab figure huddled inside the gate and signaled the coachman to stop. He opened the carriage door. "Here I am, punctual as promised. Come in out of the rain."

"You look horrible." Miss Tremayne didn't mince words. She disdained his hand as she climbed into the coach. Her cloak and bonnet were damp; she looked as though she had been out in the rain for some time.

"Thank you," Everly replied dryly. "I hope I did not keep you waiting."

She shook her head, and pushed a few damp strands of hair away from her eyes. "No, not long. Madame sent me on an errand, so I don't have much time."

He nodded. "Of course. May I see the letters?"

Miss Tremayne reached into her reticule and produced an awkward-looking bundle. When she handed it to him, Everly realized, that the letters had been bound in oilskin to protect them. He glanced up at the young woman. She perched on the edge of the carriage bench, her reddened hands clasped tightly in her lap, her heels tapping nervously on the floor. Her skin was so pale that her huge dark eyes looked like holes burned through cloth. Lines of weariness pulled at her mouth.

"You're tired," he observed.

He expected her to bristle, to deny his observation. To his surprise, she merely nodded. "I have been working late."

Everly frowned as he undid the knotted twine that surrounded the oilskin bundle. "You should at least wear gloves. The air is chill."

She folded her hands beneath her cloak, out of sight. "I forgot them at the shop. I appreciate your concern for my welfare, Captain. Now please read the letters."

She didn't want charity—she didn't even want his concern. Stubborn chit. Everly unfolded the letters and read each one in turn. When he was finished, he replaced them in the oilskin as if they were fragile pieces of porcelain. They might as well be, for if anything happened to this last link with her father, she would be desolate.

"Well?" she asked, anxious. Tremors shook her slight body.

Everly chose his words with care. "Your father was thorough in his documentation," he began gravely. "Unfortunately, I do not think these letters will prove useful to our case."

"What? How can you say that?" Anger raised twin spots of flame on her cheeks.

"We have no evidence to corroborate his claims. At this point, it would take months to track down anyone mentioned in these letters, and we don't have the time. I'm sorry, Miss Tremayne." He handed the bundle to her.

She snatched it from him. Bright tears limned her eyes. "So you're saying they mean nothing?"

"I would like to help you, Miss Tremayne, but I'm afraid you overestimate the value of your father's correspondence. I know these letters mean a great deal to you, but that is the extent of it."

The young woman bristled. She hugged the packet to her chest. "Do not patronize me, Captain. I know this information is useful. I just know it."

Everly could see her resolve crumbling. He had just scuttled her hopes, and his heart went out to her. "I do wish to help you," he said softly, "but this is no longer your battle. In a few days I will have another opportunity to find direct evidence against Locke. If I discover anything to corroborate the information in your father's letters, I will let you know."

"What sort of opportunity?" Her fingers tightened around the oilskin packet.

"Nothing you need to worry about," he assured her.

"Are you going back to Locke's town house?"

Damn, but she was a persistent creature. Beauty and endless potential for exasperation in one neat package. "As it so happens, yes. Locke is hosting a private card party."

"Take me with you," demanded Miss Tremayne.

At first her scandalous suggestion robbed him of speech. Then his indignation took command. "Out of the question," he snapped. "There will be only one sort of woman at this party, and no proper young lady would even consider attending."

Her brow puckered. "What are you talking about? What sort of woman?"

"Courtesans, Miss Tremayne," he retorted, hoping his blunt words would shock her. "Fashionable impures. Cyprians. Demi-reps."

She wasn't shocked. In fact, she seemed intrigued by the prospect. "Really? With that many women, perhaps I could—"

"No. Absolutely not. You will not go with me. That is an order."

Miss Tremayne twitched as though she'd been stung. "You cannot order me about. I am not a member of your crew."

"Aye, for if you were, I could have you flogged for

your insolence!" He paused to settle his rising temper. "If you know what's best, Miss Tremayne, you will go home and cease your infernal meddling. It's not your place to get involved." He spoke more sharply than he'd intended, but his patience was worn thin.

"I vowed to clear my father's name, and I will not rest until Locke is bought to justice." She bit off each word.

"He will be," Everly promised. Egad, arguing with this girl was like arguing with a mule. A twinge of pain erupted at his temples; his headache was returning with a vengeance.

She shot him a clever, speculative look. "What if I told you that I knew of a secret compartment in Locke's office?"

"What?" Everly demanded. She hadn't told him the complete truth, after all, and the thought infuriated him. "What did you find? And why the devil didn't you tell me about it?"

"You needn't swear at me. I didn't tell you because I didn't know if I could trust you."

"And now?"

"I'm still not entirely sure. Perhaps we are both better off with an element of suspicion."

"We share the same goal, Miss Tremayne, albeit for different reasons. Tell me where the compartment is."

Her lips thinned into a stubborn line. "No, I will not. Nor will I tell you how to open it. Besides, Captain, how do you expect to slip away from a small gambling party to rifle through your host's private belongings?"

She had a point, but he was not about to concede. "Insolent little baggage," he fumed.

"Patronizing, arrogant tyrant," she flung back.

Everly's head throbbed in time with his pulse. He rubbed his temples. "I am not taking you to that party," he insisted.

Her expression softened. "If I went with you, you could keep Locke busy upstairs while I searched his office. I know just where the compartment is, and how to get into it. No one would notice my absence."

"That's extortion," Everly said with a growl.

She made a little moue. "I regret this course of action, Captain, but you leave me little choice. Either we work together to expose Locke, or you can muddle through on your own and get caught in flagrante delicto."

Latin. He should have expected something so incongruous from this unconventional female. Everly threw up his hands. "If I took you with me, you'd run the exact same risk."

"But I'd stand a better chance than you. I'm smaller, can move quickly, and—" she glanced at his cane—"I'm far more mobile."

He winced. Ordinary females were not supposed to possess this capacity for logic. Then again, he knew by now that Miss Tremayne was anything but ordinary. He fixed her with his gimlet captain's gaze, guaranteed to wither the most hardened sailor, and tried another approach. "How can I, in good conscience, take a lady of good breeding to a place that is little better than a bawdy house? You have no idea what you're getting into."

"You needn't worry about offending my sensibilities, Captain," Miss Tremayne said briskly. "I am three and twenty years old, and quite capable of taking care of myself. I have endured the deaths of both my parents in the span of six months. I have withstood hardships I had never dreamed possible. And I have played actress before; this will not be any different."

Either she wasn't affected by his glare, or she wasn't paying attention. His lips twisted in a sneer. "I think you're mistaken. If—and I still say *if*—you were to go, you would have to play the part of my mistress. A daunting task. Are you up to the challenge?"

He had hoped to frighten her into reconsidering, but his strategy went awry. Rather than flinch away from him, she squared her shoulders and returned his glare with rebellious tenacity. "I am if you are, Captain."

Miss Tremayne as his mistress. Everly had a vision of the girl, dressed in nothing at all but a silky negligee and lounging on a bed, her dark hair curled over her breasts. Heat surged through him, and his breeches grew painfully tight. He shook himself. This was sheer folly. Why was he even considering such a foolhardy plan?

"I'm going to ask you something, Miss Tremayne," he said soberly, "and please do not take umbrage at what I'm about to say. Have you considered the consequences of this strategy? What if a prospective fiancé discovers that you have masqueraded as a courtesan and attended a party at a bawdy house? Your reputation would suffer irreparable damage. So would that of your grandmother."

Shadows clouded her eyes. "My family's name is blackened beyond measure. No one will ever wed me. Let us be realistic, Captain. Who in his right mind would want to marry a traitor's brat? My reputation cannot get any worse. I have nothing more to lose." Her voice dropped to a whisper, and she turned away. "You may think me a desperate fool, but I cannot turn back now."

These admissions took Everly aback. She was right— as it stood now, her future was bleak. Most women of her age were married already, with a family of their own. While he could not help but admire her determination, she posed a unique threat to his mission. How could he do his duty when all he wanted to do was protect Amanda? Er—Miss Tremayne.

Everly considered her elegant profile. He knew he should be suspicious of her, but she was nothing like Felicia. Felicia was beautiful, delicate like a porcelain doll, but indolent and spoiled. Miss Tremayne was lovely as well, but resourceful, intelligent, fiercely loyal, and infuriatingly independent. A little lioness. He had known her only a handful of days, and already he was torn between kissing her and strangling her. He sighed. "After this party, you must have nothing more to do with this investigation."

She turned, her lips parted in surprise. "Y—you'll take me with you?"

He smiled despite the pain careening through his head. "I believe I just said that. But only if you withdraw afterwards and let others continue the chase."

She seemed to weigh the merits of this offer; her eyes

darted from him to the packet of letters she held in her lap. "Agreed, Captain. I will not interfere in your investigation, but only if you agree to help exonerate my father, should you uncover the evidence I know exists."

He nodded warily. "Done."

She extended her hand. "Then let us shake on the bargain."

Everly took her hand in his. Her skin was warm, her grip firm. A question popped into his head and out of his mouth before he could stop it. "Where did you learn to throw a punch like that?"

She flashed a fleeting, impish smile. "I suppose my upbringing was rather unorthodox. My father taught me. I had difficulties with a bully when I was seven."

"Did you have no brothers to protect you?"

"No. I was an only child." Her smile faded. "Harry tried to defend me, but Throckmorton was twice his size."

"Who is Harry?" He dimly remembered that he still had hold of her hand, and released it.

"The lieutenant who accompanied me yesterday. Harry Morgan. We grew up together. In Dorset."

That explained the fellow's protective nature, thought Everly, if not his belligerence. "I will come for you at half past ten. We can discuss our strategy on the way."

"I shall be ready, Captain," she replied softly, then opened the carriage door. The rainfall had increased; raindrops drummed a tattoo against the roof of the carriage.

He couldn't let her go out into such inclement weather. She would be soaking wet in no time. "A moment, Miss Tremayne—may I give you a ride back to your shop?"

She started, and he could see reticence in her face. "No thank you, Captain. I am used to rain. Until Saturday, then." She exited the coach, then bounded off like a hare and disappeared down an alleyway, her cloak wrapped around her. She did not look back.

Everly watched her, unable to shake his uneasiness. Did she know the feminine power she wielded? Had he allowed her beauty to blind him to common sense, allowed her to manipulate him? He couldn't answer those questions with any certainty, and he wondered if, in dealing with Miss Tremayne, he had gotten more than he bargained for.

He signaled the coachman to head for home, then propped his aching leg on the opposite seat and relaxed back against the squabs. As cease-fires went, this one was shaky at best. He sighed. What on earth possessed him to agree to this scheme? For all the hardship she had endured, Miss Tremayne was still a gently reared young lady. She was bound to be shocked, if not traumatized, by the events at Locke's bacchanal.

Everly recalled the drab frocks that comprised her wardrobe, serviceable creations appropriate to her lowered circumstances. She'd worn green silk to Locke's party—where had she gotten it? He drummed his fingers against the leather seat, thoughtful. She said she worked for a dressmaker, and she was certainly reckless enough to have borrowed a gown for her own use. Hmmm. She might not be able to do so again. Could she dress the part for Saturday evening?

Everly's lips quirked into a grin as an idea took shape. He would provide her with a dress, one so scandalously indecent that she would refuse to wear it. Or her grandmother would refuse to let her out of the house. He'd wager that the rest of her wardrobe could not provide a suitable alternative, so she'd have to renege on their agreement. He chuckled and told his coachman to alter course. Once, long ago, he had kept a mistress with excellent—and very expensive—taste in clothing. Time to see if he could teach Miss Tremayne to look before she leaped.

Chapter Seven

The box arrived early Thursday evening, addressed to Amanda.

"Who could it be from?" Mrs. Tremayne wondered aloud. She set the last of the supper dishes out to dry, then wiped her hands on a towel and joined Amanda at the kitchen table.

"I don't know," answered Amanda faintly. "There was no card."

Something about this mysterious package generated sensations of dread in the pit of her stomach. Who would send her a box from a dressmaker's shop? Had Madame learned about the green silk, after all? Amanda chastised herself for being such a goose. She was letting her imagination get the better of her.

"Well, aren't you going to open it, dearest?" Mrs. Tremayne's dark eyes shone with excitement.

Amanda managed a nervous smile. With her sewing scissors she snipped the cords that bound the box. Then she lifted the lid. A cloud of fine white India muslin decorated with tiny gilt spangles greeted her startled gaze.

"It's beautiful," she breathed, running a hand across the diaphanous material. A note lay atop this confection, written in a bold, masculine hand:

For Saturday's festivities. You might want to damp your petticoats for greater effect.—E

Damp her . . . ? Heat bloomed in Amanda's cheeks as her mood swung wildly from surprise to pleasure to embarrassment. Her hands curled into fists. If this was Captain Everly's idea of a joke—

"How strange," murmured Mrs. Tremayne. She took the note from the box and frowned at it. "Who is this mysterious 'E,' Amanda? And why is he sending you gowns and advising you to damp your petticoats?"

Amanda's mortification grew to the point where she wished the floor would open up and swallow her whole. This was no joke, after all. Everly must have known that her grandmother would ask questions when this package arrived. He'd put her in a very compromising position. Intentionally. Damn him! He wanted to maneuver her into crying off. Of all the underhanded, devious, despicable . . .

"Amanda?" prompted the older woman.

"I need to tell you something, Grandmama," Amanda replied quietly, her eyes still focused on the dress. She unclenched her fingers and massaged her palms. She had never intended to deceive her grandmother about this latest development; she just hadn't gotten around to telling her.

Mrs. Tremayne fixed Amanda with a knowing look. "I thought you might. You've been on edge for the past two days. You needn't look so surprised, dearest. I know you far too well."

Guilt added another element of turmoil to the emotions churning in Amanda's breast. "Remember Captain Everly, Grandmama?"

The older woman nodded. "Yes, the gentleman you said was going to help us."

"Well . . ." Amanda hesitated. How was she supposed to tell her grandmother that a virtual stranger was going to escort her into unsavory, if not dangerous, circumstances?

Mrs. Tremayne scanned the note again. "Everly. Is he the 'E' who sent you this dress?"

Amanda winced. Age had not dulled her grandmother's faculties a whit. "Yes, Grandmama."

"And might I assume you're going to explain why?"

Nor had it dulled her tongue. Amanda's eyes slid to

the dress, to the sequins glittering in the candlelight. "Captain Everly is working for the Crown, searching for a traitor in the Admiralty," she said.

"Yes, you mentioned that as well." Mrs. Tremayne's impatience hovered around her.

"He suspects Admiral Locke is a member of this spy ring, and that the admiral holds the key to the ringleader's identity."

"What does that have to do with the dress?"

Amanda took a deep breath. "He has been invited to a small soirée at Admiral Locke's house tomorrow night, and I am going to accompany him."

Mrs. Tremayne put a hand to her throat. "Oh, dearest—you cannot possibly . . . !"

"It will be all right, Grandmama," Amanda soothed. "Captain Everly needs me. This is the perfect opportunity to explore that secret drawer in Locke's desk, and only I know where it is."

"You could tell the captain where to find it," argued Mrs. Tremayne. Now her dark eyes snapped fire. "You do not need to put yourself in any further danger."

Amanda shook her head. "Captain Everly recently sustained a wound in his leg, and he is not as quick or nimble as I am. Nor would he be able to slip away unnoticed from the rest of the guests to search Locke's study. He needs my help."

"Whether he wants it or not."

Amanda recognized the accusatory expression on her grandmother's face. Oh, heavens. Now she was in the suds. "Well . . . perhaps."

"I'm sure Captain Everly is perfectly capable of completing this mission on his own. You do not need to be involved. I will not allow you to risk either your well-being or your life." Mrs. Tremayne tossed the note back into the box, her hands trembling.

"But I'll be fine, Grandmama. Captain Everly will ensure my safety." A tinge of desperation colored Amanda's voice. "Nothing will happen to me."

Tears shimmered in the older woman's eyes. "Why do you insist on pursuing this folly, Amanda? You are risking everything you hold dear to search for something that may not exist."

"I do it because I still have hope, Grandmama." Answering tears seeped onto Amanda's lashes. "As long as there is hope, I must do whatever I can."

"The only thing we *must* do is accept our circumstances with dignity."

"If my Fate lies in resignation and regret," Amanda murmured, "I will not accept it. I will not stand by and wring my hands because that is what is expected of me. I have to do this."

Mrs. Tremayne drew herself up and leveled her gaze at Amanda. "Then you must decide for yourself if the ends justify the means. I want you to know that I do not approve. I cannot. It is dangerous, undignified, and unladylike, but there is little I can do to stop you. I can only pray that you do not pay too great a price for this madness." The elderly woman marched into their bedchamber and closed the door.

Amanda sank into one of the kitchen chairs, her grandmother's words ringing in her ears. Did the ends justify the means? She rested her elbows on the table, her chin in her hands. When she'd first come to London, consumed with grief and pain and rage, she would have answered that question with an unqualified yes. Now she wasn't so sure. She'd managed to anger both Harry and her grandmother, the two people she cared for most in the world. She'd put herself in peril of arrest, transportation, and bodily harm. And still she felt she had not done enough. Amanda sighed. Perhaps her grandmother was right—perhaps this was madness.

Her gaze strayed to the dress, which rested innocuously in its box. Amanda made a ferocious face. And then there was the matter of Captain Everly and his ill-timed gift. Well, perhaps ill-timed was the wrong word; she had spent the last two days wracking her brain, wondering where she would get a gown. She had not thought of that particular detail when she demanded to accompany the captain to this party. Now it seemed she had a dress.

What had prompted this show of generosity? Amanda lifted the dress from the box and held it against her body. Her eyes widened. Oh, heavens. He expected her to wear *this*? The neckline plunged to indecent depths, and the material itself was so sheer that she would have to wear several petticoats beneath it to avoid putting her body on public display.

A slow flush crept over Amanda's face. Of course. That was his ploy all along. Captain Everly thought he could humiliate her, shame her into crying off from this party. He was probably laughing at her even now, congratulating himself for being rid of her. Amanda's jaw tightened. Well, she would just have to call the captain's bluff.

Amanda reexamined the dress with a professional eye. For all its overabundant *décolletage*, the gown was beautifully made; the material was some of the finest she'd ever seen, and the sequins and embroidery at the hem were the product of hours of handwork. She'd wager that Captain Everly had paid a princely sum for it. An expensive joke.

Amanda considered her options. The gown was a little too big, so she would take in the sides. The hem was too long, but she could take up the excess material from the waist and use it to fill in the neckline, make it a trifle more modest. She smiled. Her labors at Madame's shop had not been in vain, after all. She may have to play the role of a courtesan, but she did not have to flaunt herself like one.

Her course of action determined, Amanda set the dress aside and began to clear the table. She had work to do, and very little time to do it. She glanced at the closed bedroom door, and hoped her grandmother would understand.

She hoped in vain. Her grandmother said very little to her for the rest of the evening, and even less the next day. They shared a silent supper. Amanda ate just enough to insure she wouldn't faint later on. Sandwiched between nerves and unhappiness, her appetite had evaporated.

Her grandmother, accustomed to country hours, retired early; Amanda completed her toilette as quietly as she could to avoid waking the older woman. By the light of a single candle she dressed her hair in ringlets and confined them with a bandeau of leftover spangled muslin, which she knotted below her right ear. She'd trimmed the finished ends of the muslin with gold beads, so that they lay enticingly against the curve of her neck.

She surveyed her appearance in the old, mottled mirror with a critical eye. Well, she had no rouge and very little powder, so she would have to make do. Amanda frowned at her pale reflection and pinched her cheeks. That was as much color as she could manage. She reached for the bottle of jasmine perfume. Her hand hesitated on the stopper. The last time she'd worn this scent, Captain Everly had used it to discover her hiding place. She could not take such a risk again. She sighed and withdrew her hand. Time for the dress.

Amanda slipped into the muslin gown, sighing as the soft fabric caressed her skin. This creation could only be described as . . . well . . . decadent. A shiver that was half delight, half trepidation skittered up her back. She moved in front of the looking glass to survey the full effect. A worldly, sophisticated woman stared back at her. Had she raised the neckline too far? Amanda's heart sank. In this case, sophistication did not equal seduction. She did not look nearly provocative enough to be a courtesan. Botheration. She'd have to damp her petticoats, after all.

The damping was easily done, but not so easily borne. Amanda shivered again, this time from the chill muslin skirts that clung to her legs like seaweed and outlined every curve of her legs and hips. Hmmm. Still not enough. Oh, heavens—she had hoped it wouldn't come to this. Amanda closed her eyes, took a deep breath, and ripped away the filmy fichu she'd tacked into the neckline. She peeked at her reflection—and gaped. Her breasts, barely contained by the material, looked as though they might spill from the bodice at any moment. One good sneeze would undo her altogether. Amanda put her hands to her feverish cheeks. Well, at least she now looked the part.

The clock with the cracked face registered half-past ten when Amanda gathered her gloves and fan. She donned her blue velvet cloak, a Christmas gift from her parents and the last piece of finery she owned, and settled the hood over her head. She hoped Captain Everly was punctual, otherwise she might lose her nerve.

At the doorway to the bedroom she paused, candle in hand. The dim light revealed her grandmother's sleeping form. Amanda crept to her grandmother's bedside and placed a gentle kiss on the wrinkled cheek visible above the covers.

"I love you, Grandmama," she whispered. The older woman did not stir.

Amanda rose and departed without another word.

Punctuality was a hallmark of naval service, she mused as she emerged from the lodging house. Captain Everly had just exited his coach and was approaching the building with a slight smile on his face.

"I'm here, Captain," she called.

He spotted her then, and his smile faded. Amanda kept her cloak folded around her body partially to keep herself warm, partially to keep her gown from Captain Everly's sight. Let him wonder if she'd worn the dress. She would wait until they arrived at Locke's home to reveal her attire, lest the good captain declare her too unclothed and refuse to take her in the first place.

"Miss Tremayne," he greeted her. He swept his bicorne from his head and bowed. His eyes scanned her up and down, and a slight frown creased his brow.

"Good evening, Captain," Amanda replied with breezy self-assurance. She climbed into the coach without his assistance, her smile hidden behind her gloved hand. Oh, she couldn't wait to see the expression on his face when he realized she'd called his bluff. That should take some of the wind out of his sails.

Captain Everly settled himself across from her, his brilliant blue eyes clouded with wariness. "Are you prepared, Miss Tremayne?" he asked. "You know you don't have to go through with this."

First subterfuge, now the direct approach. From what she knew of Captain Everly, he was stiff-rumped enough not to admit that he needed her help. Her shoulders stiffened. "I am quite prepared," she answered.

Captain Everly stared long and hard at her for a moment, then rapped his walking stick on the roof of the carriage. The coach started forward with a lurch.

"When we get to Locke's," he said through his teeth, "I will introduce you as my mistress, Lucy Campion. You are a former opera dancer."

"I can only imagine that being someone's mistress is far more lucrative than dancing," quipped Amanda with a little laugh. Honestly, what made her say that? She must be more nervous than she thought.

Everly was not amused; he scowled. "Pay attention, Miss Tremayne. After we arrive, we must allow some time to pass before you go in search of the secret compartment."

"Why?"

"The longer we wait, the more distracted the other guests will become. They will either be drunk, engaged at cards, or occupied with the ladies."

Occupied? Amanda blinked. Then comprehension set in, and a hot flush exploded in her cheeks. Oh. *Occupied.* She retreated into her cloak.

"I will keep Locke distracted," Everly continued. "Once you return, we can make our excuses and depart. Then I will take you home, and we shall be done with this." His gloves strained over his knuckles as he gripped the head of his cane.

"I assure you that I have no wish to remain in that house one moment longer than is necessary."

"Remember this, Miss Tremayne—you are likely to see things tonight that are contrary to every polite sensibility. Whatever happens, you must not let your emotions get the better of you. This is war; by coming with me you have made yourself a soldier. And as a soldier, you must achieve your objective at all costs. Do I make myself clear?"

Amanda flushed. She would hate to be a midshipman under Captain Everly's command; he was starting to sound like a martinet. "Perfectly clear, Captain."

"You must play your role, no matter what depredations you see, no matter how shocked or appalled you become."

Amanda scanned his taut, tense features. The man gave every impression of a captain about to sail into battle. His body thrummed with tension.

"I understand what is expected of me, Captain," she said. "I suggest that we both try to relax. If we walk into the admiral's house looking as though we expect an attack at any moment, he will be suspicious."

"I am not a spy, Miss Tremayne," he snapped, irritated. "I am not used to such underhanded machinations."

Machinations? He did not give himself enough credit for the dress, but Amanda decided not to point this out. "Neither am I, Captain, but we will do what we must. To paraphrase Nelson, England expects us to do out duty."

His face relaxed for a moment, and he almost smiled. "Quite right, Miss Tremayne," he replied. "Quite right."

When they arrived at Admiral Locke's town house, Amanda's heart increased its cadence as she stared up at the huge, elegant Georgian residence. She was about to brave the monster's den a second time. Fear flashed through her, and she took a deep breath to steady herself. Locke was unlikely to recognize her from the ball. She had been one person in a sea of hundreds, and tonight she was dressed in quite a different manner.

"Courage, Lucy dear," murmured Captain Everly as he offered her a hand down from the carriage.

It would not do for a mistress to disdain her protector's help. Amanda placed her gloved hand in his and descended with slow, deliberate steps. It would be just her luck to turn an ankle now.

In the cloakroom, Amanda removed her velvet cape and handed it to a footman. Cool air caressed her bare neck and shoulders, raising goose bumps on her flesh. A defiant smile on her lips, she turned to gauge Captain Everly's reaction, to see if she could pique his temper. The result was not what she expected.

The captain stared at her, his eyes narrowed. She could almost feel his gaze as a tangible force as it roamed over her body. She gasped. Everly was looking at her the way Lord Bainbridge had at the ball. No . . . not quite like Lord Bainbridge. Everly stared at her with the hollow-eyed fascination of a starving man who hadn't eaten in days.

"Captain?" she breathed. Her knees started to tremble.

"Jack. You should call me Jack," he said hoarsely. He approached her in two long strides and seized her bare shoulders. "I was a fool to get you involved in this. I was an even greater fool to send you that dress."

His eyes were so blue that they seemed to glow. Amanda stared up at him, mesmerized. "Does my appearance meet with your approval?" she whispered.

"Dammit, this is not a game!" he snapped.

She could see the rapid pulse throbbing at his temple. "Yes, it is. A very dangerous game. One we must play through to the end."

Everly's hot stare traveled down her neck, over her shoulders, and lingered on the white curve of her bosom. He leaned down, his face very near hers, his breath warm against her ear. "I am going to have to protect you from every man here. Including myself."

His touch did the strangest things to her senses. Amanda's flustered mind could not form a reply. She looked away. "Should we not go and greet our host . . . Jack?"

Everly's head snapped up. He shook himself like a man emerging from a dream, then retreated a step. After a long moment, he offered her his arm. "Indeed. Just be careful."

Amanda hesitated, then placed her hand on his arm. Even through layers of fabric and kidskin, the contact was electric. She ran her tongue over her parched lips.

Raucous laughter accosted Everly and Amanda as they reached the top of the stairs. Several men clustered in the hallway, framed by a haze of tobacco smoke. A few wore uniforms, a few wore evening dress, but they all turned as Amanda and Everly approached; their eyes flicked over the captain, then focused on Amanda. Like a pack of hungry wolves, she thought, alarmed. Everly nodded curtly to them before he steered Amanda into the ballroom.

The series of rooms looked nothing like it had two weeks ago. Several large tables, each covered with green baize, inhabited what had been the dance floor. The immense crystal chandelier was dark; pools of light from a few tall candelabras provided a close, intimate atmosphere. The low hum of conversation, punctuated by an occasional laugh or oath, pervaded the air, as did a profusion of scents: cheroot smoke, heavy musk, attar of roses, hair pomade, and unwashed linen—Amanda wrinkled her nose.

A number of officers sat at each table, engaged with either cards or dice. Ladies—if one could call them that—lounged against the men's shoulders. A few even snuggled on officers' laps. And the way some of them were dressed! Compared with the genuine article, Amanda thought her muslin gown too modest. Could she indeed masquerade as one of these creatures? They seemed to accept the boldest caresses, even in front of other people. Amanda's hand tightened on Everly's sleeve.

"Don't worry. You're safe with me," he murmured.

Yes, thought Amanda with a twinge, but was he safe from the sharks? Several women had already looked in Everly's direction and afforded him seductively inviting smiles. Everly smiled back.

"Ah, Captain Everly. Good of you to join us." Admiral Locke approached them, a tall, red-haired woman on his arm. Taller than Amanda, though similarly shaped, the lady carried herself with the haughty grace of a queen. A queen in an amber silk gown that left nothing to the imagination, and jewels that would make true royalty green with envy.

"Hello, Admiral. Good of you to invite me," Everly replied with ease.

"And who is this you've brought with you, Captain?" inquired the redhead.

"I didn't think you'd mind if I brought my mistress—she's a jealous sort." Everly grinned down at Amanda and tweaked her under the chin. "If I came to this party without her, I'd never hear the end of it. Admiral, may I present Miss Lucy Campion. Lucy dear, the esteemed Admiral Locke, the Lion of the Mediterranean."

He really was doing it a bit too brown. Amanda forced a smile to her lips and dipped a saucy curtsy. Locke's gaze slithered over her, a blatant evaluation of her charms. Amanda repressed a shudder.

"Well, Captain, I must say that I am very disappointed," the red-haired woman said, her lips pursed in a pout. "The admiral has told me all about you, and I do so adore enigmatic, fascinating men. I wanted us to become better acquainted."

Locke chuckled. "You'd best be careful around Maria. She always gets what she wants."

"Always," the woman echoed. She stroked the tip of her fan down Everly's jaw, a brazen gesture that set Amanda's teeth on edge. She must have made a little noise of protest, for Maria Danvers shot her a hostile, challenging glance.

"Then I shall consider myself warned." Everly inclined his head and smiled.

Locke turned to Amanda. "Have we met, my dear?" he asked, speculation in his icy eyes. "You seem familiar."

Amanda's jangled nerves shirked. Oh, heavens! She needed to think of something clever, something to put him off the scent. "I—I do not believe so," she stammered. She bit her tongue. So much for cleverness.

"She used to be the darling of Covent Garden," Everly added smoothly. He snugged a possessive arm around her waist. "Although you can hardly fault me for keeping her to myself. I don't need any competition for her favors."

Locke's good-natured laugh turned a few nearby heads. "She is a fetching creature. Perhaps when you tire of her, we might come to an arrangement."

"Perhaps." Everly's hand tensed on Amanda's waist.

The admiral gestured to the rest of the room. "For tonight though, enjoy yourself. I hear the vingt-et-un table is particularly lucky."

"Will you not join us, Admiral?" Everly asked.

Locke gazed speculatively at Amanda. "In a few moment, perhaps," the admiral answered. With a nod and another genial smile, Locke started back across the ballroom, his hostess affixed to his side. Mrs. Danvers spared them both a watchful glance over one bare shoulder.

Amanda exhaled in a long, slow sigh. Her limbs quivered, but there was little she could do to stop them. "What do we do now?"

"We take the admiral up on his suggestion. This way."

His hand still at her waist, Everly steered Amanda through the crowd to a table occupied by four other officers. "May I join you, gentlemen?" he asked.

The men looked up. The dealer, a young man in a lieutenant's uniform, smiled a humorless smile. "I'm not sure if we can afford you, Everly," he drawled.

Amanda felt the captain stiffen, though his pleasant expression never wavered. "That's Captain Everly to you, Mr. Hale," he replied. "You might do well to remember the formalities of rank, even in your patron's home. And you can always go somewhere else if you're afraid to wager against me."

The young man's face darkened. "Sit down, then, *Captain*. Your luck has to change sometime."

Everly seated himself at the table and shrugged. "But perhaps not tonight."

As he shuffled the cards, the lieutenant's eyes slid to Amanda, who stood close by Everly's right shoulder. His smile turned venomous. "Who's your ladybird, Captain? Sillsby was right about one thing—you must pay her well indeed to endure your deformity. Perhaps she fancies someone younger . . . and unblemished. Shall we make her favors the stakes for this game?"

Terror strangled the breath from Amanda's lungs. Everly would never consider—

"I think not," she heard Everly growl. "She's with me."

Just as Amanda's heart began to resume a normal pace, Everly snaked out an arm and swept her onto his lap.

"What are you doing?" she whispered, shocked.

"You called this a game, didn't you?" His expression was pleasant, but his eyes blazed with a dangerous, angry light. "Play along."

"But this is—"

"Is your ladybird having second thoughts, Captain?" taunted Hale as he dealt the cards.

"Not at all," Everly retorted. He drew a finger over her lips. "Are you, Lucy?"

"Of course not . . . Jack." His touch, though featherlight, thrilled her down to her toes. Awareness of his body flooded through her—his muscular thighs, his broad chest, the clean scent of his skin. A warm ache pooled low and deep within her. Such strange sensations—what was happening to her?

"That's my girl." Everly barely glanced at his cards. His hand drifted down her throat, down to her neckline, tracing a maddening line on her bare skin.

Amanda jumped when his fingers stopped at the hollow between her breasts. "Stop!"

He silenced her with a kiss, his mouth hard and unyielding. His arms tightened around her, crushing her to him. If she struggled, the other men would grow suspicious, but for the moment she could do nothing, even if she wanted to. The feel of his lips against hers froze her limbs and set her blood on fire. At last Everly pulled away, his eyes leveled at hers like loaded cannon.

"Why are you doing this?" She squirmed and pulled back as far as his arms would allow.

He held her fast. "You demanded to come along, knowing full well what sort of party this was," he murmured. He nibbled at her earlobe. "It's time you learned that your rash actions have consequences."

Consequences? Amanda's eyes narrowed. He was doing this to punish her for defying him. Part of her wanted to slap him, but more disturbing was the part of her that wanted him to kiss her again.

"Your wager, Everly," prompted one of the officers at the table.

The captain muttered an oath under his breath. The bright fury dimmed from his eyes, and he loosened his hold on her. "No more of this, sweetheart, or you'll distract me."

In one fluid movement he lifted Amanda and set her gently on the ground. Amanda didn't try to move right away; she didn't trust her legs to support her. The captain sat down again without looking at her.

"Jack?" she ventured.

"Don't go far, love," he replied without glancing up. "I wouldn't want anything to happen to you."

He was right; it was too early for her to sneak down to the study. Her eyes flitted across the room. Locke and Mrs. Danvers were still making the rounds, conversing with the other guests. She would have to wait awhile.

Amanda returned her attention to the vingt-et-un table. Lieutenant Hale had just upped the wager again. Everly concentrated on his cards, not on her. Amanda copied the pose of a few other courtesans and leaned negligently against Everly's shoulder. She felt him stiffen. Good. A tight smile curved her lips. It would serve him right if she *did* distract him.

"It seems your play is not up to snuff, Captain," Hale announced at the end of the hand. With a smirk, he gathered in his winnings.

"There's always the next round," Everly retorted. "Deal."

Amanda continued to hover above Everly's shoulder, keeping one eye on the room as the evening progressed. Servants made the rounds with port, Madeira, and champagne, but Amanda refrained; her stomach was in enough distress already. The men at the vingt-et-un table imbibed freely, all save Everly. He kept a glass of brandy at his elbow and seemed to take a sip from time to time, but Amanda noticed that the level of liquid in the glass went down very slowly.

After another few hands, Amanda decided that she could wait no longer. The noise level in the room had increased appreciably, as had the general *joie de vivre* of the guests. Locke seemed to be engaged in a boisterous conversation at the other end of the room.

She leaned down to Everly's ear, her lips close to his golden curls. "I'm going for the study," she whispered.

Everly nodded, an almost imperceptible gesture. "Be careful," he murmured. "I'll keep Locke busy up here." Then, more loudly, he said, "You do that, sweeting. I'll join you when I'm finished here. I promise I won't be long."

As she turned to leave, she felt Everly pat her derriere. "Oh!" she exclaimed. Rude laughter sounded from the table. Over clenched teeth, she flashed what she hoped was a smile at Everly. Then, fanning herself, she exited the room with as much decorum as she could muster.

The corridor outside the ballroom was empty. Amanda sighed and put a hand to her pounding temples. She would be so glad when this was all over, when her life could return to normal. No more intrigue, no more disguises, no more nerve-wracking escapades. She looked down the hall in both directions, then crept to the back staircase.

Downstairs, all was quiet. She tiptoed to the door of Locke's study and opened it just far enough for her to slip inside, steeling herself against the squeal of the hinges. For once her small size played to her advantage; she squeezed through the crack, and the door never opened far enough for the hinges to protest. Amanda closed the door behind her.

Tonight a fire blazed on the hearth, enough to illuminate most of the room. Good—she shouldn't need a candle. Her heart drummed an excited tattoo in her breast as she crossed the room. Now, to work. She didn't have much time.

Out of the corner of his eye Everly watched Amanda depart, absorbed by the gentle sway of her hips and the way the muslin skirt accentuated her voluptuous curves. Heat rose through him.

Laughter from the other officers at the table startled him, and brought his attention back to the game.

"You should bring your ladybird to every game, Everly," crowed Lieutenant Hale. "She's made me luckier tonight than I've been in months."

Everly scanned his cards. He had played with all the finesse of a drunkard, judging by what he held in his hand. Disgusted with himself, he laid his cards facedown on the table. A slow flush crept over his face. Damnation. Never before had he been so easily distracted.

"Another hand, or will you be leaving us for . . . other pursuits?" Hale prodded.

Everly tossed his cards toward the sneering lieutenant. "I have a few moments. Deal."

Hale shrugged. "As you will. But are you sure you can trust your little mistress to go off by herself?"

Everly's eyes narrowed. "I am certain she will be fine, just as long as you stay away from her."

Hale smirked and began to shuffle the deck. "Ah, you're the jealous sort, are you, Everly? Do you have reason to doubt your ladybird's loyalty?"

"No more than you have reason to doubt your skill at cards," Everly retorted. "I should say you require opponents who are drunk or besotted in order to win."

Tension vibrated across the table as this comment sunk in. Hale's face twisted into a mask of fury.

"Ah, our gracious host. Good evening, Admiral," said one of the other players in a nervous voice.

Everyone at the table turned at the approach of Locke and Mrs. Danvers. The admiral walked with his chest puffed out, a jovial smile on his face, evidently very pleased with himself.

"Good to see that you are enjoying yourselves, gentlemen," he said. "How is your luck holding, Captain Everly?"

Everly relaxed back into his chair. "Well enough, sir."

"Better now that he has no distractions," said Hale in a thin voice.

Locke looked between the two men and arched a questioning eyebrow. "Yes, where is your little opera dancer, Captain? I would have expected to see her here."

A forced smile bloomed on Everly's lips. "She started to complain that she hasn't had a moment alone with me in weeks, so I told her to find us a suitable trysting place. Must keep her happy, at least for the moment."

Locke laughed. "Ah, women. Predictable creatures, are they not, Maria?"

At his side, Maria Danvers cocked her head and regarded Everly from beneath lowered lashes. "You seem to go to great lengths to keep your mistress contented. You bring her here, and cater to her every whim. Should it not be the other way around, Captain?"

Damnation, but that woman had a viper's tongue. Everly pretended indifference to her sting. "What would you suggest, madam?"

Mrs. Danvers walked behind Everly's chair and toyed with the curls at the nape of his neck. "I suggest that you find a mistress who is more willing to satisfy *your* desires, Captain."

Everly tried very hard not to shudder with revulsion.

"Enough, Maria," Locke said with a laugh. "You'll put the poor man off his game."

At last, the cue Everly needed. "Have you come to join us, Admiral?"

Locke considered the invitation. "Very well. But only for a moment."

The admiral settled himself in the chair next to Everly, but Maria Danvers made no move to join him. She remained at Everly's shoulder, her hip brushing against his epaulets, watching him with her intent, poison green eyes.

Hale, now somewhat subdued, dealt the next hand. Everly examined his cards, but his mind was still far from the game. Even with Mrs. Danvers so close to him, all he could think of was Amanda. He should never have let his temper get the better of him like that. Yes, he was angry with her, but he should never have pulled her onto his lap as though she were a common dolly-mop, and he certainly should never have kissed her. Her body had been so warm, her skin so soft beneath his fingers. Her curves had fit so well against him. Everly gritted his teeth and shifted in his chair as his body responded to such provocative thoughts. A fine sheen of sweat dewed his brow.

The wagering began, and Everly wrenched his attention back to the cards. He had to keep Locke occupied long enough for Amanda to open the secret compartment and examine its contents.

Play continued for several rounds, and although the admiral was discreet about it, Everly noticed the man checking his pocket timepiece.

"Enough for me, gentlemen." Locke set his cards on the table and rose.

"Leaving so soon, Admiral?" Everly asked. He had to give Amanda more time. "The game has just begun to get interesting."

Locke straightened his cravat. "I regret that my other guests require my attention."

"I never thought you one to shy away from the chance to recoup your losses." Everly sat back to observe what effect his provoking statement had on the admiral.

Locke's pale blue eyes grew cold. "Continue without me, Captain."

"Are you certain?" Everly let his insolence tinge his words.

"I insist," Locke replied, with more than a hint of impatience. "Come, Maria."

Mrs. Danvers pouted and detached herself from Everly's shoulder. "Let me know if you change your mind," she breathed in his ear.

Everly could not unclench his teeth in time to give her an answer. Damnation—he could do nothing more to delay them, short of accosting Locke and calling unwanted attention to himself. As he watched his host and hostess depart, he could only hope that Amanda had retrieved the information and was far away from the study by now.

*   *   *

Amanda went right to Locke's desk and opened the drawer. Everything looked as it had before. At this rate, she would have the papers in her possession and she and Everly could leave the house within the next few minutes. She carefully removed the papers from the drawer, then felt toward the back for the spring. She pressed it, and a small door popped open at the bottom of the drawer. Amanda's heart leaped into her throat. This was it! She removed her glove and reached into the secret compartment. What would she find? Papers? Charts? Correspondence?

Nothing.

The compartment was empty.

Amanda withdrew her hand and stared blankly at the drawer. She hadn't imagined things, had she? There *had* been something in this drawer. In response to her burglary attempt, Locke had probably moved the documents from his desk. A prudent move. Botheration! The last thing she needed was a prudent enemy. Amanda fought back her disappointment as she closed the compartment and replaced the papers in the drawer. Where could he have put them? Her eyes scanned the room. Perhaps he hadn't moved them very far.

Not in any of the other drawers. Behind the portrait? No. A secret compartment in the fireplace? Amanda investigated every crevice and knob on the mantelpiece, down the ornate molding along the sides, but found nothing. If Locke didn't hide the evidence in this room, the only other likely hiding place would be . . . his bedchamber. Amanda shuddered. No, it had to be here in the study. It just had to be.

Voices sounded from the hallway. Fear tripped icy fingers down Amanda's spine. Someone was coming. Coming to the study? No way to tell. She looked wildly around the room. The curtains. No, she'd been found there before. Besides, Locke would notice if the curtains were closed, rather than open as he'd left them.

The voices came closer. Two men. Amanda muffled a little shriek. There was nowhere else to hide, not even so much as a decorative screen. If not the curtains, then perhaps the balcony . . . Amanda scooted through the French doors and out into the chill night air. She flattened herself against the dank stone wall next to the railing and tried not to think about the cold. Wisps of fog escaped her parted lips with each breath. She shivered. Her damp petticoats wrapped her legs in layers of ice. Goose bumps covered every inch of her exposed skin. Oh, let them pass, let them pass. . . .

She heard the study door open; the hinges squawked. Her heart pounded like a kettle drum as the two men came inside. Amanda heard the faint click as the door closed behind them, and her eyes widened with horror. She was trapped.

Chapter Eight

The voices, muffled at first, became more distinct as the men came into the room. On the balcony, Amanda could see the shadows they cast, and she willed herself to stay out of sight and motionless. Then, with a sudden clatter, someone yanked the curtains closed. The noise made Amanda jump, and she bit her tongue to keep from crying out.

"Now we are safe from prying eyes," said one voice. Amanda recognized the speaker: Admiral Locke.

"You are . . . (mumble) . . . will miss you?" asked the second. Amanda could hardly hear him. She crept toward the French doors; with the curtains closed, the men inside would not be able to see her. She pressed her ear to the cold glass.

"No. They're all involved in their own pursuits. We can proceed with our business, and none will be the wiser."

"You are taking unnecessary risks," declared the other man. "You realize that the person who rifled through your desk during the ball might make anther attempt."

Amanda wrinkled her forehead, perplexed. The man's guttural tones sounded familiar. She had heard his voice before, but she couldn't place it. She leaned into the glass as much as she dared, straining to catch every word.

"I doubt a navy man was responsible," the admiral replied. Amanda heard the clink of glassware. "Such an act would violate an officer's code of honor. At any rate, there is nothing here for anyone to find."

Amanda stiffened. Nothing to find? Botheration—he *had* moved them.

"Good," said the second voice, pinched with sarcasm. "I'd hate to think you had endangered our operation by keeping any incriminating documents in your possession."

"You know I wouldn't do that." Locke's irritation was unmistakable.

"I am pleased to hear it. Now, we must assume that our activities are still under suspicion, and move with caution. I have just received our orders: the next navy packet arrives at Portsmouth on Tuesday, with information vital to our cause."

"Your cause. Not mine."

"Let us not bandy semantics. It is your cause, Locke, because you work for us."

"Not by choice."

Outside, Amanda's jaw dropped in shock. The second man must be the traitor from the Admiralty! His voice sounded so familiar. If only she could place it.

"Nonsense. We have paid you very well for your services. From the way you've redecorated your house I can see that you've become accustomed to extravagant living."

Admiral Locke mumbled something, too soft for Amanda to hear, but the tone was definitely unpleasant.

The traitor did not seem impressed. "Your disposition worsens with each passing day, Admiral. I'd be more careful, if I were you. You are not irreplaceable."

"You need me," Locke argued.

"Yes," the traitor agreed, "you have been a valuable asset. But even you can push too far."

Locke hesitated a moment before answering in a tight voice, "Quite a choice you've given me—the hangman's noose, or a knife in the back."

"I see we understand each other. Now, can I rely upon you to deliver that information to our agents?"

"Yes, damn you. But after this, I'm done," Locke growled.

The traitor guffawed, a harsh sound. "I think not. You're done when I say you're done."

A long pause fell over the room. Amanda held her breath. What was going on in there?

"I'm warning you," Locke said harshly. "I want no more part of this. I've seen too many men die as it is."

"You've never struck me as the squeamish type, Locke. Is that business about Captain Tremayne still bothering you? Ah, I see that it is."

The edges of Amanda's vision began to blacken. Her father . . . they were talking about her father. Her fingers curled against the glass.

"He was a decent man," Locke said. "A good officer. He didn't deserve what happened to him."

"Of course he did," countered the traitor. The cold cruelty in his voice made Amanda's skin crawl. "He pried into our affairs and endangered our mission. We had to get rid of him. It was his life or yours, and both you and I know that your sense of self-preservation is greater than your sense of honor."

Another long pause, broken by a crash and the tinkle of shattered glass.

"No need for such displays of temper, Admiral," said the traitor. "This affair will work to everyone's satisfaction. Our mission is nearly finished. Deliver the information from the packet to our man at the George and Dragon, and Le Chacal shall reward you handsomely. A few days later you shall have your new command."

"Good," Locke muttered. From the placement of his silhouette, Amanda realized that he stood right in front of the curtains. She tensed. Her heavy breath fogged the windowpane.

"But in case you are tempted to double-cross me," the traitor continued, "I feel obliged to tell you that I am prepared to send those raving letters of yours to the First Lord. Should anything happen to me, my men have instructions to deliver them immediately. You'll hang for murder."

"My life is ruined either way. You bastard." Locke was angry. She didn't need to see his face to determine that.

"You won't be ruined if you continue to follow Le Chacal's instructions."

"By God, what a supreme stroke of irony—I must atone for my sins by committing treason."

"As sins go, yours is particularly heinous. I wonder how society would react if they knew you strangled your wife in a jealous rage."

Nausea swept Amanda in a wave. She squeezed her eyes shut. First treason, now murder.

"I did not mean to kill her," Locke said thickly.

"Whether you meant to kill her or not, the fact is that she's dead. But for those letters, her death seemed like an accident," the traitor continued. "You should have been more careful."

"Why did you choose me to be your cat's paw? Why not someone less conspicuous?"

"Because of your influence as an admiral, and because your particular vices made you an easy target. As it turns out, we've proven to be an effective team, you and I."

"Go to hell, you hypocrite. You betrayed your country, then blackmailed me into helping you."

"My country," spat the traitor, "betrayed me first. But I did not come here to argue with you. You have your orders, Locke. Defy us once more, and you'll regret it."

Amanda heard one set of heavy footsteps head toward the door. The hinges protested, the door clicked shut again. She pulled away from the window and squinted through the panes. One silhouette still remained in the room. She put her ear back to the glass. What was Locke doing now?

Another clink of glass. "My dearest Emily," Locke murmured, "I am so very sorry. Forgive me."

A pause. Then footsteps, headed away. The hinges screeched, then the study door closed with a snap.

Amanda sagged against the door frame and put a trembling hand over her mouth. She didn't need to find the documents Locke had hidden away. She hadn't heard the traitor's name, but she had heard his voice, and knew when and where they would make their next move.

She gingerly opened the doors into the study. Warmth flooded through her. She peered through the part in the curtains—the room was empty. Rubbing her hands to restore the circulation, she stumbled over to the fireplace. Cold, she was so cold. She pried off her gloves and held her numbed fingers before the flames. What had just taken place within these four walls chilled her more than the night air. She didn't know the traitor's name—Locke had never mentioned it—but she knew she would recognize his voice if she heard it again.

She wriggled her toes inside her slippers as feeling began to creep back. She'd wait a little longer, just to make sure no one saw her leave. Her mind reeled with a million questions. Who was Le Chacal—another French agent? Heavens, she'd discovered an entire nest of them. Whoever this Frenchman was, it sounded like the traitor from the Admiralty took orders from him. Locke played only a small part in this treasonous web, but that had not diminished her desire for vengeance. For justice. She had to find Captain Everly—Jack—right away.

Amanda thrust her hands into her gloves, then hurried to the door. She opened it a crack, then cocked a cautious ear. Good, there was no one in the hall. She opened the door a little further, mindful of the hinges, and slipped out into the corridor.

A burst of falsetto laughter froze her where she stood. Someone was coming down the hall from the main stairs. Startled, Amanda lifted her skirts and raced to the back staircase, praying that she wouldn't run into anyone else.

The clamor of raised voices caught her attention as she neared the first floor landing. She peeked around the corner. A few offices stood in the hall, not far from her. Amanda ducked back into hiding. It would seem suspicious if she suddenly appeared from the servants' stairs. Better to go up one more flight, then come back down the main stairway. She watched the officers nervously, but none of them so much as noticed her as she sneaked across the hall and up the next set of stairs. Amanda's knees wobbled as she hurried upward.

The second floor of the town house held the family and guest bedchambers. Amanda ran this gauntlet as quickly as she could, willing herself to ignore the moaning and the rhythmic thumping that came from some of the occupied rooms. *Occupied.* Heat flooded her face. The sooner she found Jack, the sooner they could leave this horrible place.

At the head of the stairs, she paused to take a deep breath. How she wanted out of this house! She concentrated on each step as she descended, for her shattered nerves had turned her limbs to jelly. She must be calm, she told herself; she must do her duty. So intent was she on her footing that she didn't recognize the men standing by the newel post until she was upon them.

Admiral Locke looked up, and his icy blue eyes impaled her.

"Prospecting the bedrooms, Miss Campion?" he asked, one brow lifted in a suggestive arch.

The question caught Amanda off guard. She was fumbling for a reply when Everly's admonition ricocheted through her skull. *You must play your role, no matter what depredations you see, no matter how shocked or appalled you become.* She was supposed to be a strumpet; she would act like one. She tossed her head and smiled at her enemy.

"I did not think you would object." She hardly recognized the low, throaty laugh as her own.

Locke shrugged. "Not at all, my dear. But I fear Everly is still engaged at cards. I do hope he hasn't forgotten about you."

"I doubt that, Admiral." A knot of arctic cold gathered beneath Amanda's heart. He was playing with her. Why?

"Do not fret—I'm certain this young man could divert you for a time. Could you not, Lieutenant?"

Amanda turned and found herself the focus of Harry Morgan's astonished stare. From the bumper of brandy in his hand, as well as the golden cast to his hazel eyes, she could see he was well and truly foxed. Oh, heavens, what else could go wrong?

She pirouetted and latched coquettishly on to Harry's arm. "Yes, I'm sure Mr. Morgan will keep me amused for a time. If you'll excuse us?" With a flutter of her lashes, Amanda pulled Harry away from Admiral Locke.

She could feel the admiral's gaze drilling into her back, and willed herself not to run.

"What . . . what're you doing here, Amanda?" demanded Harry. He wobbled and stumbled against her.

"Shh! Not so loud," Amanda hissed, propping him up with one shoulder. She maneuvered him down the hall. The door to a side parlor stood open, and she headed for it. She needed to explain before things got any worse.

Harry ignored her. "I said, what're you doing here?" He shook off her touch, and his eyes flared with a golden glow as he scanned her up and down.

"Not now, Harry. I'll tell you everything later, I promise." Amanda darted a panicked glance over her shoulder, but Locke had disappeared.

"No, you'll tell me now!" With an oath, Harry seized her arm and propelled her into the parlor.

"Harry, you're hurting me," she protested. She tried to pull away, but Harry tightened his grip. She winced. "You're bosky."

The lieutenant downed his brandy in three gulps and set the glass down with a bang. "So what if I am a lil' cup-shot? I'm not so disguised that I can' see the way you're dressed. You look like a wh . . . a doxy. What the hell're you doing here?"

She had never seen him like this. His slurred, accusing tone sliced through her. "I promise I'll explain everything later. Please, just let me go."

"No. No more promises," Harry muttered. He leaned down, his nose almost touching hers. "Tell me—now!"

Amanda coughed as brandy fumes engulfed her. "You know exactly what I'm doing—I'm here to find my proof."

He waved a finger in her face. "Dammit, Amanda, I told you to go home. You don' belong here."

She batted his hand away. "Stop ordering me about, Harry."

"Stubborn. Always so stubborn. You just keep pushing, don' you? You don' care who you hurt." Harry ran a hand through his tousled hair. "Well, I'm not goin' to stand by and let you do this. You're goin' home."

Amanda recoiled from the strange glitter in his eyes. "No, Harry, I can't. I'm here with Captain Everly."

Harry's brows shot skyward. "Everly? Cap'n High-an'-Mighty? You're here wi' him?"

A bitter mixture of alarm and impatience mingled on Amanda tongue. "Yes, I am, but it's not— "

The young lieutenant didn't wait to hear the rest. "That whoremonger. I'll call him out!" he roared. He released Amanda, pivoted, and all but lunged for the door.

"Harry, no!" Amanda managed to grab his sleeve. "Stop this!"

"Why're you protectin' him?" Harry spun about and grabbed her by the shoulders, his fingers digging painfully into the tender skin. "You wanted to be here, didn't you? You wanted to be here with *him*."

"Don't be ridiculous. I needed his help to get into the house."

"Did he give you that dress?" he demanded. "Has he kissed you? He has, hasn't he?"

Alarm raked its way up Amanda's throat. She couldn't reason with Harry, not when he was like this. Neither could she tell him the truth. "N–no, of course not."

Harry stared at her, his eyes narrowed to golden slits. "You're lying."

"Harry, please let me go."

"Not until you kiss me the way you kissed him." Intent, he bent down and tried to plant his lips against hers. Amanda gasped and twisted away; Harry's mouth skidded across her cheek. He frowned at the evasion. She tried to struggle free of his embrace, but he tightened his grip and tried to kiss her again.

"Stop it!" Amanda cried. Panic warred with reason; panic won. She slapped him. Hard.

The young lieutenant, caught off his guard, teetered backward and landed sprawling on an overstuffed chair. He raised a hand to the angry red mark on his cheek, his face clouded.

"I thought you were my friend, not a drunken sot whose only thought is to maul me." Amanda trembled

from head to toe. The coldness beneath her breastbone
was back, a terrible black void. So much had happened
tonight . . . she wasn't sure what to think anymore. Tears
sprang to her lashes as she backed toward the door.

"Amanda, wait!" Harry sputtered, struggling to rise
from the chair.

"Just forget you ever saw me," Amanda whispered as
she made her escape.

Desperation drove her as she dashed into the hallway.
She needed to leave! She barely saw Admiral Locke by
the parlor door, barely saw the assessing look he gave
her. She slowed only when she reached the ballroom; the
sight of the assembled guests made her pause. She
needed to collect herself. If she dashed through the room
like a Maenad, all wild eyes and flying hair, she would
become an instant cynosure. She'd already withstood
quite enough attention.

"Why, here she is, Lord Peverell," came a sweet voice
at Amanda's elbow. "Dearest Lucy, where have you
been? We've been looking everywhere for you."

Amanda, startled, met the venomous green gaze of
Mrs. Danvers. With the hostess was a tall, dandified man
whose capucine-colored waistcoat glowed like a bright
orange signal beacon from beneath his black evening
jacket. Dark, carefully pomaded hair framed his sharp,
pointed face. The dandy smiled wolfishly at Amanda and
licked his lips.

"She is everything you said she was, Maria," he
drawled. "Fine as fivepence."

The hairs on the back of Amanda's neck stood at attention. "Excuse me, Mrs. Danvers, but I must find Captain Everly."

"Oh, you needn't worry about Captain Everly. He is
well looked-after." She twirled one bottle red curl
around her finger. "Viscount Peverell has been very anxious to make your acquaintance. He's a friend of the
admiral's, and quite a man of influence. I suggest you be
very, very nice to him."

Nice to him? What the devil was the woman up to?
Amanda scanned the room with anxious eyes, trying to

spot a glimpse of Everly's golden head, but to no avail. "I'm afraid, my lord, that Mrs. Danvers has misinformed you. I am with Captain Everly."

"A spirited filly, eh? Even better." Lord Peverell chuckled. His high, starched collar points framed his pointed chin like an extra set of canine teeth as his smile broadened. "Come along, m'girl, and I'll make it worth your while. I'm certainly more flush in the pocket than an upstart baronet."

Mrs. Danvers spread her fan and bent behind it to whisper something to the viscount. The man uttered a sharp bark of laughter.

"Quite so, Mrs. Danvers. A firm hand, indeed. I believe I shall enjoy this."

His laughter cut across her nerves like a blade over a wound. Intuition told her to flee, whether she looked like a wild woman or not. She retreated a step. "Captain Everly is waiting for me," she said, less firmly than she would have liked.

"Oh, I wouldn't be so sure of that." With a low, knowing laugh, Mrs. Danvers glided away.

Lord Peverell was suddenly by Amanda's side, one arm snaked around her waist, his hand pressed indecently against the curve of her bottom. The tension knotted in her shoulders rose into her throat and came out her mouth as a shriek.

"Come, my dove. No need to play the innocent." Peverell nipped at her earlobe.

"No!" Amanda looked wildly about, searching for someone who might come to her aid, but all she saw were amused expressions—if they even noticed her at all.

"Go ahead and struggle," murmured Lord Peverell. His whiskers tickled her ear. "It makes the conquest all the more satisfying."

The cold, gaping pit in Amanda's stomach gaped wider as she realized she had to get herself out of this coil. Her fingers balled into a tight fist; she no longer cared about appearances.

*   *   *

Too long. She'd been gone far too long. This arrangement brought to mind the uncertainty of steering ships through a fog bank—no one knew where the others were, what was going on, or if they'd sailed too close to the enemy. Time for him to reconnoiter. He threw his cards on the table and rose.

"I'm out, gentlemen," Everly declared.

A sly grin stole across Lieutenant Hale's face. "What, leaving already, Captain? A pity—I've almost recouped my losses from our last encounter."

"As much as I'd like to continue this diversion, I'm afraid I have something better waiting for me. I pray you excuse me." He inclined his head to the group, then took his leave.

"No wonder he seemed so distracted," one of the other officers said with a chuckle.

"You'd be distracted too, Maitland, if you had that particular bit o' muslin to warm your bed," said another.

The nape of Everly's neck grew hot, but he forced himself to maintain a sedate, nonchalant pace. He scanned the other tables, but saw no sign of Locke. His eyes narrowed. Where was the admiral? Had Amanda been discovered? Damnation—he should have been the one down in the study, the one taking this terrible risk.

The captain wrestled to keep his imagination in check, and his mind focused on facts. Having Amanda—Miss Tremayne—on his lap had scrambled his instincts. To institute an effective search, he must be methodical. He would make sure she wasn't on this floor before he went downstairs.

"You're not leaving us so soon, are you, Captain?" purred a female voice close to his ear.

Everly turned just as Mrs. Danvers attached herself to his arm. The redhead was intent on mischief; Felicia used to get that same cunning look in her eyes whenever she was up to something. A look that set off warning bells in his head.

"Not at all, Mrs. Danvers—"

"Maria."

"Maria." Everly's polite smile grew tight at the edges. "I'm going to join Lucy. She's expecting me."

The woman parted her ruby-painted lips and ran the tip of her tongue over her lower lip. "Are you so sure of that?"

Everly frowned. Egad, the woman was like a leech—once she latched on, she was nearly impossible to shake off.

"What do you see in that die-away chit anyway, Captain?" continued Mrs. Danvers, without waiting for his reply. Jeweled rings flashed as she ran a hand over his chest. "I know an older, more experienced woman who would know how to fulfill your desire."

Everly thought of Amanda's sweetly curved backside pressed against his thighs, remembered the feel of her lips, the scent of her hair. Another rush of need engulfed him like a tidal wave. He shook himself and tried to conjure visions of snowstorms and ice to cool his ardor. What was he thinking? He should never have taken such liberties with her, and he knew it.

Mrs. Danvers must have seen his flush and mistaken it for anticipation; with a laugh, she twined her arms around his neck. "That's better. Much better. I knew you'd come to see it my way."

The captain stared down at the woman with narrowed eyes and disengaged himself from her embrace.

"Madam, I suggest you display your wares elsewhere—dockside comes to mind. Good evening." Ordinarily he would use fire or a knife to remove a leech from his skin. This time, he hoped cutting words would suffice.

He heard Mrs. Danvers's gasp of outrage just before a shriek split the air. Everly's head snapped toward its source. Two figures—one tall and masculine, one petite and distinctly feminine—stood just inside the main doorway, locked in a close embrace.

"You seem very certain of your mistress's affections," snapped Mrs. Danvers. The angry red in her cheeks warred with her coppery hair. "It would seem she has other ideas."

Closer scrutiny revealed that the woman in the doorway was struggling against the taller, more powerful man. With a jolt of alarm, Everly recognized her raven curls and spangled muslin gown. He muttered an evil-sounding curse and launched himself toward the door.

He was no bear-garden bruiser, but he was handy enough with his fives; at the moment he wanted nothing more than to floor that jack-a-dandy who dared molest Amanda. As it turned out, the lady had no need of rescue. He watched as Amanda, pale-faced and terrified, cocked back her fist and planted the fop as sweet a facer as he had ever seen. The man screeched and covered his bloodied nose. Everly grinned in spite of himself; he should have seen it coming.

"You little bitch!" the dandy yelped, his voice muffled by his kerchief. "How dare you strike me!"

Amanda backed against the door frame, her eyes huge and wild. Her fist remained clenched, her muscles tight.

Everly stepped between them. "She gave you exactly what you deserved," he said with no little heat. "I suggest you leave her alone."

The viscount stared at the captain as though he'd lost his senses. "What does it matter to you? She's a whore. Less than nothing."

"You were poaching, Peverell. You're lucky she didn't serve you any worse." Everly turned to Amanda. "Are you all right?"

"Get me out of this terrible place, Jack," she replied in a low, strained voice. "Please." She was shaking, although he could not tell if fury or hysteria were the cause.

Coldness gripped his vitals as anger and frustration warred with concern. If she had not blackmailed him into bringing her here, this would never have happened. Damnation!

"Did you find what you came for?" he rumbled.

Amanda nodded and gripped his arm. "Just get me away from here before I scream and run straight to Bedlam."

Her skin was clammy, her face white as a new topsail. If they didn't leave now, he wasn't sure how either of them would react to any further complications.

Mrs. Danvers was tending to the still-yelping Lord

Peverell with a semblance of great sympathy. The other guests gawped and laughed at the spectacle, allowing Everly and Amanda to slip, unnoticed, to the main stairs. Perfect.

"Look lively," Everly murmured in her ear. "We'll slip away before Locke comes to investigate."

Everly escorted Amanda down the stairs as quickly as his injured leg would allow, although she wanted him to move faster than he was able; she rushed ahead and tugged at his arm to hurry him along.

Everly resisted. "Trim your sails, before you break both our necks."

He spoke more harshly than he'd intended, and she looked up at him like a frightened doe, tensed and poised to flee. A raucous caw of laughter erupted from the ballroom, and she flinched.

"Steady," he murmured. He took her cloak from the footman and draped it over her shivering shoulders.

She nodded, and her curls bounced with the movement.

"Once we're away, you can tell me everything," he said as he led her down to the carriage. "Especially what has frightened you so."

"It is worse than I imagined, Jack," she breathed, her voice a hollow whisper. "Much, much worse."

Chapter Nine

Once in the carriage, Everly did not mince words. "Well, what did you learn?"

"You're vexed with me." Amanda's thin voice came from the corner, where she huddled in the velvet folds of her cloak.

"What do you mean?" The captain frowned as he considered her response. He had to admit that he had been more of a crosspatch in the past few days than he'd ever been in his entire life. All due to the influence of Miss Amanda Tremayne. She had a special talent for turning everyone's life upside-down.

She stared at the floor. "The way you looked at me when we left. The . . . the way you kissed me."

"I should not have done that. I was less than a gentleman, and for that I apologize." Everly expelled his breath in a rush. He *had* been angry. Angry that she had put them both in such a precarious situation. Angry with her for being so attractive, and jealous of the way the other men had looked at her. And he had been afraid for her, fears which had been justified. Whatever the reasons, he should never have taken his frustrations out on her. Everly removed his bicorne and tossed it on the seat across from them. He shoved a hand through his hair.

She edged further away from him, pulling herself into a tight ball. "You had every right to be angry. I should never have tricked you into taking me to that party."

The muscles at the back of Everly's neck drew taut. "What do you expect me to say, Miss Tremayne? 'Of course not, you were perfectly justified?' What you did put both of us at risk. You are an innocent. You went into that house knowing nothing about a courtesan's trade, yet you were determined to play the part."

"I realize that now. I thought I . . . that I could . . . Those men thought that I was just a pretty . . . thing . . . and they could do whatever they wanted to me."

A soft sob came from the depths of her hood, and Everly realized that she was weeping. Sympathy and shame blindsided him. She was overwrought, and he had given her the full volley of his fury. Had the disaster with Felicia so hardened his heart? Had he become as ugly inside as out?

"Gently, now. Everything is all right." He reached out a hand to her, and she did not pull away. He brushed back the edge of the hood to reveal her face. Moisture gilded her lashes. She tried to fight back the tears; she squeezed her eyes shut, but a solitary droplet escaped and trailed liquid silver down her cheek.

"I was . . . so . . . frightened. You were right. I should never . . . never have . . ." Gasps punctuated her words. Another tear followed the first. She raised a trembling hand to cover her face.

Everly reacted without thinking. With long arms, he reached out and drew her closer. To his surprise, she uttered a little cry and clung to him, her fingers clutching his lapels. She shivered within his embrace as he stroked her hair and murmured gentle words. "It's over, Amanda. You're safe. You'll never have to go through an ordeal like that again."

She snuffled and nodded, her face buried in the fall of his cravat.

Everly lifted her chin. Her eyes glazed with shock, Amanda stared at him, seemingly unaware of the tears streaming across her bloodless cheeks. Everly smiled and pulled his kerchief from his pocket. "Why do women never have a handkerchief when they need one? My cravat makes a sad substitute."

"I fear I've wilted it." Amanda took the kerchief and smiled back at him through her tears, a smile that hit Everly in his vitals like a shot. She was truly innocent. Unlike Felicia, nothing about Amanda was contrived.

"And I fear I'm going to kiss you again." Everly drew his thumb over her quivering lower lip, fascinated by the lush curve of her mouth. He bent his head and tenderly brushed his lips over hers.

She did not stiffen, or pull way, or turn her head. He heard her soft gasp, felt her shift closer to him. That was enough to tempt him into a second kiss.

"Amanda," he murmured.

Everly had every intention of controlling himself, of maintaining a chase and gentle embrace, but never before had a kiss tasted so sweet. He claimed her mouth and savored the salty sheen of tears that clung to her lips. A tiny moan escaped Amanda and she leaned into his kiss, her breasts pressed against his chest. Everly's self-control began to shred like old sails in a storm.

This felt so . . . so right, even in this awkward pose—knees bracketed together, shoulders braced against the padded squabs, bodies twisted at strange angles to clasp each other more closely. That didn't matter. All he could think about in that moment was her. Desire heightened every awareness; he reveled in the seductive scent of her skin, the feel of her body snuggled so intimately against his, the intoxicating softness of her lips. Heat surged through him and ignited a passion he had thought long dead. He shifted one hand beneath her cloak, laid it on her hip just above her pert, rounded derriere. He wanted her, and not just in a physical sense. True, her form was attractive. Very, very attractive. But what he felt went deeper than that. Everything about her—her loyalty, her volatile temper, her stubborn independence—combined to form the unique treasure that was Amanda. The woman he held in his arms. Damnation—she was a feast for the mind as well as the senses, and at the moment he wanted nothing more than to devour her. In a distant corner of his conscience, the remnants of his self-control nagged at him, but at the moment he was quite willing to throw all sense of caution overboard.

His conscience persisted. Everly drew back and gazed down at Amanda. Her eyes heavy-lidded, her lips swollen from his kisses—she had all but surrendered herself. So much trust. Such innocence. Everly swallowed hard. He mustn't do this. With a great effort, he set her away from him.

"Jack? What's wrong?" Her voice echoed the confusion on her dainty features.

He could still feel the warmth radiating from those lush curves. He imagined running his hands over that lovely pale skin, caressing her narrow waist and flaring hips, her body against his without the constraints of fabric between them. . . . Cynicism slapped him. She didn't know what she was doing. She had been distraught, and he had just taken advantage of her. Again. He cringed. Would he never learn?

"I seem to forget all sense of propriety where you are concerned, Miss Tremayne." Addressing her in a formal manner helped put some distance between them, but it was not enough. Everly levered himself over to the opposite bench. Both of them would be safer this way.

"One would suppose me a bad influence." Her smile was a pallid version of its normal self, not even enough to evoke her dimples. She rubbed a finger over her lips and slid her gaze away.

Disappointment pricked Everly with sharp, spiteful fingers, and he shifted his expression to blank neutrality. She had come to her senses; she was trying to remove the traces of his touch. What on earth had possessed him to kiss her like that? Felicia had screamed and run from his shambling form. Other women had curled their lips in disgust. At least Miss Tremayne was more polite. Everly damned himself for a fool.

He offered her a weak smile of his own. "Nonsense. Tonight you did what few others could have accomplished—you managed to get the information from Locke's study."

Amanda bit her lip. "Well, not exactly."

"What do you mean?"

She fingered the drawstring of her reticule. "Locke moved whatever had been in that secret compartment. It was empty."

Everly bit back an oath. "But you said you found what you came for."

She nodded. "By accident, really. I was looking around the study, thinking that Locke had hidden his secrets somewhere nearby, but I heard voices coming down the hall."

Everly tensed. He remembered what had happened the last time she'd tried to hide in that room.

Amanda saw his expression and gave an odd little laugh. "No, they didn't catch me—I fled out onto the balcony."

"Small wonder you were shivering. You could have gotten pneumonia."

"It was the only safe place, and a fortunate choice—I overheard their conversation, Captain. I heard every word they said."

"They? They, who?"

"Locke, and the traitor from the Admiralty."

Everly sat back, stunned. "The traitor? How do you know it was him?"

"He gave Locke orders, but Locke didn't want to follow them. They argued."

Something alive stirred within Everly, something he hadn't felt since the battle of Lissa. He realized how much he missed the excitement of incipient combat. "Did Locke mention the traitor's name?"

"No." Amanda's brow furrowed. "But there was something familiar about his voice."

"How so?"

"I know I've heard it before, but I just can't remember where. The more I think about it, the more it slips away from me."

Everly gestured impatiently. "Don't concentrate on that right now. What else did you hear?"

Her eyes lost their focus. "I know their next move."

The hairs stirred at the back of Everly's neck. "Go on."

"Information important to their cause is coming in on the next navy packet; it arrives in Portsmouth on Tuesday. The traitor ordered Locke to retrieve the information and deliver it to their contact at the George and Dragon Inn."

"Good God."

"There's more." She swallowed hard. "The traitor said that someone named Le Chacal would reward Locke once he completed his mission."

"The Jackal," Everly translated. "I should have suspected that the man in the Admiralty wasn't the ringleader."

"No—he gets his orders from this Frenchman."

"This conspiracy runs deeper than we imagined," he muttered.

Amanda leaned forward, a strain of urgency in her voice. "But the traitor said that this will be Locke's last assignment. After this, he departs for a new command, and the traitor will leave for France soon afterward. We have to tell someone about this, Captain, and quickly."

Everly rubbed his jaw. "And so we will," he stated. He'd take her to Lord Carlisle. . . . Everly caught himself. He did not know where Carlisle lived, nor did he think the spymaster would want Everly dragging this business into his home. With the earl's penchant for secrecy, Everly wagered that few others in London knew his vocation. The captain gazed at Amanda, at her pale, drawn face. Where else could he take her? To Admiral Lord St. Vincent? Everly grimaced. Given his patron's prejudice against Amanda's father, he did not think that a viable option. He would be able to convince the admiral of the veracity of their story, but Amanda would not be a credible witness in the old man's eyes. No, it had to be Carlisle.

Everly thought of Grayson MacAllister, dressed in livery and riding at the back of the carriage, keeping careful watch. By the time he had the young Scotsman send word to the earl, then set up a time and place for the interview, it would be morning. Amanda—Miss Tremayne—needed to rest and recover from this evening's events. They had over two days until Locke was to meet the packet; they could afford a few hours' delay.

"I will send a message directly," he said. "I imagine

my superior will wish to speak with us both. I shall arrange a meeting for first thing tomorrow morning."

Amanda frowned. "Why not now?"

"I will need time to reach him. Besides, you have had enough excitement for one evening. You will make a much more credible witness after you've rested and changed into something more appropriate. As it is, I will have a difficult time explaining how you became involved in this whole affair."

"Oh. Of course." Amanda pulled her cloak more securely about her, hiding all traces of her gown beneath the velvet folds, then pulled the hood over her head. Her features disappeared into shadow.

He had embarrassed her. Somewhere in the course of these events he had evolved from a charming man into a complete oaf. At least he wouldn't have to worry about his lack of manners when he was back at sea. Everly leaned out the window and ordered his coachman to change course.

They journeyed in painful silence broken only by the sound of the horses' hooves and the jingling of the harness. The streets in this part of London were all but empty at this hour, and they soon arrived at Amanda's lodging house. Not soon enough, judging by the way she hunched into the corner and avoided his eyes.

"Allow me to escort you up," said Everly as they pulled to a halt.

"That is not necessary, Captain," Amanda replied in a stilted tone. She did not even wait for the footman to open the door; she reached for the door handle.

He put out a hand to stop her, but she drew back. Everly's jaw flexed. "Try to get some sleep. I will come for you midmorning."

"I shall be ready." The footman opened the door, and she was gone from the carriage. Everly descended behind her and watched her small form dash into the building. He waited until she was safely inside before he climbed back into the waiting coach. His leg twinged; more rain was imminent. Damnation. He glanced back at the drab lodging house and sighed. Tomorrow morning he could finish this business and get back at sea, where he belonged.

When Everly arrived home, he gestured to Mr. Mac-Allister. "Come with me, Thomas. I require your assistance."

"As you wish, sir," answered the younger man. He followed Everly into the study and closed the door behind them.

"Thomas. Hmph. I'd never take you for a 'Thomas,' MacAllister." Everly spared a glance at the young Scot, who looked out of character in livery and a powdered wig, before he went to his desk. He pulled out a sheet of paper and began to scribble a hasty note.

"My disguise must be complete, down to an assumed name. Besides, every household has a footman named Thomas." The Scotsman's smile dimmed. "You seem concerned, Captain."

"As well I might be. Were we followed from Admiral Locke's house?"

"No. I would have informed you if we were."

This piece of news, while reassuring, did little to loosen the tight knot of tension in Everly's shoulders. "Thank goodness for that, at least."

"I take it that your foray into the admiral's house was successful?"

Everly nodded, still focused on the letter. "Indeed."

"And Miss Tremayne is well?"

Now Everly's eyes flew to meet the Scotsman's bland gaze. "What do you mean by that? Explain yourself."

"She seemed quite upset when you left the admiral's house."

"As well she might, given what went on there."

MacAllister cleared his throat. "I have been riding around in your carriage for nearly a fortnight, Captain, and although you have never said as much, I am aware that Miss Tremayne is involved in this affair—she's in it up to her pretty neck. No, I have not mentioned this to Lord Carlisle. But I do wonder why you haven't told him about her."

"It hasn't been important until now," Everly growled. "She was seeking information to clear her father's name, and to prove Locke's guilt, but tonight she discovered a great deal more. She knows who the traitor is."

"What?" All traces of color vanished from MacAllister's face.

"She overheard Locke talking to him. She didn't see the man or hear his name, but she knows his voice, and she knows where they'll strike next. I need to get her to Lord Carlisle immediately. I assume you know where to find him." The captain's tone suggested he would accept nothing else.

"I can get the message to him at once," the young man asserted.

"Good."

"Ah, Captain . . . ?"

"Yes?" Everly folded the vellum and affixed his seal.

MacAllister clasped his hands behind his back. "I mean you no disrespect, sir, but are you certain you can trust the girl?"

Everly sat up, his brows pinched together in a line. Trust her? She had lied to him, manipulated him, and badgered him. She'd jeopardized his mission and ruffled his temper, not to mention wreaking havoc in his precisely ordered life. Yet, after all that had happened, he realized that he *did* trust her. He trusted her completely. Then again, he amended with a wry smile, Amanda Tremayne had a way of casting anyone's wits adrift.

"Yes, Mr. MacAllister," he replied, his smile fading. "Miss Tremayne is as loyal to the Crown as I am."

The younger man seemed to accept this assurance; the tense lines of his shoulders relaxed.

Everly handed him the letter. "Deliver this to Lord Carlisle at once, and return with word of our rendezvous point."

MacAllister tucked the message into his breast pocket. "Yes, sir."

"One more thing." Everly drummed his fingers on the arm of his chair. "Do you have other men at your disposal?"

The young man's expression turned wary. "I can arrange it, sir. Might I ask why?"

"I want you to have them keep watch on Miss Tremayne's rooms at the lodging house, just to make sure she remains out of harm's way until morning. I do not know if Locke suspects her true identity, but right now we cannot take any chances. Her safety is vital to our mission; she alone can make a positive identification of the traitor."

The Scotsman nodded. "I'll see to it, Captain."

"Look sharp, then. Too much time has passed already."

MacAllister inclined his head in salute, then departed.

Everly slouched back in his chair; the leather creaked a vague protest, as did his injured leg. Amanda—Miss Tremayne—would be fine. He'd take her to Carlisle in the morning, they would expose Locke, unmask the traitor, and he'd have a new command before All Hallows' Eve. It was all quite straightforward.

Right. And he was the Queen Mother.

With an ungallant snort, Everly heaved himself out of his chair. He limped up the stairs to his bedchamber, his humor getting worse with each step, and bellowed for Stubbs.

"Confound it, man, where are you?" he roared.

"In a fine temper tonight, ain't ye, Captain?" the grizzled servant muttered, carrying a laden tray into the room. "With the rain comin', I thought ye might do with a nip o' the hellbroth."

Everly grunted his thanks and poured himself a glass of whiskey. Laudanum would leave him groggy in the morning; for tonight, alcohol would have to take the edge off his pain. "Here's to an end to this blasted business."

"Summat amiss happen at the admiral's house, sir?" Stubbs asked, his lined face etched with worry.

"No. The mission was successful. We know who the rogue is. Now we have to catch him, and nab the French agent responsible for compromising our national security."

"Sweet Jasus!" Stubbs's jaw sagged.

A humorless smile stretched Everly's lips. "Exactly."

Stubbs cocked his head, his eyes clouded. "Then if ever'thing went so well, Captain, why the blue-devils? Wimmin trouble then, eh?"

"What the hell are you rattling on about?" grumbled Everly. He shrugged out of his jacket and tried to remove his cravat with a series of impatient tugs.

The servant picked up the coat and brushed it off. "Beggin' yer pardon, Captain, but ye're never this out o' sorts unless a female's involved."

Everly shot the smaller man a quelling glare. "You've become quite an expert on my moods these days."

Stubbs helped unknot the tangled neckcloth. "Aye, sir. Just an observation, sir."

Everly harrumphed. "Well, it so happens that a young lady *is* involved."

The servant shook his head. "No good will come of it, Captain. Females mean nothin' but trouble."

"Spoken like an old tar." Everly chuckled dryly. "And a bachelor, to boot. That will be all for now, Stubbs— enough of your fussing. Wake me when Mr. MacAllister returns, and again at dawn."

Stubbs's gnarled brows lifted skyward. "Dawn, Captain?"

Everly lobbed his waistcoat at the nearest chair. The shirt followed, but missed and hit the floor. "What, are you deaf as well as impertinent?"

"No, sir. Dawn it is, sir." Muttering something about land-bound captains with bees in their bicornes, Stubbs retrieved the fallen clothing and left.

Everly hobbled to the washstand and poured cold water into the basin. This uneven temper was unlike him. An image of Amanda in that nigh-unto-indecent dress flashed through his mind, and his body responded. He splashed his face vigorously to douse the heat. Perhaps Stubbs was right. Females—certain females, at least— were nothing but trouble. If only she weren't so bloody attractive . . .

The captain remembered their first meeting at the ball, then their encounter outside Admiral Lord St. Vincent's home. What would she do when this was all over? Perhaps that young lieutenant—Harry Morgan—would marry her. Everly scowled as he reached for a towel. Amanda deserved more than an overprotective bantam. She deserved—

He straightened, a warning tremor arcing through his body. Amanda's lieutenant—Everly remembered seeing that young officer's face at Locke's soirée. He rubbed his jaw. Was he imagining things? No, he recalled seeing that face in profile at one of the gambling tables, just before Locke had come to greet them. Damnation! Everly ran damp fingers through his hair. He should have recognized that ginger head at once, but he had been distracted.

His curse blistered the air. How could he have discounted something so important? Had the young man seen Amanda—or worse, recognized her? What was he doing there in the first place? Locke had invited some of the worse sorts into the house: debauchers, rakes, gamesters of the lowest order. Where did the red-haired lieutenant fit into that scheme, and how had he come by an invitation?

A muscle twitched at Everly's temple. He did not know how much Amanda had told her friend, but she seemed to trust him. How loyal Harry would be to her, he could only guess. Everly stripped off his remaining clothing and forced himself to crawl into bed. He entertained thoughts of returning to Amanda's rooms, of relocating her and her grandmother to his house, but dismissed the idea as nonsense. He would not give in to foolish paranoia.

Everly pounded one of the pillows, leaving a fist-sized indent. He was turning into a character from one of those dreadful romances Felicia had been so fond of—a crotchety old wigsby who had nothing better to do than fret and worry. Amanda would be fine until morning; there were no hordes of French agents in the shadows, waiting to murder her. Everly sank back into the bed, his head now throbbing in time with his leg.

He just wanted her out of harm's way. After their

meeting with Carlisle, he hoped she would remember her promise and let him finish the investigation. He snorted and rolled onto his side. Not bloody likely. He'd ask Lord Carlisle if he could spare Mr. MacAllister for one more mission: to see Amanda safely back to Dorset. Everly grinned suddenly, imagining the outraged expression on Amanda's face when she found herself outmaneuvered.

Amanda. Miss Tremayne. Try as he might, Everly could not get to sleep; he saw her face even beneath his eyelids. He rose and poured himself another glass of whiskey. This was going to be a long night.

Chapter Ten

Amanda lay awake in the darkness of her bedroom, watching as the patch of sky visible through the small garret window lightened from black to deep purple to steel gray. A pretty-enough sight, until clouds rolled in like slow tide and blotted out the glimmer of the last morning stars. Amanda listened to the soft, even cadence of her grandmother's breathing, then rolled onto her side and burrowed further under the covers. Weariness bore down on every inch her body; the marrow of her bones had turned to lead. The series of fitful naps she'd managed during the night had given her little rest. Too many images writhed within her memory.

Admiral Locke's conversation with the traitor. His suspicious, icy stare. The wolfish anticipation on Viscount Peverell's face. Her frigid sojourn on the balcony. Mrs. Danvers's sneer. Harry's drink-suffused anger.

Jack's kiss.

More than anything else, her mind lingered on the tender, passionate embrace she and the captain had shared in the carriage. She pressed her palms to her face and fancied she could still detect the faint scent of his skin, feel the sinewy strength of his arms around her and his broad, muscled chest pressed against her breasts. The sensation of his lips over hers had been blissful.

Amanda groaned and pulled the covers over her head. The memory of that kiss alone was enough to ignite the same strange, fluttery warmth that she'd felt last night. Her skin still tingled from his touch. What madness had possessed her? She had *wanted* him to hold her, to comfort her . . . to kiss her. And she had clung to him like a wanton. No lady would behave as she had. Small wonder he had wanted nothing further to do with her.

Amanda sighed and bit her lip. She would not cry! Jack—Captain Everly—was right to set himself at a distance. If only it didn't hurt so much. It would not have, if it were not her fault. His stern visage and stilted, formal address had spoken volumes; her indiscretion had cost her his respect, and any hope of his friendship. Or more.

She chastised herself for being such a goose. He was a war hero. She was a nobody. A nuisance. What could he possibly see in her? Amanda thought about the dress and flushed. Aside from her physical charms, that is. Oh, could she do nothing right?

Botheration!

Amanda flung back the covers and rose. Sleep was a lost cause, and she refused to languish in bed; she may as well face the day and whatever it would bring. She fumbled in the half darkness until she found the clothes pegs, then pulled down a petticoat and a dress without bothering to determine which one she had chosen. All her dresses were similar—plain, prim, and practical. Besides, it didn't matter what she wore, as long as it was clean. As she drew off her night rail, the air pressed against her bare skin like an icy blanket. She shivered and dressed as quickly as she could, careful not to wake her grandmother. Several harsh strokes with a hairbrush tamed her torrent of curls, which she pinned into an awkward chignon without the benefit of her looking glass. She couldn't bear to see her reflection this morning, anyway; she must look a fright.

Amanda tiptoed from the bedroom, still shivering. A damp chill lingered in the air, a forecast of rain. Amanda's hands shook as she lit the fire in the stove. As warmth began to penetrate the room, she put on her work apron and began her morning chores. She was in the middle of stirring porridge when a knock at the door startled her. A glance at the cracked-face clock told her it was only half past seven. Who would be here at this hour on a Sunday morning? Her heart leaped. Was Jack—Captain Everly—here already?

She ventured to the door. "Who is it?" she called.

The voice that came from the other side was frustratingly familiar. "Amanda, open up. It's Harry."

Amanda scowled. "I don't want to see you. Go away!" she snapped.

"Amanda, please. This is important."

She leaned her forehead against the stained wooden door. "So important that it couldn't wait for a more decent hour?"

"I need to speak with you right away. I—I'm sorry about last night."

"So am I."

She heard the shuffling of booted feet. "Dammit, Amanda, if you don't open this door, I'll make a row that will wake the Devil himself."

He'd do it, too. Amanda sighed and opened the door. Harry stood before her, hat in hand, his hangdog expression made worse by his ill-used appearance. Bloodshot eyes and a pasty complexion, however, were no cause for sympathy. She glared at him. "Come in then, but be quiet about it. Grandmama is still asleep."

Harry shambled into the room, casting a cautious glance at the closed bedroom door.

"Well, what do you want?" asked Amanda, her arms folded across her chest.

The young lieutenant fiddled with the brim of his bicorne. "I came to apologize. The way I behaved last night was inexcusable."

"Yes, it was," agreed Amanda. The genuine misery on Harry's face blunted the hard edges of her indignation. "You may as well sit down, Harry. No, not that one— it's got a broken brace. Use one of the others."

"Thank you," murmured Harry as he gingerly lowered himself into the worn-looking chair.

Without ceremony, Amanda poured a cup of tea and plunked it down before him. A few drops sloshed over the edge and into the saucer. "I'd never seen you three sheets to the wind before."

Harry brushed the errant droplets from the bottom of his cup and took a careful sip. "Ugh. Insipid stuff. I don't suppose you have any coffee?"

She scowled with disapproval. "Too expensive."

The young lieutenant avoided her eyes as he took another sip. "Of course. I'm sorry."

"Whatever were you doing at Admiral Locke's in the first place, Harry?" She sat down across from him.

"I went with a former shipmate of mine, Lieutenant Edward Hale. He said this party would be just what I needed to"—he flushed deep crimson—"to loosen me up."

Amanda remembered Lieutenant Hale all too well, and she shuddered with revulsion. "Hale? The man is a knave, Harry. And out-and-out rotter."

"He knows a great many important people."

"That may be so, but why the admiral's house, of all places? You know the man's a traitor." Amanda saw the doubt flash across Harry's face, and ice replaced the blood in her veins. "Don't you?"

"We're not certain of that." Harry tried to hide his expression of discomfort in his teacup.

Amanda sat back, stunned. "You never believed me, or what was in my father's letters, did you?"

"That's not—"

"How could you?" Her chair scraped against the wood floor as she pushed it away from the table. "To say you'd help me find evidence against Locke, only to associate with him on the sly. I never took you for a hypocrite, Harry. I never thought you of all people would patronize me like this."

Harry set down his cup with a clatter. "Cut line, Amanda. I didn't want to go, but Hale said there would be men of influence present. You must understand that I'll never get a captaincy unless I have a patron, and I thought I might find someone there."

Harry had talent, but a patron would more easily grease the wheels of the naval promotion system. Why would he search for someone in that crowd? Amanda recalled the callous leers, the atmosphere of casual license at the party. "And did you?" she asked, struggling to keep her voice level.

Harry must have read the skepticism in her face, for he drew himself up indignantly. "Well, it just so happens that I did. I told him about you."

"You what?"

Harry reddened anew. "I told him about your father, about the letters. He wants to help you, Amanda. He thinks he can clear your father's name."

Amanda's inherent skepticism was not enough to temper her surge of eagerness. "Really? How?"

"He needs to see Captain Tremayne's correspondence. If you give them to me now, I can take them to him straightaway—I'm supposed to meet with him this morning."

She shook her head. "I can't do that, Harry. It's not that I don't trust you, but I know nothing about this man. Who is he?"

"An admiral. A man of influence, just as I said. He asked me not to reveal his identity to you."

A slight hesitance in Harry's demeanor made Amanda pause. "Odd. Why not?"

"He said that if anything goes wrong, he didn't want you involved, that you'd been through enough already."

"How very discreet of him," muttered Amanda. She drummed her fingers on the tabletop. Something about this offer didn't seem quite right, but she knew Harry would not deceive her. "All right. But I still can't give you the letters, Harry. I want to deliver them myself."

Harry picked up his teacup, frowned at it, and set it down again. "Well . . . I suppose that would be all right. But we'll have to leave right away—my meeting's at eight o'clock, sharp."

"This morning?" Her question came out as an incredulous squeak.

"Of course this morning. 'A rolling stone gathers no moss,' and all that. The sooner we clear this up, the sooner you can go back home, where you'll be safe. Besides, my patron leaves soon for a new command. We have very little time."

"But I can't go with you," she protested. "Not this morning."

"Whyever not?" Harry frowned.

Amanda's mouth opened to reply, then thought the better of it. To explain, she would have to tell Harry about her other appointment. Or at least part of it. But she could trust him, couldn't she? She plunged ahead. "I'm waiting for Captain Everly."

She regretted those words immediately, for as soon as she'd spoken them, a change came over Harry. He scowled, his face darkening like a summer storm. His eyes flashed amber fire.

"Everly again," he growled. "What is your connection with him, Amanda? First, he all but kidnaps you from the street, then you show up at the soirée with him. What haven't you told me?"

Amanda drew back, alarmed. "I won't tell you if you get yourself into a pother about it."

Like a summer storm, his anger faded as quickly as it had come, replaced by a pleading look. "Forgive me. I . . . I'm concerned for you."

This jealous outburst made Amanda uneasy, but this was Harry, her childhood friend and confidant. "Promise me that you won't repeat what I tell you to another soul. Not even your patron."

"You have my word," Harry affirmed.

"Captain Everly is on a mission to uncover a traitor in the Admiralty. He thinks Locke may be involved— that's why he was at the party."

Harry's eyes widened with shock. "A traitor? By Jove!"

"He let slip about the party when he took me home from St. Vincent's. Once I found out, I used it as a chance to get back into Locke's study. The captain didn't want to take me; I forced his hand." She peered at Harry. "Are you all right?"

The young lieutenant put a hand to his head. "I'm a little muzzy from last night, that's all. So why do you need to see him this morning?"

"I need to tell his superiors what I know, that's all."

She hoped Harry would not wish to pry any further. Although he had given his word, she didn't want to put him at risk. At least she had learned that much from this maddening mull.

"Amanda, I want you to listen to me. I overheard something about Captain Everly at the soirée."

"What did you hear?" she asked cautiously.

"I heard that Everly wants a new command, but that he's had difficulties obtaining one. He's desperate to be back at sea, so desperate that he'll do anything to get a new ship."

"That's utterly ridiculous," she breathed, but Harry's words had put her mind in turmoil. A lead weight settled in her stomach as she remembered Everly's anger toward her for her interference, and his distance after their kiss. Would he use her knowledge of the traitor's identity to get his new command? Would he leave and forget about his promise to her? She gripped the edge of the table to steady herself.

"It is true, Amanda," Harry insisted. "I also heard that's why he was at St. Vincent's house—he's hounding the old man for a ship, but the admiral doesn't have the power he once did, and ships are hard to come by these days. Don't trust him, Amanda. He wants only what's best for himself, I'm sure of it."

"I can't imagine this to be reputable information, coming from that crowd," she scoffed, although she did not sound convinced.   ·

Harry persisted. "Once this is over, what do you think will happen? Everly's a decorated officer—a success will boost his standing in the navy, so he's sure to get a prime command. How well do you know him? Do you think he'll want to concern himself with you and your grandmother when he's got a ship waiting for him?"

"I . . . I don't know."

Harry reached across the table and took her hands in his. "I know how much you want to believe him, Amanda. Part of me wants to believe him, too, but you must consider the facts. He's a career navy man, and a baronet to boot. He doesn't have time to deal with bumpkins like us."

Amanda hesitated, her lower lip caught between her teeth.

"You trust me, don't you?" asked Harry gently.

"Yes, of course."

"Then come with me, and bring the letters. You're much better off with me than you are with Everly. If you still want to help the captain after we meet with my patron, I'll bring you straight home."

Amanda swallowed the lump in her throat, torn between her duty to her country, and her duty to her father. Couldn't she do both? As much as she was drawn to Captain Everly, and as much as she wanted to trust him, Harry had a point. Everly's mission was to expose both Locke and the traitor, nothing more, and he had said he'd help her only if they found information linking Locke to her father. They'd found none. Well, nothing concrete. All she had was snippets of conversation between two traitors—information she had obtained by eavesdropping while hiding out on a balcony. What magistrate in his right mind would take her at her word? She had not even told Jack about what she'd heard; although it was unlikely, he might think her desperate enough to invent such a conversation. She needed hard evidence to prove what she had discovered. If she didn't take the opportunity that Harry offered her, she might lose forever any chance to clear her father's name.

She took a deep, shuddery breath. "All right. I'll go with you."

Harry beamed at her. "Capital!"

Amanda rose slowly from her chair. "But I must not be gone long. I have a responsibility to Captain Everly. I may be nothing but a country miss, but I know the meaning of duty and honor."

Harry's smile lost some of its luster as he, too, climbed to his feet. "You're not a nobody. I'll always be here to take care of you. You know that, don't you, Amanda?"

Amanda fidgeted beneath his intense gaze. "You've always been my best friend, Harry."

Harry took a step toward her, an odd expression on his face. "I want to be more than that." He leaned down, one hand on her cheek, and kissed her.

As kisses went, this was a fairly nice one, Amanda supposed. Much nicer than the one he had attempted last night. His lips were dry, and his breath no longer smelled of spirits. Still, she could not help but remember Captain Everly's passionate embrace, and the hot, heady sensations he had kindled in her body. Compared to that, Harry's kiss was tepid and decidedly strange—as if she'd been kissed by her brother. She pulled away and retreated, her face aflame.

"Let me write a note for Grandmama. She should be up at any moment, and I don't want to go haring off without leaving word." Amanda busied herself with pen and ink and avoided Harry's eyes, her jangled nerves making her hands shake. She almost upset the inkwell, but saved it before it could capsize. Botheration. She scribbled the note as quickly as she could, then read it over. Though worse than usual, her handwriting was still legible.

Leaving the note on the kitchen table, Amanda fetched her cloak and bonnet, then stuffed the oilskin-wrapped bundle of letters into her reticule.

"I'm ready," she announced.

"Good. My carriage is below." Harry offered her his arm, and after a moment's hesitation, Amanda took it. She was doing the right thing, she told herself as they descended the stairs. So why did she feel as though she were sailing straight off the edge of the world?

Everly tossed the ruined neckcloth aside with an oath.

"That's five," Stubbs grumbled. "Ye've set a new record, Captain."

"Devil take the bloody thing," Everly muttered as he reached for a fresh cravat.

"Let me, sir," Stubbs interjected. "If ye're wantin' to weigh anchor on schedule, that is."

With a grimace, the captain handed the strip of linen

to his servant. "Nothing fancy, Stubbs. Don't make me look like a peacock."

"When have I ever?" Stubbs scowled up at Everly. "Ye're in a fine mood this morning—cross as crabs."

Everly sighed and forced himself to stand still while Stubbs arranged his cravat. "Lack of sleep, I suppose," he explained in a heavy voice.

Well, that wasn't entirely the truth. He had slept—long enough to have nightmares about being thrown overboard and swimming in vain after his ship. In the next, he tried to save Amanda from the clutches of dark, shadowy figures. He even had a dream in which he tried to kiss Amanda, only to have her turn into Felicia, who then screamed in horror and fled. Amanda, always Amanda. Even unconscious, he couldn't get the little vixen out of his head. Small wonder he was grumpy.

"Ye'll be able to rest once this to-do is over. There, Captain. Right as rain." Stubbs stepped back to admire his work.

Everly glanced at the mirror and smiled for the first time that morning. "Well done, Stubbs. You've saved me again."

"Part o' my job, sir." Stubbs picked up the captain's jacket and held it out for him.

Everly shrugged into the coat. "Just don't let it go to your head."

Stubbs grinned as he began to collect the host of rejected, wrinkled neckcloths. "Aye, sir."

The mirror caught his attention. Everly stared at his reflection, at his handsome face, so incongruous with his crippled form. "That will be all for now, Stubbs. I need some time to think."

"Hmph. Ye been doin' entirely too much thinkin' of late," was Stubbs's acerbic comment as he vanished through the door.

Everly shoved a hand through his hair, rumpling the guinea gold waves. He limped to the window and back, then checked his pocket timepiece. A quarter past eight. Grayson MacAllister had arranged for Everly and Amanda to meet with Lord Carlisle at nine. He shifted the weight off his aching leg. He had time to spare, but the last thing he needed was to fritter it away in fruitless pacing. Amanda would understand if they were early and had to wait. Besides—it would enable him to spend a few more minutes with her.

He did want to see her again, he realized. To see her, and make sure she was safe. Egad, he was even anxious about it, like a lovestruck schoolboy. Not even Felicia had smitten him so, and that thought worried him. Everly shut his timepiece with a snap. His regard for Amanda would mean nothing when he was back at sea. It meant little enough now; her reaction to his kiss told him that. How could she hold any affection for someone as lame as he? Everly squared his shoulders, angry with himself. He was still getting his hopes up. He should have learned his lesson by now.

The sea was the solution. He would forget about Amanda, and she about him. A patent argument. So why was he not convinced? Everly grimaced and reached for his bicorne.

Rain fell in shimmering sheets by the time he climbed into his carriage. Damnation. That's why his leg hurt so ferociously. At least he'd had the foresight to bring his cane along with him. With any luck, Carlisle would not keep them waiting. Perhaps he wouldn't even have to climb any stairs.

The carriage drew up before the lodging house, which looked even more dreary in the gray morning light. His hand on his walking stick, Everly opened the door and lowered himself to the pavement. Raindrops pattered a steady cadence on his high-crowned hat. He squinted through the downpour at the building's coal-darkened walls and grimy windows. No doubt about it—Amanda would be much better off, and much happier, in Dorset. Sea air and sunshine was what she needed.

"Captain!" Grayson MacAllister, his footman's livery discarded in favor of rough workingman's clothes, detached himself from a doorway and hurried to Everly's side. The Scotsman's sea green eyes glittered with a feverish light.

Everly stiffened. "What is it? What's wrong?"

The younger man drew Everly aside, away from the few passersby. "She's gone," he croaked.

"What?" Everly demanded.

"Miss Tremayne left a little before eight with a young navy lieutenant—"

A navy lieutenant? Everly knew of only one such officer connected with Amanda. "Did he have red hair?"

MacAllister nodded.

"Damnation!" the captain exclaimed. The orange seller on the corner cast a curious glance in their direction, but he paid scant attention. "Was there anyone else with them?"

"No—just the lieutenant."

"And she went willingly?"

Again, a curt nod. "She seemed to."

"Then where did they go? Why didn't you send word to me?"

"I sent a man to tell you, but he was too late to catch you before you left your residence. I sent another to Carlisle, and the rest to follow Miss Tremayne and the lieutenant."

"How many men do you have?"

"Enough." The Scotsman's lips quirked in a tight, humorless smile.

"And how can they tell us where Amanda went?"

If MacAllister was startled by Everly's use of the lady's Christian name, he gave no sign. "They work in a relay, Captain. They'll mark the trail so we can follow it, then the last two will join us in case we need the extra support. Wherever they've gone, we can find them."

Everly clenched his teeth. So the ginger-haired lieutenant had proved to be a factor in this intrigue, after all. Damnation! What was he up to? And why had Amanda gone with him, knowing that Everly was coming to fetch her? Whatever the lieutenant's game, Everly needed to locate them, and quickly. Every instinct in his body told him that she was in danger.

"Then we haven't a moment to lose," he snapped. "How are you at the ribbons, MacAllister?"

"I'm a member of the Four-in-Hand Club, sir."

So, the Scot claimed to be no good with horses, eh? Everly gave a bark of laughter. Carlisle's agents were a talented lot, down to their strategic manipulations. "Excellent. You saw where Amanda and the lieutenant went; you can recognize the signs your men left to mark their trail. And you're driving." Then, to his coachman's astonishment, Everly ordered the man to get into the carriage.

"A moment, Captain." MacAllister reached beneath his jacket and produced a loaded pistol. "I hope you won't need this."

Everly jammed the weapon into his belt. "So do I." Face set with pain, he climbed up to the driver's box.

The younger man sprang up beside hm and grabbed the reins. "Hang on, then." He whipped the horses, and they were off.

Chapter Eleven

Amanda watched out the rain-spattered window as the carriage passed St. James's Park, traveled eastward along the Thames, down Fleet Street, then crossed the Blackfriars Bridge. Her alarm grew as they progressed into the warehouse district of Southwark.

"Where on earth are we going?" she asked, her brows knit together in a frown. "I thought we were supposed to meet your mysterious patron."

"We will be," Harry assured her with a smile. "He wanted to rendezvous in a discreet location."

"Discreet?" murmured Amanda, still staring out the window at the multitudes of docks and warehouses, the dirty streets and disreputable-looking shops. "Dangerous, perhaps, but discreet?"

Harry's smile frayed around the edges. "Don't worry, I'll keep you safe."

Amanda twined her fingers in her lap and turned back to the window, lest Harry see the cloud of doubt that hovered on her brow.

The carriage threaded through the streets of Southwark, traveled into Bermondsey, passed the southern end of London Bridge, and halted in front of a dingy warehouse. The street outside the building was all but deserted. Small wonder—Sunday morning, in the pouring rain—most sane people would be indoors. As Harry helped her from the carriage, Amanda could see the top of the Tower of London, across the river from them, and her trepidation increased fourfold.

She turned her head against the driving rain and scowled at her companion. "Why does your patron want to meet at such a location? A warehouse? I don't like this, Harry, not by half."

"He told me it belongs to a friend of his. Come on, Amanda. We're late." Harry bunched his cloak closed with one hand, took Amanda by the other, and hurried up the short set of stairs to the warehouse office.

Once inside the small room, Amanda slid her hand from his possessive grip. Wet tendrils of hair clung to her face; she pushed them aside with impatient fingers.

"You haven't given me a single reasonable explanation as to why we are here," she accused, shaking the water from her cloak.

"I told you my patron wants to be cautious," replied Harry with a sigh of exasperation. "Who would suspect the presence of navy officers around a dock?"

Amanda evaluated their surroundings with a jaundiced eye. This warehouse had not been kept in the best of repair, if this office area was any indication. Two books propped up the truncated leg of one of the desks. Tattered papers and other refuse littered the floor, and the air was saturated with the smell of rotting wood and river water, punctuated by the heavier odors of cinnamon and cloves. Her nose twitched. A spice importer's facility, unless she missed her guess. A rustling came from the ominous shadows at the end of the narrow corridor, followed by a shrill squeak. Amanda paled and turned back to Harry.

"Ordinarily I would agree with you," she said, a trifle breathless, "but this particular portion of the docks is all but deserted. There is no one to be seen besides the rats. And if your patron is here and expecting us, why is it so dark?"

Harry glanced toward the source of the rustling, and his expression soured. "He wanted to meet me here, Amanda, for reasons he would not reveal. Considering the favor he's going to render you, shouldn't you give him the benefit of the doubt?"

Amanda swallowed her apprehension and wrapped her cloak around her to ward off the chill, dank air. "All right. Let's get on with this."

"Stay close," Harry advised. "I know how you detest rats."

"You needn't remind me." Amanda shuddered again and stepped carefully around the piles of refuse on the floor.

She followed Harry down the dim corridor, then through another, larger door and into the warehouse itself. The squawk of the door hinges ricocheted up to the ceiling and back, disturbing the pigeons roosting in the rafters. Amanda winced; they might as well announce their presence at the top of their lungs. She surveyed the place with a sinking heart. Pallid light filtered through the grimy windows on the upper floor, which did little to dispel the pervading gloom. A combination of dirt, straw, and pigeon feathers swirled around their feet as they traversed the rough wooden planking. The warehouse itself was about half full; a number of wooden crates and barrels lay stacked along the dockside wall near the loading door, and a larger group of crates occupied the center of the floor. A few bales of straw languished by the stairs leading up to the loft.

Movement caught her eye. A man sat atop one of the barrels, in the deepest shadows beneath the edge of the loft. Amanda's eyes narrowed with concentration as she peered through the dusky air. The silhouette was not that of a naval officer—she saw no bicorne, no scarlet-lined cape, no contrast of blue jacket against white breeches. The man seemed to be a civilian, with a high-crowned beaver hat and caped greatcoat.

Harry cleared his throat. "Admiral, I brought Amanda with me. She insisted on delivering the letters herself."

The figure rose from the barrel, dusting off his breeches. "Come closer, Lieutenant. I would like to meet this remarkable young lady."

As they approached, the man lit a lantern and set it on the barrel. Amanda suddenly grasped the reason behind this morning's secrecy. The moment she saw his face, her body stiffened in shock. She knew now why there were no lanterns lit when they had come in—this man had wanted to keep her from recognizing him until the very last moment.

Rear Admiral William Locke.

The Lion of the Mediterranean.

The traitor.

Rage and loathing consumed Amanda. She spun to face Harry, her lips contorted in a snarl. "What have you done?" she spat.

Harry retreated from her anger, his hands raised in front of him. "Easy now, Amanda. No need to be at daggers drawn. Let me explain—"

"*This* is your patron?"

The young lieutenant shot an uneasy glance at Locke, his face pale. "Give the admiral a chance. He will tell you his side of the story—he's innocent, Amanda. It's not what you think."

Had he been within range, Amanda would have slapped him. "What I think, Harry, is that you're the greatest looby who ever lived! You've delivered me right into the enemy's hands. I shall never forgive you for this!"

"Calm yourself, my dear Miss Tremayne," said the admiral in a weary tone. "No histrionics are necessary, especially so early in the morning. Since you were so obliging as to accompany Lieutenant Morgan, I will make this process as easy as possible. May I see the letters?"

Amanda clutched her reticule. "No."

Locke took a step forward; she retreated. He held a hand out to her. "Come, child, I will not harm you. I merely wish to read your father's correspondence. Perhaps they will give me a clue as to who committed these crimes."

Amanda stared at the hand as though it were a snake, poised and ready to strike. "Do you take me for a fool?" she demanded, incredulous.

Locke sighed, removed his hat, and set it on the barrel behind him. When he turned back to Amanda, his pale eyes were warm and full of concern. "You seem convinced of my villainy, my dear; it pains me to see you so upset. I explained my situation to your young friend last night, and he believes me. Is there nothing I can say to convince you that I am not your enemy?"

Amanda began to shake with the force of her fury. "There is nothing you can stay to redeem yourself, sirrah. I don't know what lies you told Harry, but they won't work on me."

The lines of Locke's face softened, his expression became almost paternal. "You are overwrought, my dear. You and your family have suffered a great tragedy. Come, let me help you."

"It won't fadge, Admiral," Amanda snapped. "I believe every word my father wrote. You're a traitor to the Crown. I know what you're capable of."

Locke cast an amused, knowing look at Harry, as if the two of them shared a private joke. "Is she always like this?"

Harry flushed. "Yes, sir."

A roaring began in Amanda's ears. She stood, her breath coming in painful gasps, her reticule clutched to her like a talisman. A red haze consumed her vision, and the words came out before she could stop them. "I heard you! I head you talking with the man from the Admiralty. You're going to intercept navy intelligence and give it to the French. You monster! Too many good men have died because of you!"

A pregnant pause settled around them.

"Amanda?" Harry's complexion turned the color of moldy cheese. "What are you saying?"

Locke glared at Amanda, his eyes glittering like chips of crystal. "She's saying, Mr. Morgan, that she knows too much."

The admiral's chilling gaze ripped the breath from Amanda's body, and she berated herself for losing control of her temper. Oh, now she'd gotten them in the suds.

"What . . . what are you going to do?" She took another step backward.

"You're not going anywhere, Miss Tremayne, until you give me those letters." Locke held out his hand again.

Gone was any pretense of patience or good humor. The man who faced her was cold and relentless. When she hesitated, he pulled a pistol from his belt.

"Don't do this," protested Amanda. "I know the hold he has over you, but you must not let him make you his cat's paw. You're betraying your friends, your shipmates. You cannot allow more innocent men to die."

Locke advanced on her. "Military men know the consequence of war," he rasped. "The letters, Miss Tremayne. I will not ask you again."

Amanda shook her head.

The admiral's brows drew together in a harsh line. "I remember now. You were at the ball." A statement, not a question. "Mrs. Seagrave—I should have guessed. Very clever, my dear. You might have succeeded, had you chosen your second disguise with more care; anyone with eyes in his head could see that you did not belong with members of the muslin company."

"I did what my conscience dictated," Amanda snapped back, her jaw tight. "Something you will never understand."

"Enough of this," said a gray voice from the shadows.

Amanda froze. She knew that low, gravelly tone—it belonged to the other man from that fateful conversation: the traitor from the Admiralty. She glanced fearfully toward Harry, who seemed rooted where he stood, his hand white-knuckled on the hilt of his sword. He made no move to draw it; he seemed to know as well as she that a blade against pistols was a forlorn hope.

"Kill them both, you fool, and destroy the letters. Weight the bodies and throw them into the Thames," commanded the unseen traitor.

"I won't kill a woman in cold blood," Locke growled over his shoulder.

"You weren't so particular when you killed your wife. Do it, or I'll do it for you."

"I am supposed to meet Captain Everly this morning," Amanda announced. Try as she might, she could not keep her voice from shaking. "If I disappear, he will come looking for me. And he will not come alone." An empty threat, but she had to try. There was no way Everly could know where she had gone. Oh, heavens, if only she'd waited for him!

"So Captain Everly is involved?" Locke's mouth twisted. "I'll deal with him when the time comes."

Footsteps sounded from the shadowed pile of crates, and three men walked into the light. The two larger ones were bruisers, mountains of human flesh dressed in rough, stained clothing. One of them grinned at Amanda, displaying the yellow, rotted stumps that were once his teeth. She shivered all the way down to her toes.

"Surely you don't think that Captain Everly will come riding to your rescue," scoffed the traitor. "Such a quaint notion."

Amanda's attention snapped away from the two thugs to the figure who stood between them. The traitor was slender and slightly dandified, a young man with thinning brown hair and a hawkish nose. Lusterless black eyes, glassy and cold like a shark's, stared back at her with such callous cruelty that Amanda bit back the urge to scream.

Then the puzzle of voice and face came together.

"You!" She pointed a trembling finger at him. "You're the clerk who ordered me thrown out of the Admiralty!"

"Stephen Garrett, at your service." The traitor sketched a mocking bow. "But I am no clerk. No mere clerk could get access to secret orders and other documents, or do what I have done. I am a man of singular talent, Miss Tremayne."

"Yes," she snapped, ashamed of herself for showing fear. "A talent for blackmail, murder, and treason."

The self-satisfied smile vanished from Garrett's face. "Her meddling is your fault, Locke. You should have dealt with her earlier."

"I had no idea she'd seek me out," Locke argued.

Garrett rolled his eyes. "Just get on with it."

Locke raised his pistol and set the hammer back to full cock.

Amanda backed away, her eyes fixed to the barrel of the gun. A hard lump of panic wedged itself into her throat. "No—you can't do this," she said in a hoarse whisper.

"Wait . . . what if we swear never to tell anyone?" Harry edged over to stand at her side. "We will give you our word that we'll keep silent, and you can let us go."

"I don't think that's an option for these men, Harry," Amanda murmured.

"She's right, Mr. Morgan," Locke replied. "I'm truly sorry, but I'm afraid there is no other alternative. Stand still, and I will make your deaths quick and painless."

Harry stepped in front of her. "This is insane. You can't betray your own country," he stated, glowering at Locke and Garrett.

"My country," snapped the traitor, "betrayed me first. My father was an officer in the Flanders campaign of '95; he was accused of allowing his men to run riot, to loot and burn an entire Flemish village. He was innocent, but no one would listen to him. He blew his brains out, leaving his wife and six-year-old son to get out of that hellhole on their own. I will spare you the rest of the sordid details, but suffice to say that the French were more sympathetic to my plight than England would ever be. I came back to England a few years ago under an assumed name, and proceeded to exact the perfect revenge. You are an even greater fool than I thought, Lieutenant, if you expect any consideration from me."

Harry turned to Locke, desperation ragged in his voice. "Admiral, these are your countrymen! This is unconscionable!"

Locke sighed. "I had no choice. I'm doing you a favor, Mr. Morgan. You may be a talented officer, but you are hopelessly naïve. Step back. Now."

Harry did as he was told.

"He has only one shot," Amanda whispered to Harry, her horrified eyes never leaving the gun. "You could make it to the door before he can reload."

"I'm not leaving without you," he hissed back.

Locke aimed his weapon straight at Amanda. "You first."

Amanda's breath came in short gasps, every muscle in

her body drawn taut to the point of numbness. Images flashed before her eyes: her father, her grandmother, Jack Everly. She would never see him again, never hear his warm, deep laugh, never feel his strong arms around her. Before she met him, her only thought had been to avenge her father. Now she envisioned a life with him, having his children. An impossible dream. She had held her tears in check until now, but could do so no longer. Jack proved to be her undoing, and the tears flowed freely.

The barrel of the pistol wavered.

"Bloody hell!" Garrett exclaimed in disgust. "Give me that. You may not have the stomach for this, but I do." The traitor grabbed the pistol from Locke's shaking hand, pointed it at Amanda, and fired.

Amanda felt herself shoved aside at the same time as she heard the pistol's deafening report. Thunderous flapping erupted from the rafters as the host of pigeons took wing. She staggered and realized with horror what had just happened.

"Harry!" she cried.

Harry crumpled to the floor with a grunt of pain, a rapidly expanding patch of darkness staining the breast of his lieutenant's uniform. He put a hand to the wound; it came away wet and crimson.

"Damnation!" shouted Garrett. He ripped another, smaller pistol from beneath his own jacket.

Harry turned to Amanda, his eyes rimmed in white. "Run, Amanda!" he gasped. "Run!"

Everly planted his booted feet and held on for dear life as the carriage careened around a corner and onto Fleet Street. The wheels skidded on the wet pavement, throwing him hard against the railing. Agony shrieked through his injured leg, but he fought the urge to cry out. Raindrops pelted into his eyes; he dashed them away with a wet hand. He was soaked to the bone, his wool cloak weighted down with water, but he paid scant attention. Like a lookout in the rigging, his eyes strained against the weather, desperate to catch any sight of Amanda's coach.

Next to him, MacAllister handled the ribbons like a master, deftly threading the team in and out of traffic, unmoved by the oaths of other drivers and passersby. He slewed them through spaces Everly thought were too narrow, without even scratching the glossy black finish of the coach's exterior. Despite the seriousness of the situation and the pain in his leg, the captain could not help but smile; as a coachman the young Scot was either a child prodigy, or a complete and utter lunatic.

Amanda's trail was leading them toward the heart of the City; if they continued in this direction, they would pass St. Paul's Cathedral, the 'Change, and eventually the Tower of London. Everly scowled, then clamped his bicorne more securely to his head as they rocketed around a slow-moving dray. Where was this lieutenant taking Amanda? They had already passed the more fashionable neighborhoods, and the Admiralty was back in the opposite direction. Everly cursed himself for his lack of foresight. If only he had given in to his paranoia and brought Amanda to spend the night under his roof, she wouldn't be in danger now. She'd be hopelessly compromised, but she would be safe.

Everly's eyes glazed over. If he had compromised her, he'd have to marry her, honor would demand it. Much to his surprise, he found this thought appealing. Amanda, his wife. Amanda in his home, raising his children.

Amanda in his bed.

He blinked. What was he thinking?

The carriage hit a pothole, and the resulting jolt sent a stronger spasm through his leg. Everly welcomed the pain; it brought him to his senses. Amanda would never consent to marry him, the stubborn chit. She despised him. Even if by some great stretch of imagination she did agree, Everly would be away at sea for the remainder of the war, and God only knew how long that would be. He could not ignore his duty to his country. Either way, he would have to leave her, and they would drift in separate directions.

Damnation!

Everly pinched the bridge of his nose, partly to ward off the throbbing from his leg, partly to divert his thoughts away from Amanda. Where was she? What sort of danger had she gotten herself into now? She was a clever and capable minx, but if Locke were involved in her disappearance, she was in over her head. In the worst case, she might be dead already. The thought nauseated him. He couldn't bear to lose her. . . .

"Are you all right, Captain?" shouted MacAllister over the pounding of the horses' hooves and the rumbling of the wheels. The Scot's blond hair was plastered to his head; water ran in rivulets down his pale face.

"I'm fine," Everly yelled back. "How much further?"

As if in reply, MacAllister hauled on the reins, bringing the team to a neighing halt. A short, scrawny man in a flapping greatcoat and outdated tricorne rode up on a lathered horse, both of them breathing hard.

"Blackfriars Bridge," the man wheezed. His nervous horse threw up its head and danced sideways, and the agent fought for control. "Bingham is on the other side; he can take you the rest of the way."

Everly and MacAllister exchanged a worried glance.

"They've gone into Southwark," the Scot said, his jaw set at a grim angle. "Damn. That place is a rabbit warren of warehouses, narrow streets, and blind alleys."

"And docks," added Everly. "We should check the riverfront. Maybe this lieutenant had a ship waiting."

"In which case, let us pray we're not too late. Follow us, Evans. We still have need of you." MacAllister flicked the whip over the lead horse's ears, and the carriage lurched forward through the steady curtain of rain.

"Run!"

No sooner had Harry uttered that word than Amanda took to her heels. She had to get out, to find help! Her skirts bunched in one hand, she darted around the cluster of crates. She could see the stairs up to the loft, which meant the exit was close by. Behind her, she heard the traitor curse.

"Get after her, you beef-brained idiots," he howled. "I want her dead!"

Fear spurred Amanda to greater effort. With a burst of speed, she rounded the last set of boxes . . . only to see a third brute enter the warehouse. The man was smaller and thinner than the other two, more of a mole-hill than a mountain, but the large, wicked-looking knife in his belt made up for any differences in size. Amanda skidded to a stop.

" 'Ere now, wot's all this?" he demanded. "I 'eard shootin'!"

"Stop the girl!" Garrett ordered. His shout rang to the rafters.

"Come 'ere, missy," the third thug said with a malicious grin. His dark, ferrety eyes glittered as he crooked a finger at her. "I won't 'urt ye none."

Amanda cast a wary glance around the man; there was not enough room for her to try to slip past him out the door. It was either the stairs to the loft, or double back through the warehouse and try to get out through the main doors. If they were unlocked. And unguarded. She edged toward the stairs.

"Oh, no ye don't." Molehill lunged for her and caught hold of her cloak.

Amanda screamed, her reaction instantaneous. She balled up her fists and tried to hit him, but her aim was off, and she missed. In return, Molehill backhanded her across the face. Her oversized bonnet caved in over her forehead; he ripped it away.

"Uppity, ain't ye?" he growled, his breath hovering between them in a fetid cloud. "Lemme show ye wot I do t' uppity wimmin."

Amanda's head spun from the force of the blow. This had never happened before; a stiff facer had dissuaded most bullies. But when she was still in the schoolroom her grandmother had advised her of another, more po-tent form of defense. She'd never had to use it, but now was as good a time as any. As the thug hauled her toward him, she brought her knee upward into his groin.

"Ooof!" The man's eyes crossed with pain and he staggered backward against the wall. He let go his hold on Amanda's cloak, but he didn't fall over. Instead, he snarled at her and took a shambling step forward, his face a mask of murderous rage. "Bitch!"

Oh, heavens—she hadn't hit him hard enough.

Now the loft was her only option. Amanda lurched for the stairs, one hand gripping the flimsy railing for support. The thug swore again and swiped at her. Amanda felt his grimy hand brush her arm, and it galvanized her to greater speed. She clattered upward as fast as her skirts would allow.

"There she is!" yelled the traitor.

Another gunshot resounded through the warehouse, and a track of burning pain spread across Amanda's ribs. The blow spun her around and threw her against the wall. She cried out and crumpled to one knee, one hand pressed to her side. Stunned, she realized the shot had sliced into her flesh; her fingers came away red.

Keep going—she must keep going. The bullet must have just grazed her, and she must not give Garrett an opportunity to better his aim. She kicked her sodden skirts out of the way and lunged awkwardly toward the landing, keeping frantic watch on the men below.

On the warehouse floor, the traitor cursed and threw his spent weapon aside. He yanked a second from his belt and pointed it up at her. His glittering eyes smiled at her as he sighted down the barrel. Amanda had nowhere to hide. She screamed.

"No!"

The word had not come from her throat, but from someone below. Amanda watched, shocked, as Admiral Locke tried to grab Garrett's pistol. With a snarl, Garrett shoved Locke aside. Amanda heard the tinkle of shattered glass. The admiral staggered back, and Garrett shot him at near point-blank range. Locke sank to his knees, his eyes wide with disbelief as his chest bloomed red. Then he collapsed, facedown, on the straw-strewn floor.

Garrett looked up at Amanda again, his expression a dark promise of pain and death. Heavy footsteps sounded behind her; the mountainous thugs had reached the stairs. Amanda reached the loft, panting. A broken barrel caught her eye. The top had been staved in, but it would serve her purposes. Ignoring the spreading numbness in her side, she wrestled the barrel to the top of the stairs and shoved it downward. It tumbled straight into the two brutes, knocking one of them through the railing and off the stairs with a crash. The other, who had flattened himself to the wall to avoid the barrel, growled at her and resumed his ascent.

Amanda gulped. Aside from the barrel, sawdust, a few broken boards, and pigeon nests, there was little else in the loft. She began to back away from the stairs.

Then Amanda heard the crackle of flame. Acrid smoke curled up from between the loft floorboards. She coughed.

Oh, heavens—the lantern! Garrett or Locke must have knocked it over during their struggle, and now the straw was on fire. That tinder, combined with the dry, rotted wood of the walls and floor, meant the whole warehouse could burn down around their ears in a trice.

Harry! He was still down there!

"Harry?" she called, frantic. "Harry!"

"I'm afraid your companion is indisposed," called the traitor in that cold, emotionless voice. "But don't worry; my associate will see that he's taken care of."

"You monster," she hissed, but the man couldn't hear her over the crackle of the flames. Fresh tears stung her eyes.

The smoke increased in volume, drifting up to the loft in huge black plumes, stinging her eyes and throat. Amanda coughed again, grabbed her kerchief from her reticule, and held it over her mouth. There was no other way out of the loft besides the stairs. She glanced to the railing, but knew she wouldn't survive a jump to the bare floor below. Well, she wouldn't survive a pistol shot from close range, either. Her choices were decidedly unappealing: death by falling, pistol, or fire.

The first set of footsteps heralded the approach of the traitor; the set behind him was probably Molehill, for it did not sound heavy enough to be one of the larger cutthroats.

"There is nowhere to run, Miss Tremayne," Garrett called as he stalked up the stairs.

Amanda, flattened to the wall, her heart in her throat, found that she had to agree with him.

Chapter Twelve

Throughout the morning's ordeal, Everly had done his best to keep his emotions confined behind an impassive mask—a mask which might as well have been made of wax, for it melted now with alarming speed. Seething with rage and frustration, the captain thrust his face into the agent's with a snarl. "What do you mean, you lost them? Well, man, speak up!"

Startled, the slender youth drew back, his horse curvetting beneath him. He turned to MacAllister, hesitant. "Sir?"

"You heard the captain, Mr. Bingham," rapped MacAllister. He laid a restraining hand on Everly's arm. "Explain yourself."

The agent looked between the two men and managed to turn paler still. "W-well, after they crossed Blackfriars Bridge they followed Clink Street, but once they came to London Bridge they turned off into an alley. Then my horse stumbled and threw me, and by the time I searched the surrounding streets, there was no trace of them. It was as if they vanished."

"Damnation!" Everly exclaimed. To have come so far only to lose them . . . this was unacceptable. The sensation of impotence was as unfamiliar as it was unwelcome. Amanda's life might hang in the balance. His body tensed.

"We'll find them, Captain," MacAllister insisted. He turned to his agent, face grim. "Are you all right, lad?"

"A little bruised, sir, but well enough." The young man swallowed heavily, his Adam's apple bobbing. "My apologies, Mr. MacAllister."

MacAllister dismissed his subordinate's remorse with an impatient wave of his hand. "There will be time enough for you to amend your mistake, Bingham. Do you still have your pistols?"

The agent brightened. "Yes, sir."

"Then come with us. I still have need of you." MacAllister again took up the whip, but engaged the team at a slower pace. "Dockside is still the best place to begin; I believe your instincts are correct, Captain."

Everly inclined his head in a curt nod. "Let us hope we are not searching for the proverbial needle in a haystack."

Lead by Bingham, MacAllister guided them along the route Amanda's carriage had taken. Once the trail ended, however, the Scotsman advised them to begin a methodical search.

"I know that time is of the essence, Captain." MacAllister's sympathy was unmistakable. "But you know as well as I that we cannot simply start beating on doors all the way down the street, hoping to find her. My men and I are doing all we can, but I am neither magician nor miracle-worker."

Everly growled a brusque agreement under his breath and shifted on the hard driver's bench. His throbbing leg did little to sweeten his temper. Better at this point that he simply kept his mouth shut.

With the mounted agents acting as scouts, they continued through the dockside warrens of Southwark. As they passed London Bridge, Everly shifted his straining eyes from the colorless rows of buildings to the horizon.

"There!" The cry tore from his lips. No, he hadn't been mistaken. He *had* seen it.

MacAllister drew the team to a halt, his brow furrowed in a puzzled frown. "I don't see anything."

"Smoke. Just a wisp. It's wood smoke, not coal, coming from somewhere up ahead." Everly stood and scanned the nearby buildings, ruthlessly ignoring the protests of his injured leg. The steady rain kept any telltale plumes from rising too far into the air, and obscured his vision, as well. At this distance, and without his spyglass, he couldn't be certain of its exact origin. He hated to think that Amanda's welfare depended on his best guess.

"Smoke? Where? I don't see anything," said Mr. Evans from beneath his battered tricorne.

"Use your nose, man," MacAllister snapped. "I can smell it, Captain, but can you spot its source?"

Everly's leg nearly gave way beneath him; he sat down harder than he intended. Pain shrieked a scarlet path behind his eyes, and the skin at his temples drew taut as he quashed it. "I cannot say for certain until we get closer, but my estimate is about five to six blocks ahead."

MacAllister paused, as if selecting his reply with care. "What makes you so certain Miss Tremayne is there? We will lose valuable time if you're wrong."

Everly shook his head, water running out from the tasseled ends of his bicorne. "I am no magician either, Mr. MacAllister, but every instinct tells me she's there."

"I pray you're right." The young Scotsman turned his anxious attention back to the horses.

Everly drew a long, deep breath. "So do I."

The measured footsteps neared the head of the stairs. For a frantic moment, Amanda imagined herself a doe cornered by hounds. She gritted her teeth and gathered her wits; she was no frightened animal to be driven mindlessly to her death. There had to be another way out. She darted to the row of windows and peered through the dirty panes. Perhaps there was an overhang, something above the dock onto which she could jump. She squinted until her eyes were the barest slits, but could barely make out the shape of the pier through the glass beneath the first window. She went to the next window, and the next, until she came to the corner of the loft. She saw nothing below but the dark water of the Thames. Amanda gulped. If only she could swim.

"Impressive sight, isn't it?" came the traitor's hollow voice. "The tower, that is. I assume that's what you were observing. You couldn't have been searching for an escape route. I told you there was no way out of here."

The skin at the small of Amanda's back crawled upward to her neck. Heavens, the man might as well be conversing over tea.

"Come, Miss Tremayne. This will be much easier for everyone if you cooperate." Garrett stood at the top of the stairs, hands on his hips, watching her every move with dead eyes. Molehill padded up behind him, his mouth split in a wide grin.

"Cooperate?" Amanda's lip curled in disdain. "I will not."

The traitor sighed. "Oh, very well. Jigger, keep watch. I'm going to do this myself."

A look of keen disappointment crossed Molehill's—Jigger's—rough countenance. "Do ye want me knife, guv?"

Garrett made a dismissive gesture. "No. Too quick. Our redoubtable Miss Tremayne deserves something special for her trouble. A more . . . personal experience."

Amanda's breath caught in her throat. Personal? For whom? Heavens, the man was mad. Jigger thought so too, judging from his queer expression. Amanda saw a chance to reason her way out. Jigger may be a thug, but he was an English thug. "You can't let him do this! He works for the French—our enemy!"

Jigger shrugged his narrow shoulders. "Frogs or English—it don't much matter to me, missy. Gold is gold, and 'e pays me well enough so's I don't ask questions."

"But he's mad! Can't you see that? He'll let this place burn down around us! We must get out while there's still time."

The ruffian hesitated and looked toward Garrett.

"Stay where you are, Jigger," warned the traitor. "You know what will happen if you disobey me."

Jigger paled and nodded.

So much for reason. Hungry flames popped and crackled on the warehouse floor below. Amanda's eyes watered from the smoke.

The traitor crossed the floor in deliberate strides, seemingly unaware of the growing conflagration beneath them, untying his cravat as he came.

"What . . . what are you doing?" The hard lump of panic lodged in Amanda's throat made speech difficult.

Garrett snapped the strip of linen taut between his hands. "Since I have no more bullets, I shall have to improvise."

Amanda's eyes saucered. "You can't!" she gasped.

A thin smile stretched Garrett's lips. "Did I ever tell you how much trouble your father caused me? He was far too inquisitive for his own good, a trait you seem to have inherited. Although I do admire your motives, and your exasperating determination. Few have the stomach or the intelligence to exact a proper revenge. Perhaps we are more alike than you would choose to admit."

"I am nothing like you," Amanda spat through clenched teeth.

The traitor sighed. "As you will."

Still he came forward, as inexorable as the tide. Amanda retreated from him until the wall pressed against her back. Trapped. Harry was wounded, perhaps even dead. No one else knew where she was. No one would come to rescue her, like the heroines in penny fiction. Amanda stood frozen, mesmerized by Garrett's terrible lifeless eyes, too terrified even to scream.

Everly's heart beat a drummer's call to arms within his chest as they neared the next row of warehouses. Rain streamed into his eyes, and he pulled his bicorne further onto his brow to shield himself against the drenching spray. The smell of smoke was much stronger on this street. They must be close.

"Ahead, sir!" cried Mr. Bingham. He pointed up the street. "The second to last warehouse in the row—that's where the smoke is coming from."

Everly squinted against the downpour. "There's no carriage waiting outside."

"A bad sign," muttered MacAllister. Another flick of the whip, and they rocketed forward.

The captain gripped the head of his cane as indecision gnawed at him. Instinct was not science; it had nothing to do with facts. If he was wrong . . . No. He would not even consider the consequences. They would succeed. They must. Everly tightened his already ferocious grip, the sinews of his hand standing out beneath the taut surface of his gloves.

Sudden movement caught his eye. Through the pervasive gray curtain of rain, Everly spotted two figures emerging from the warehouse, one dragging the limp body of another. His heart gave a titanic leap as he recognized Amanda's lieutenant—just before the man collapsed in the street.

"Whoa!" MacAllister sawed on the reins with frantic haste. The horses slipped on the slick pavement, whinnying, but the Scotsman managed to swerve them around the prone forms of the two men. He pulled the foaming, wild-eyed team to a halt.

In that instant Everly leaped down from the coach, his focus riveted on the body of the lieutenant. The captain knelt by the young man's side, horrified to see a spreading bloodstain on his soot-begrimed uniform. Harry moaned and tried to fight off Everly's touch.

"Be still!" Everly opened the youth's jacket and assessed the wound; the ball had struck him just below the collarbone. He thought nothing vital had been hit, but the lieutenant was losing blood at a rapid rate. The captain wadded up his handkerchief and pressed it against Harry's shoulder to staunch the flow.

MacAllister appeared at Everly's side and turned over the body of the second man. "Locke," he pronounced. He felt for a pulse. "Alive, but barely."

"Amanda," muttered Harry. He struggled to sit up.

Everly restrained him. "What about Amanda? Where is she, Lieutenant?"

Harry raised one hand and clutched weakly at Everly's jacket, his hazel eyes aglow with panic. "Still . . . inside. Trapped!"

The captain spun around and grabbed MacAllister by the sleeve. "Amanda's inside. I'm going after her."

"I'm going with you," answered the Scot.

Everly grunted. "Watch your back. I'll wager that who-

ever shot Locke and the lieutenant is still in there with
Amanda."

MacAllister nodded in quick agreement, then ordered
his men to get the wounded officers into the carriage.

Everly drew the pistol from his belt and hobbled to
the warehouse door.

"Will you be all right, Captain?" the Scotsman asked.

A half chuckle, half growl rumbled from Everly's
throat. "Well enough for what we need to do. Look lively
now, Mr. MacAllister."

A thick, choking miasma of black smoke and a blast
of infernal heat greeted the two men as they entered the
warehouse itself. Everly flung an arm over his nose and
mouth. Egad, this place was a veritable tinderbox! The
fire had spread from the barrels at the back of the warehouse to the crates at its center, and now threatened the
bales of dirty straw beneath the loft. The captain narrowed his watering eyes and peered through the dense
smoke. Where could she be?

"Amanda!" he called, then coughed as he breathed in
a lungful of heat and ash. His only answer was the increased roar of the hungry flames. "Amanda!"

"Any sign of her?" yelled MacAllister.

"None," Everly shouted back.

MacAllister pulled out his pistol and disappeared between the smoking stacks of crates. Then the sound of
breaking glass reached Everly's ears. The loft! Energy
surged through him, and any twinges of pain vanished as
he focused on the stairs. The boards groaned beneath
his booted feet as he began his ascent. A cold sweat
broke out on his brow. The mere suggestion that the
stairs might collapse beneath him brought back images
of the *Hyperion,* of the agony he endured after crashing
through the splintered deck. He shook his head and berated himself for his weakness. Amanda's life depended
on him, and he must not succumb to fear.

"Amanda!" he cried again as he reached the landing.

A slight figure appeared at the head of the stairs,
wreathed in smoke. Everly's heart leaped, then tumbled
again when he realized that the figure was not Amanda,

but a grimy, evil-eyed little man. In the span of a heart-beat, the fellow whipped the knife from his belt and launched it at Everly's chest.

The captain saw the glitter of the blade in the man's hand and dodged aside. The knife thudded home into the wall mere inches from his shoulder, pinning his cape to the rough wood. Dismayed, the scrawny ruffian reached into his sleeve. Before the man could draw another weapon, Everly's pistol barked a harsh reply. The thug doubled over, eyes bulging, and fell forward. Everly avoided the body as it rolled down the stairs, limbs limp and flailing. With an oath, he shrugged out of his heavy cloak.

Amanda must be in the loft; the presence of the knife-wielding ruffian made it a certainty. The crackle of the fire took on a different pitch. Looking down, Everly saw that the stacked bales of straw were now ablaze. Greedy tongues of flame licked at the boards beneath his feet. Heart scorched the soles of his Hessians. He jammed the empty pistol back into his belt and raced up to the loft.

"Amanda!"

The loft was a nightmarish inferno of haze and heat, the gloom punctuated by flickers of orange light from the blaze below. Smoke and ash clogged his nostrils. His eyes watered from the acrid fumes. He squinted through the choking miasma, but could make out no distinct shapes. No, wait—was that movement he saw in the corner?

Two figures stood, locked together in struggle. Dread knifed through Everly's heart as he realized that the smaller of the two combatants was Amanda. And she was not fighting, she was thrashing about, trying to free herself from the grip of her attacker. She pulled at her throat. Egad, the bastard was choking her!

"Amanda!" he yelled, and lunged forward.

Her attacker heard him, and darted away into the smoke. Amanda's small form crumpled to the floor by the far wall near a shattered window.

"Amanda?" The blood congealed in his veins. Dear God, she wasn't moving. Was he too late?

Smoke swirled off to his right; he thought he heard the click of boot heels. As he spun around, the wall of inky smoke spewed forth a human shape. Everly's sword did not have a chance to clear the scabbard. He caught a glimpse of a young man's baleful, soot-smudged face just before the man tackled him. The impact drove them both to the floor. Everly's forehead struck the wooden boards; his bicorne flew off, and a battery of brilliant explosions flashed before his eyes. The stranger drove a knee into his ribs. Everly's breath left his body in a rush of pain.

Everly tried to lift his sword, to backhand the man with the hilt, but the stranger felt the movement. With a snarl, the man grabbed Everly's wrist and smashed it against the floor. The captain's fingers went numb. His blade skittered across the boards, out of reach.

"How good of you to join us, Captain," panted his attacker. The man thrust his grimy face into Everly's, his teeth bared. "Your arrival is fortuitous—Miss Tremayne was so afraid she'd have to die alone."

Everly growled and heaved himself onto his side, trying to unseat the stranger from his back. His attacker had the advantage of position, but he was larger and stronger. He twisted and lunged upward; he would have grabbed for the cravat, but the stranger's shirtfront was open and bare. Everly seized his attacker's lapel, then used that leverage to thrust the man aside and flip himself over.

This move unbalanced the stranger for a moment, but only a moment. Before Everly could lift himself from his prone position, the man leaped upon him again, his knees straddling Everly's body. Damnation—whoever this bastard was, he moved like a spider.

"I'll not let you ruin everything I've worked for," the man spat, each word dealt with a blow. "I have waited my entire life for this, and they will pay!"

Flat on his back like a turtle, Everly found himself again at a disadvantage. Blood sang through his head. In a dim corner of his awareness, he could feel the heat from the fire below them. What started as an unpleasant

warmth on his back increased to a burning. The glow
from the fire intensified. Flames darted up between the
floorboards, which groaned and popped beneath them.
Sweat trickled down Everly's brow, down his back. The
heat pressed against his skin like a living thing. His lungs
burned from the smoke.

The barrage came to a sudden halt as the young man
wrapped long, slender, and surprisingly strong fingers
around Everly's throat and squeezed. "Time to join your
dear little Miss Tremayne," he grated between clenched
teeth. "She died well, if that's any consolation."

Rage and grief sang through Everly's blood as he tried
to pry the man's hands away from his throat. His enemy
began to smile, and recognition struck the captain like a
lightning bolt. He had seen this man before, on the Admiralty staff. Everything came together. This was the
traitor the government had sought for so long. Traitor,
and murderer. Amanda was dead. Everly's anguished
eyes looked to the small, unmoving body in the corner.

Something snapped within him, and he lashed out with
his fist. The blow caught the traitor under his jaw; the
man fell backward and tumbled off Everly's body. Everly
breathed deeply, filling his starved lungs—and coughed
as smoke clawed its way down his throat. He struggled
to his knees. Where was the traitor? There he was—a
few feet away, struggling towards the stairs.

The traitor must have heard Everly's attempted pursuit, for he looked back at the captain with narrowed
eyes.

"Adieu, Captain," he panted. "Forgive me for taking
French leave."

Amanda came awake to the sensation of her head ringing like a giant ship's bell. Pain throbbed behind her eyes
with every peal. She moaned and shifted; rough wood
scraped against her cheek. What—where was she? As her
eyes focused, she realized that she was lying facedown on
a wooden floor, and that she felt intense heat all around
her, like the inside of a great oven. Her mouth was dry,
her tongue cleaved to the roof of her mouth. A cloud of

smoke wafted into her face. She coughed, and agony exploded in her throat. With it came memory.

Garrett—the traitor—had tried to strangle her. Amanda raised a hand to her neck. The last image she remembered was the eerie glitter of pleasure in Stephen Garrett's eyes as he tightened his cravat around her throat. She had struggled, and shattered one of the windows. Then she remembered hearing someone shouting her name. Garrett had heard it, too. His features had contorted into a mask of feral rage and he had pulled harder on the garrote.

Amanda held her head and struggled to sit up, wracked with pain as her abused body protested even the slightest movement. What had happened? She remembered nothing after that. She should be dead—shouldn't she?

A grunt and several thuds distracted her. She turned groggily toward the source of the noise. Two figures were grappled with each other, not far from her. Amanda's eyes watered from the acrid smoke. Garrett—one of the men was Garrett. And the man fighting him was . . . Her heart skipped a beat as she recognized the golden hair that gleamed above the navy captain's uniform.

"Jack!" The name emerged from her tortured throat as the merest whisper of sound.

A crash reverberated from the vicinity of the stairs, and Amanda realized that the stairway had collapsed, or at least a portion of it. The two men heard the noise, as well; Garrett grinned at Everly and bolted for the stairs. Everly snarled and gave chase, catching up with the traitor in a few long strides. He leaped upon the smaller man, and the two of them fell hard to the floor.

Amanda heard the floorboards snap beneath them.

"Jack, look out!" Her warning was nothing more than a hoarse croak.

Everly didn't hear her, didn't move out of the way in time. Amanda watched, horrified, as the boards buckled and gave way. The traitor shrieked as both men disappeared through the floor. Flames shot up into the breach.

"No!"

Tears scalded Amanda's eyes. She had lost him, just like that. Lost him without telling him that she loved him.

"Jack . . ." Amanda laid her head on the floor and wept.

"Bloody . . . hell!"

Amanda's head jerked up. Through the veil of her tears, she spied a figure struggling up through the broken boards. Everly's golden hair was singed, his jacket smoked, his face twisted in pain and exertion—but he was alive.

"Jack!" she cried.

But only for a moment. Everly faltered; his eyes went wide. Despite his efforts, he was slipping backward, back into the flames.

She wouldn't let him die! Amanda crawled and stumbled over to where Everly clung, then grabbed hold of his smoking sleeve. She braced herself and began to pull. Slowly, inch by agonizing inch, Everly began to emerge from the fiery pit. Sweat poured down Amanda's face, down the collar of her dress. Hair got in her eyes and in her mouth. Her muscles shrieked, but she refused to let go.

Once Everly's torso was free, he kicked his feet over the edge and levered himself up onto the floor. His coattails were on fire; Amanda ripped off her cloak and threw it over him to smother the flames. Everly moaned and rolled onto his back, then opened his eyes.

"Amanda?" Everly stared at her as though he'd seen a ghost.

"I'm here," she croaked.

"Dear God." He sat up and reached for her, drawing her tightly against him. Amanda felt him shake. "I thought you were dead."

Amanda closed her eyes and laid her head on his broad chest, not daring to speak for fear she'd break the spell. So close—she had come so close to losing him. Tears slipped out from beneath her lashes.

The floorboards groaned an ominous warning. Both Everly and Amanda jumped.

"We need to get out of here." Everly released her and

looked toward the stairs. Amanda followed his gaze and saw nothing but a wall of flame. So much for that route.

"I have an idea," she rasped, and struggled to her feet.

Everly tried to rise, but his right leg buckled beneath him. He cried out and clutched his hip.

"Take my arm." Amanda helped him to his feet, then drew his arm over her shoulders and led him to the shattered window. Below them, two stories down, roiled the murky waters of the Thames.

The singed remainders of Everly's brows drew together in a frown of concentration. "Can you swim?"

Amanda's knees began to quake. "At this point, it hardly matters."

Everly did not seem to have heard her. He shrugged out of his coat, wrapped the material around his arm and used it to sweep away the shards of shattered glass that remained in the window frame.

"Up you go." Everly lifted Amanda to the casement.

She stared down at the water, her face ashen.

"Go on, Amanda," Everly urged. "I'll be right behind you. Jump!"

Amanda took deep breath and leaped from the window. The world turned into a gray blur as she plummeted down toward the water. She seemed to fall so far, and so fast; the fear in her belly clawed its way out her throat as a hoarse, choking scream.

She hit the surface with a titanic splash, and her scream ended abruptly as the cold, dark water closed over her head. She tried to kick for the surface, but her heavy skirts wrapped themselves around her legs and pulled her further under. Unbearable weight pressed against her chest. Air—she needed air! She flailed desperately upward, but the cold water sapped what strength she had left. As she tried to call Everly's name, nothing but a trail of silvery bubbles escaped her lips.

Everly watched Amanda plummet, hair streaming behind her, and splash into the river. Behind him, more of the loft fell inward as the fire consumed it. The captain swallowed heavily, said a quick prayer, and launched himself from the casement.

He hit the water hard; pain ricocheted through his body. His leg radiated sheer agony. Everly forced himself to concentrate on swimming. He broke the surface and gasped for breath. After the infernal heat of the warehouse, the cold of the river shocked his body, penetrating his skin with a thousand icy needles.

"Amanda?" He flipped the wet hair from his eyes and looked around. The perpetual cascade of rain ruffled the surface of the water and made it difficult to spot anything on the surface. Everly squinted against the downpour. Where was she? A knot of panic formed in his throat. He took several strokes toward where he thought she'd gone in. "Amanda!"

He glimpsed movement at the periphery of his vision: a flailing arm, a dark head, a feeble splash. Everly swam toward their source as quickly as his exhausted body could manage, but Amanda had disappeared into the black depths of the river.

With a shout, Everly dived beneath the surface. Silt and muck clouded the water and made it difficult to see. The cold current pulled him down into its insidious grip. His lungs began to burn. He groped about like a blind man, his vision turning gray, then red for want of air. His blood pounded in his ears like the crashing of the surf, then he emerged at last. He gasped and drank the air in great gulps. He heard another feeble splash; Amanda bobbed to the surface, not far from him.

Galvanized, he swam forward and seized Amanda just as she went under again. Ignoring the throbbing of his burned fingers, he hauled her to him.

She lay limp in his arms. He rolled onto his back to keep her head above water.

"Breathe," he commanded as he pushed the seaweed strands of her hair away from her nose and mouth.

No response.

He slapped her. "Breathe!" he shouted. He hadn't found her only to let her slip away again.

There was little else he could do here in the middle

of the river. Despair had begun to overwhelm him when Amanda suddenly coughed. Her body spasmed. She spat out river water. "Ugh."

Hope flooded through him. "Thank God," he said hoarsely. "You should have told me you couldn't swim!"

"It . . . wasn't important." Her eyelids fluttered. "So . . . tired."

"Amanda, wake up. You have to stay awake." He shook her, and she made a vague protest. Damnation. He had to get them out of the water. Rain pelted them in a merciless torrent; both of them were chilled to the bone.

Determination injected energy into his limbs; he swam for the nearby dock, shouting MacAllister's name as he went, hoping that someone would hear him over the combined din of rain and fire.

Never had the shore seemed so distant, so unattainable. His limbs had turned to lead. Everly struggled to the dock just as his reserves of strength began to ebb; any longer in the water, and they would both be in grave danger.

"Captain!"

Someone thrust a hand down to them. Everly, his eyes narrowed against the rain, stared up into the youthful face of Mr. Bingham. Grayson MacAllister appeared over Bingham's shoulder and added his hand in support.

The agents pulled Amanda, then Everly from the water and onto the dock, where they lay like a fisherman's catch. MacAllister bawled at his men to grab some blankets from the carriage. Everly crawled closer to Amanda. His leg was numb, his ribs ached, his hands were red and blistered—dammit, his whole body hurt, but none of that mattered at the moment. Amanda was safe. *His* Amanda.

She moaned and lifted a fluttering hand to her neck. Everly's eyes widened. Dear God. A hideous purple bruise encircled her throat like a grotesque necklace. Everly suddenly remembered his attacker's open shirtfront. The bastard had used his neckcloth to strangle her. That she was still alive was a miracle in itself. All this, and she had pulled him from the clutches of the roaring flames.

"Stubborn minx," he murmured, and winced. Even the smallest hint of a smile sent pain lancing through his face. No matter. He pulled Amanda toward him, wanting nothing more than to hold her. Her skin was so cold; her lips were tinged with blue.

Then he saw the blood on her side. His hand came away red where he touched her. Upon closer examination, he spotted two bullet holes in her dress—one an entry, the other an exit. He blinked. Dear God, she'd been shot! She was so pale. Fear constricted around Everly's heart.

"Amanda?" Water ran in rivulets down his face, dripping from his nose and chin, streaming into his eyes, but he felt none of it.

The light in Amanda's eyes faded. Everly's arms convulsed around her and he shouted for MacAllister. After so many narrow escapes, after all that they'd been through together, he wouldn't surrender her now—not even to death. Not his Amanda.

"Amanda!" He turned her head and forced her to look at him. "Stay awake, love. Please stay with me."

"Jack . . ." she whispered. Her eyes rolled back in her head, and she lay still.

Chapter Thirteen

Fire.
Gunshots.
Pain.
Blood.
Terror.
"Jack!"

Amanda awoke on the hoarse scream, her heart a frantic flutter in her breast. Her wild eyes stared at the pleated damask canopy above her. Where was she? Where was Jack? She tried to sit up, and pain exploded through her body. Her head, her throat, her side—all radiated agony. She uttered a little mew of pain.

Hands restrained her; Amanda looked up into a man's stern, unfamiliar face. Memories of cruel-eyed ruffians loomed in her mind. Panic surged. She shrieked.

"Amanda! Dearest, I am here!"

Her grandmother appeared at the other side of the bed. She grabbed Amanda's flailing hands and stilled them.

"You are all right, Amanda. You are safe." The older woman's face was lined with worry, her hair disheveled, her dove gray dress wrinkled and creased.

Amanda took several deep breaths. Her heartbeat slowed. "Grandmama? Where . . . where are we?" Amanda's throat throbbed with each guttural-sounding word.

Mrs. Tremayne seated herself on the edge of the bed, one of Amanda's hands gripped tightly in her own. Amanda saw the glint of tears in her grandmother's eyes.

"We are guests of Admiral Lord St. Vincent,

Amanda," Mrs. Tremayne said, her voice quavering. "This is Dr. Harrington."

Amanda scrutinized the stoop-shouldered man at her bedside and wondered how she could have mistaken him for one of Garrett's ruffians. The physician wore a wig in the style of the previous century, doubtless the fashion of his youth. His dark coat and breeches likewise reflected an earlier age. Kind gray eyes shone from his lined face and belied the gruffness of his demeanor.

"He has been looking after you," Mrs. Tremayne explained. "You have been unconscious for almost two days, dearest."

"Two . . . two days?" As guests of St. Vincent? Amanda stared at her grandmother in disbelief. After the way he had treated her earlier, this development was nothing short of miraculous.

"Indeed," said the physician, his brow furrowed. "Your condition was most serious. I do not see many cases like this one. To have a patient be shot, nearly asphyxiated, and drowned all in one day is astonishing. Your were very fortunate not to develop pneumonia, an infection, or worse as a result. How do you feel now?"

"Terrible," Amanda wheezed. Her face felt lopsided; she fingered her swollen and tender right cheek.

The doctor arched a bushy eyebrow. "Something more specific, if you please."

Amanda thought a moment. "My face aches, and so does my side, but not too much. My neck hurts most of all."

Dr. Harrington peered down at her neck. "Hmmm. The bruising seems to have reached its peak. It should start to subside in a few days."

"And my voice?" Amanda cringed at the guttural sounds coming from her throat.

The physician cast her a knowing glance. "Your voice will recover if you do not overuse it."

"I was so afraid I would lose you, dearest," whispered Mrs. Tremayne.

Amanda gave her grandmother's fingers a gentle, reassuring squeeze.

"Come now, madam, no need for tears," Dr. Harrington said curtly. He took Amanda's free hand and measured the pulse at her wrist. "Your granddaughter has an excellent constitution. The bullet merely grazed her. Her lungs are clear, and her wounds are healing well. She will be fine, given a week's rest. Be sure to keep her calm. No excitement, mind you."

"I assure you, Doctor," croaked Amanda. "I have had as much excitement lately as I could ever want in my life."

The doctor harrumphed and rummaged through his bag. "I have done all I can for now. I must visit another patient this afternoon, but I will leave you a vial of laudanum for the pain. Twenty drops every four hours. No more than that, mind you." He placed a small, dark container on the bedside table.

"Thank you, Doctor," Mrs. Tremayne said with a tear-edged smile. "You have been very kind."

"I am a physician, madam," replied Harrington, as if that explained everything. "I will be back tomorrow to check on the young lady."

Once the doctor was gone, Amanda turned to her grandmother, dread knotted in her stomach. Memory trickled back, and she was full of questions to which she wasn't sure she wanted the answers.

"Grandmama," she began in a low voice, "what happened? How is Jack—Captain Everly? And Harry—what about Harry? He was shot. Oh, please let him be all right—"

"Slowly, dearest. One thing at a time." Mrs. Tremayne released Amanda's hand and rose, but not before Amanda saw the reluctance in her grandmother's face.

"Grandmama?" Amanda asked. She ran her tongue over her dry lips.

"I fear it is all a muddle to me," Mrs. Tremayne answered. "I will leave the explanation to Lord St. Vincent; he knows more about what happened than I. And Harry . . ." Her voice trailed off.

Amanda tried to sit up. "Oh, heavens—Harry is not . . . dead?"

Mrs. Tremayne restrained her. "No, dearest. He is quite well. He has been camped outside the bedroom door ever since you were brought here, and refuses to leave until he knows you are out of danger."

Amanda sighed with relief. Brave, naïve, sweet, infuriating Harry. She didn't know if she could still be angry with him after he had saved her life. Well, she would deal with that conundrum later. "Thank goodness. And Captain Everly?"

Mrs. Tremayne poured a glass of water and handed it to Amanda. "From what I understand, he will recover." The older woman paused. "While you were unconscious, you called his name several times."

"Oh, heavens. Did I?" She hoped she sounded innocuous.

"From what Lord St. Vincent has told me, both you and Captain Everly were instrumental in discovering the identity of this traitor."

Amanda sipped the water, her attention fixed on the glass. Her grandmother was never this circumspect unless something was wrong.

"Dearest, do you have a *tendre* for him?"

Then again, her grandmother could be quite blunt. She met the older woman's gaze, half afraid of what she would see there. "Would you disapprove if I said yes?"

Mrs. Tremayne's lips curved in a wan smile. "I would not disapprove, dearest. Captain Everly is a very charming man. I would only advise you to be guarded in your affections."

Guarded? Amanda set the glass aside. "What do you mean, Grandmama? Is Jack . . . is Captain Everly here?"

The older woman shook her head. "Not at the moment, I believe."

Amanda bit her lip. Such a foolish hope, to think that Jack would be here when she woke up. And yet Harry was waiting outside her door, and had been for two days. Where was Jack? And why did her grandmother hesitate when she spoke of him? Uncertainty and worry added more loops to the knot in Amanda's stomach. Perhaps he was wounded more seriously than her grandmother would tell her. She remembered his injured leg, and the burns. . . . Was he well? She put a hand to her aching temples.

A knock at the door interrupted her chain of anxious thoughts. Mrs. Tremayne went to the door; Amanda heard the muted buzz of conversation. Then her grandmother returned.

"Lord St. Vincent would like to speak with you, Amanda, if you feel well enough," Mrs. Tremayne said, her lips pursed in a thin line. "He is most insistent."

"Knowing the admiral, you will not be able to put him off for very long, Grandmama," Amanda replied. St. Vincent would hold the answers she sought. The protestations of her wounds had diminished to a dull ache, so she could ignore her pain for a short while. "I shall speak with him."

"Are you certain, dearest?" Concern hovered over the older woman's brow.

"If he becomes overbearing, you need only quote Dr. Harrington's orders and usher him out." Amanda smiled, then winced as her bruised face renewed its protest. She fingered her swollen cheekbone. Botheration. She must look as terrible as she felt—an absolute fright. "Although I fear I am less than presentable at the moment."

"You look fine, dearest," Mrs. Tremayne insisted with a fond smile.

Amanda made a vain attempt to keep the tears from her eyes. "Oh, Grandmama, I . . . I never meant to cause you such distress. I am so sorry!"

The older woman placed a gentle kiss on Amanda's forehead. "There, there, dearest. It has all worked out for the best, and you are safe. That is what matters most. Here, dry your eyes before I show the admiral in."

Amanda took the proffered handkerchief and did as she was told.

When Mrs. Tremayne opened the door, Admiral Lord St. Vincent strode in as if taking his place on a quarterdeck. Hands clasped behind his back, he walked across the fine blue-and-rose shaded Aubusson carpet, through the afternoon sunshine which slanted through the windows, and came to stand by Amanda's bed.

"Well now, Miss Tremayne," the admiral blustered by way of greeting. "My physician tells me you shall make a full recovery."

Amanda cleared her throat in the hope that it would improve her voice. "Yes, thank you, my lord," she replied, then grimaced. So much for improvement. She still sounded like the loudest frog in the marsh. "And thank you also for your hospitality. You were most gracious to open your home to my grandmother and me."

"Nonsense, nonsense," said St. Vincent. The redness in his cheeks stood out in stark contrast to his white curls. "The least I could do."

If he thought he could buy her forgiveness, he was wrong. "Or was it the least you could do to assuage a guilty conscience, my lord?" She did not care if she sounded shrewish. At this moment, that was the least of her worries.

"Amanda." Her grandmother favored her with a sharp, quelling look before turning back to St. Vincent. "Do sit down, Admiral."

The admiral's flush deepened. "No, thank you, madam. Given your granddaughter's delicate state of health, I shall be brief." He returned his gimlet gaze to Amanda. "Your father, Captain Alexander Tremayne, has been cleared of the charge of treason, and all lands, honors, and properties belonging to your family have been restored by royal decree."

The admiral had a reputation for forthright speech, but Amanda had never expected anything like this. Her jaw sagged. "H—how . . . ?"

"Before he died, Admiral Locke confessed his part in this traitorous charade to Lieutenant Morgan, and admitted framing your father for treason. He revealed the location of several documents that corroborated this story. Apparently, the traitor was blackmailing Locke to do his dirty work; Locke kept copies of what papers he had as insurance, lest Garrett try to betray him. Hmph. No honor among thieves, indeed. Dirty business."

Amanda blinked. "Locke is dead?"

St. Vincent beamed with pleasure. "Quite so. Took a ball in the chest, and there was no saving him. Knocked off shortly after Lieutenant Morgan dragged him from the warehouse. Eh . . . ahem. Your pardon, madam. Did not intend to shock you." He sketched a brief bow to Amanda's grandmother, who sat wide-eyed and motionless, her hands over her mouth.

Amanda swallowed hard. "Pray continue, my lord."

St. Vincent harrumphed. "Ah . . . yes. The traitor, the man who called himself Stephen Garrett, died in the fire, and with him the threat to the Admiralty's security. Captain Everly told us what transpired at Locke's party, and at the warehouse. Never would have discovered the blackguard were it not for you. I owe you an apology, Miss Tremayne. I don't know what made you come to me for assistance, but I should never have treated you in such an abominable fashion."

Amanda paused to steady herself. "I came to you because my father admired you, my lord. He said you were a man of integrity and honor."

"Did he now?" St. Vincent's ears glowed crimson. "Eh, I misjudged him. 'Pon rep, I misjudged him badly."

Amanda raised her chin. "Yes, you did, Admiral. And you misjudged me, as well."

"So I did, Miss Tremayne. You are a most extraordinary young lady."

A soft sob drew Amanda's attention. She had never seen her grandmother cry since they left Dorset, but now teardrops flowed down the older woman's careworn face. Numbness spread through Amanda's body. Instead of elation, thankfulness, or joy, she felt hollow. She closed her eyes. Their ordeal was over. The honor of Captain Alexander Tremayne had been restored; they could bring his body home, where it belonged. They were traitor's kin no longer.

Admiral Lord St. Vincent glanced between the two women and shifted uncomfortably. "Well," he said, "that is the crux of the matter. I shall take my leave. Of course, you and your grandmother are welcome to stay until you are feeling much better, Miss Tremayne."

"Thank you." Amanda struggled to gather her wits. "One more thing, my lord?"

St. Vincent paused in the doorway. "Yes?"

"Is Captain Everly here?"

The admiral's brow furrowed in a quizzical frown. "Everly? No, not at all. He's at the Admiralty, I imagine."

"Oh. Thank you, my lord," Amanda repeated, this time in a whisper.

The chamber door clicked shut.

Amanda lay back on the mound of pillows and stared at the pleated damask canopy of the bed. Jack was at the Admiralty, doubtless receiving new orders. With his mission a success, he was assured another command. He would be leaving soon. Leaving England.

Leaving her.

Amanda blinked away her incipient tears. Damn Jack Everly. Why did she have to fall in love with him? The captain had to do his duty; she was a thorn in his side, a hindrance. What information she had managed to uncover was by accident, and in the end he had needed her only to finish his mission and get what he really wanted—a new ship. A means to an end.

The memory of his kiss resurfaced, taunting her. She squeezed her eyes closed and tried to think of something else, but the disturbing sensations persisted. She remembered every touch, every seductive glance. But even that was an illusion. What man could have resisted her, dressed in that infamous scrap of spangled muslin? The gown alone was responsible for his reaction, not any depth of feeling on his part. Her grandmother had been wise to suggest caution, but her words had come too late. What folly, to think that a career navy man, an officer of his caliber, would ever return her regard. Her, a traitor's daughter.

She turned her head and muffled her gasp of anguish in the edge of a pillow. No—she must not think that! She was no longer a traitor's daughter. Her father had been exonerated and Locke, the man she had hated and pursued for so long, was dead. Justice had been served. A portion of the burden she had borne for so long lifted from her shoulders. Why was it not gone completely? And why did she feel so . . . miserable?

Garrett had murdered Locke, shot him before her eyes—and robbed her of her own revenge. The thought disturbed her. Had she become so single-minded in her pursuit? Had vengeance so corrupted her morals? She had gone to great lengths to expose Locke, to ruin him the way he had ruined her father and her family. To exact retribution at any cost. Just like Garrett. A shudder of revulsion cascaded down her spine. Garrett had goaded her about their similarities. She was loath to think he had been correct.

Amanda watched her grandmother's frail shoulders shake with silent sobs. She had put her family through such an ordeal, all in the name of revenge. She had hated Locke. And yet, when she thought about it, she could not bring herself to hate him now. He had saved her, prevented Garrett from killing her, and died doing so. At death's door, even though he was not compelled to do so, he had confessed everything in order to clear his conscience and her father's name. He had found a way to redeem himself. Unlike Garrett, who had not been able to pardon those who had caused him harm, Amanda forgave Locke for what he had done. She and the traitor were *not* alike. Her quest was over; they could go home. Despite her best attempts to suppress it, she surrendered at last to her grief. The tears she had held in check spilled over her lashes and down her own cheeks.

"Dearest—it is all right." Mrs. Tremayne, her eyes red and swollen, crossed to the bed and embraced Amanda. "Everything is all right."

"I want to go home," whispered Amanda through her tears. She laid her head on her grandmother's shoulder.

"We shall, dearest, we shall. As soon as you are well."

For Amanda, that day would not come soon enough.

* * *

"Amanda?"

The hesitant voice cut through Amanda's drowsy trance. She roused herself with a start; the book in her lap fell to the floor.

With his good hand, Harry Morgan retrieved the fallen volume and handed it to her with a sheepish smile.

"Harry!" Amanda cried, delighted. She set the book aside and tried to rise from her chair.

"No, no—do not get up," Harry admonished. "Your grandmother said she would have my head if you overtaxed yourself. She is furious enough with me as it is."

Amanda smiled, ignoring the sting from her bruises, and squeezed her friend's hand. "Nonsense. I am feeling much better this morning. I am glad you've come. Please, sit down."

Harry flushed with pleasure and lowered himself into the Hepplewhite chair across from her. The midmorning sun glinted off his auburn hair. His uniform was rumpled and much the worse for wear; consequences, no doubt, of having camped on her doorstep for two days. Dear Harry. Aside from the sling on his left arm, he appeared to have suffered no ill effects from Sunday's ordeal. No, that was not entirely true, Amanda realized. Shadows lingered in his hazel eyes, and he seemed older, more world-weary.

"You look well," he said.

Warmth crept over Amanda's cheeks. "What rubbish," she countered. "I look a fright, and I sound even worse." She fiddled with the fringe of her lap robe. "But I would not be alive at all if not for you. What you did was very brave."

A muscle flexed in the young man's jaw. "None of this would have happened if not for me," he said with an abundance of self-loathing. "I was an idiot, a drunken idiot, to believe Locke's Banbury tales and all those false promises. You were right about him all along, and I wouldn't believe you. I nearly got you killed. God in heaven, Amanda—can you forgive me?"

Amanda looked away from the urgency in Harry's eyes. "I should be angry with you. Part of me still is. We both could have died. We would have, were it not for . . ." She shook herself away from that thought and drew herself up. "But you saved my life."

"Does that mean you forgive me?"

Amanda fought back her smile; Harry was nothing if not persistent. "Yes. I forgive you."

Relief flooded the young man's face, and he took her hand again and kissed it. "Dearest Amanda! I was beside myself . . . I don't know what I would do without you."

Amanda's smile froze in place. She would have pulled her fingers away, but he held fast. "Harry, there is no need—"

"Please, Amanda, hear me out." He fixed her with his intense gaze. "These past few days have been agony, sheer torture. It made he realize what I want from my life."

A lump rose in Amanda's throat. She drew breath to speak, to stop what was coming, but Harry plowed onward.

"It made me realize how much you mean to me, Amanda. I never want to lose you again. I want to be there to protect you."

Amanda made a moue. "I do not need protecting, Harry."

The young man did not seem to hear her. "I love you, Amanda. One word from you will make me the happiest man in the world. Marry me. Be my wife."

She slid her gaze away from his earnest face. "Harry, I—"

"My parents adore you, and I know they will approve of the match."

The room seemed to lurch sideways; Amanda gripped the arm of the chair with her free hand. "Harry, are you certain this is what you want?"

His eyes softened. "I have overset you. I know this is sudden, but I could not wait a moment longer. You don't have to give me an answer now, Amanda. Just promise me you'll consider my offer."

Amanda needed several moments to find her voice. "I . . . I will consider it."

Harry beamed at her and pressed another fervent kiss to her hand. "May I call upon you tomorrow?"

"Of course," she replied faintly.

Harry kissed her hand yet again and departed with a spring in his step.

Amanda sat back in her chair. Once she had contemplated spinsterhood; now she was faced with a monumental decision. A grimace distorted her mouth. Harry would never have offered for her while the stigma of treason blackened her family's name. Now that everything had worked out, he could not wait to propose. She could understand Harry's concern for his career, but how much affection did he truly feel for her?

That hardly mattered now. She did not love Harry, and the man who held her heart was gone from her life. Marriage to Harry would please her grandmother, who wanted nothing more than to see Amanda's future secured. But her grandmother also wanted her to be happy. So should she marry a man she did not love, or pine away for the man she loved but could never have? Either way led to unhappiness. The question was, how much unhappiness could she live with?

Everly thrust his head out the carriage window. "Faster, damn you, faster!"

Traffic around the Admiralty was congested this morning, and although he knew his coachman was doing the best he could, Everly could not restrain his impatience. He stared at the crumpled note in his hand, at the few lines of St. Vincent's cramped and spiky lettering. She was awake. Amanda was awake, and asking after him.

Damnation—he should have been there. Well, he *would* have been, had he not made a nuisance of himself in the admiral's household. He had lost his temper and started an argument with Lieutenant Morgan, and the two of them had kicked up one hell of a row in the hallway before St. Vincent himself separated them. His patron had been furious with Everly's lack of control; as senior officer, he should know the value of prudence and keep his temper in check. St. Vincent had ordered Everly to find another outlet for his nervous energy—namely, his new assignment—and promised to send word when Amanda regained consciousness.

Still, he should have been there. Everly sat back against the leather squabs, deep in thought. Now that she was awake, what was he going to say to her? For a man with a reputation for glib charm and witty speech, Everly found himself at a loss. Should he go in with his heart on his sleeve? Out of the question—he'd tried that with Felicia, and look where it had gotten him. The captain made a face, then fingered his bruised jaw. He hoped his phiz didn't frighten Amanda out of her wits; all the cuts and bruises he had garnered during his fight with Garrett, not to mention his singed hair and whiskers, made him a gruesome sight.

A declaration might frighten her just as much, so he would have to be cautious. If her reaction to his kiss was any indication, he must leave himself room to retreat. Bah. He tugged his bicorne further down on his scowling brow. Such indecision was anathema. He knew what he must do, even if it meant risking hurt and rejection.

He arrived at St. Vincent's town house to see Lieutenant Harry Morgan strolling down the steps. The youth had his bicorne cocked back to a jaunty angle, and he whistled a merry tune into the cool breeze. A muscle twitched in Everly's temple.

"Lieutenant," he said stiffly.

The younger man favored Everly with a slight, superior smile before he touched the brim of his hat in salute. "Captain," he replied as he sauntered past.

Everly watched him depart, suspicious. Why was that insolent pup so pleased with himself? Well, no time to wonder about that now. Amanda was waiting.

He limped up the great mahogany staircase as fast as he was able, pain singing through both his leg and his bandaged hands. Equal parts of dread and excitement mixed in his blood as he neared Amanda's room.

"Good morning, ma'am," he said to Mrs. Tremayne when she opened the door. "How is Aman—Miss Tremayne?"

"She is as well as can be expected." The elderly woman's lips thinned in a disapproving line. "Fortunately, she will suffer no lasting effects."

This statement eased the knot of tension at the base of Everly's neck. "May I have a word with her?"

Mrs. Tremayne stepped out into the hallway and closed the door behind her. She folded her hands together and looked at him with sharp, expectant eyes. "Amanda knows nothing of our previous conversation, Captain, as you requested, but I must again voice my reservations. Both you and Harry Morgan put my granddaughter in a situation that nearly took her life."

Everly's jaw tightened. "I agree that I should never have gotten her involved, Mrs. Tremayne. I would not have, but she worked her way around me. Short of tying her hand and foot to a chair, there was little I could do to stop her, and even now I think I would have been justified in such tactics."

"Amanda is very headstrong, I fear," Mrs. Tremayne stated with a frown. "Too much so for her own good."

The captain shifted more of his weight to his cane; standing in one position for so long made his leg throb. "Yes, she is rather willful, but I find that to be one of her more endearing qualities."

"And what of your career? Amanda will not be happy with a husband who is away at sea for most of their marriage."

Everly arched an eyebrow. "I received confirmation of my new assignment this morning, Mrs. Tremayne. I will be able to provide a good home for Amanda."

"Hmmm. I see. Well, Captain, I have but one more question, and I wish a straightforward answer. Do you love my granddaughter?"

His face softened into a smile. "I do."

Mrs. Tremayne peered intently at him, as if to judge the truth of his statement, then nodded. "Very well, Captain. I shall announce you to my granddaughter. But a word of warning—she may not wish to see you."

She disappeared back into the bedchamber. Everly stared at the panels of the door, his heart starting a downward slide. What did she mean? Why would Amanda not wish to see him? She had asked after him, according to St. Vincent's message. Doubtless she was upset about what had happened in the warehouse; he could not fault her for that. He would have to put her at ease, tell her that everything had turned up trumps.

He had considered a hundred strategies when Mrs. Tremayne at last admitted him to Amanda's room. The older woman cast a significant glance at Everly before she departed. The door closed, and Everly was alone with Amanda.

She sat on a chair by the window, framed by a ray of morning sunlight. Everly was startled by her appearance. The drab gown she wore accentuated her pallor and made the purpling bruises stand out all the more on her fair skin. She remained with her face turned toward the window, one hand toying with the curls at the end of her long, thick braid.

She did not look at him. "Captain," she began, her voice hoarse and rough. "How kind of you to take time from your duties to see me."

This aloof greeting stopped Everly dead in the water. "Hello, Amanda. How do you feel?"

"Does it matter?" she asked in hollow voice.

He frowned. "Of course it matters! I was worried about you."

"The doctor tells me I will recover."

"I am relieved to hear it." Egad, he felt like an unlicked cub, tongue-tied and nervous in the company of the fairer sex. So much for his vaunted charm. He tried again. "I apologize that I was not here when you regained consciousness. I came as soon as I got word."

Was that the glimmer of tears he saw in her eyes, or was it a trick of the light? "Your arrival is fortuitous, Captain. You can be the first to hear the news."

"News? What news is this?" Everly drew nearer and perched on the chair across from her. This was not going at all as he had planned. He tried to catch her eye, but she sat like a statue, her gaze fixed on the street below.

"Harry has asked me to marry him."

Everly could not have been more shocked had a be-laying pin struck him between the eyes. "What? Are you joking, Amanda?"

"My father's name has been exonerated, and I am free to marry whom I will. Harry comes from an excellent family, and we have known each other for years."

So *that* was the reason behind the lieutenant's self-satisfied smile. Everly ground his teeth together. That insolent puppy had stolen a march on him! After what had happened, after the way Morgan had betrayed her, Everly could not believe that Amanda would ever consider such an offer.

"This is ridiculous. You cannot possibly marry that—that . . ." Everly's voice trailed off under the influence of his fraying temper. The thought of her married to Harry Morgan was enough to curl his liver.

Amanda wrapped her arms around herself. "I must consider my future, even as you have," she said with a trace of bitterness.

His brows snapped together. "What do you mean?"

She blinked several times, and her eyes grew bright. "When do you leave for your new command, Captain? What ship did they give you? Now that your mission is over, I imagine that you are anxious to return to sea."

"Who told you that I was in line for a new command?"

She ducked her head. "Harry told me."

Morgan again, the interfering twit. Everly's anger siz-zled. A wave of heat colored his cheeks. Across from him, he saw Amanda bite her lip and turn toward the window. He forced himself to take a deep breath. Panic and anger weren't getting him anywhere with Amanda; if anything, they were driving the wedge further between them. He had to discover the real reason behind her sudden decision.

"Now *you* are vexed with *me*. Will you not tell me why, Amanda?" Everly leaned forward, intent on her answer.

A soft sob escaped her. "It is of no importance."

She was crying, although she tried to hide it. Did the

thought of him resuming his post make her so unhappy? Dare he hope . . . ?

"I am not going back to sea, Amanda," he said gently.

"What?" She clutched at her skirt "You—you're not . . ."

"I was wounded during the fight with Garrett," he explained. "The burns on my hands will heal, but the injury to my leg is permanent; I will never be able to walk without pain, and the limb will always be weak. My injuries, combined with the scarcity of command positions these days, render me unable to return to sea duty."

Amanda gasped and looked over her shoulder at him, her eyes rounded in shock, one hand over her mouth. She began to tremble. Fresh tears edged her lashes. "This . . . this is all my fault!"

Everly started to reach out a hand to brush the tears away, but remembered himself. He let his hand drop. "Nonsense. If anyone is to blame, it is the French, not you."

She took a great, shuddering breath and shook her head. "Don't you see, Jack? If I had not gone with Harry, this would never have happened. I am so sorry!"

Everly cast caution to the wind and seized her hands, heedless to the pain in his burned, bandaged fingers. "Stop blaming yourself. It is not your fault!"

"But I know how much you wanted a new ship." She sobbed. "I know how much you miss the sea. If I had not been so reckless, you would not have been hurt."

Her grief struck him with the force of a full broadside. "What's done is done, Amanda," he said soothingly. "I chose to go into the warehouse after you, remember?"

How lost she seemed. Her anxious gaze scanned his face. "What will you do now?"

"As it happens, I have been offered a position on Admiral Lord Kenworth's staff at the Admiralty. I may not be at sea, but I will be occupied with naval matters." His career as a seafaring captain may have been scuttled, but given the choice of a life at sea without Amanda, and a life on land with her, he would gladly make the same decision all over again.

"The Admiralty? Is that where you've been all this time?" she asked in a hurt tone.

He nodded. "I would have been here, but St. Vincent ordered me out of the house after I came to fisticuffs with Lieutenant Morgan."

"You fought with Harry?" Egad, she had turned paler still.

Everly had the good grace to be ashamed of himself. "Like two schoolboys," he admitted. "I chastised him for getting you into such a dangerous situation, and he took offense."

"So you're not . . . you're not leaving?" her voice quavered.

"No. I must remain landbound, at least as far as the Royal Navy is concerned." Everly attempted a reassuring smile. With his face such a bruised mess, he had no idea if he would be successful.

Amanda swiveled away from him once more and did not answer. She covered her face with her hands. Her shoulders shook.

Everly reached out and took gentle hold of her chin, lifting her head so she had to meet his gaze. "Would it matter to you if I were leaving?" he murmured.

She looked away, determined to evade him. "Perhaps."

He skimmed his unbandaged thumb over her lower lip. "And what about Mr. Morgan's offer—will you accept him? Once he matures a bit, he will have a promising career ahead of him."

Amanda twisted her hands together. "I cannot say."

Another trail of tears spilled down her cheek. He smoothed them away.

"You do not love him, do you?" he asked.

She shook her head. "No."

"Good. I would hate to have to call him out," Everly replied. He hoped he sounded as grim as he felt.

She stared up at him, shocked. "Jack—you wouldn't, would you?"

"Not unless you give me a reason not to. I won't let you marry him, Amanda. He will not make you happy."

"Why are you saying this?" She tried to wipe the tears from her cheeks.

"Why do women never have a handkerchief when they need one?" Everly's harsh demeanor melted; he smiled and pulled his kerchief from his breast pocket. As Amanda dried her eyes, he studied her delicate profile. How he'd come to adore that uptilted nose, those sweet lips, those irresistible dimples, and the quixotic combination of innocence and hardheaded resolve that was Amanda Tremayne.

"I suppose I should explain all this bluff and bluster." Everly tried to run a bandaged hand through his hair, failed, and flushed with embarrassment. There was no more time for roundaboutation. If he was going to do this, he had to do it now, for he'd be damned if he lost her to the likes of Harry Morgan. "I love you, Amanda. I think I've loved you since you landed on me that night in Locke's garden. I did not want to admit it at first. You see, I was engaged to be married once before. When I returned home from Lissa, my fiancée took one look at my limp, then ran from me and broke off our engagement."

Amanda uttered a little gasp of outrage and crumpled the kerchief. "That jilt!"

Everly smiled. That was his Amanda.

"I didn't want to give another woman the chance to break my heart," he continued, "but then I met you, you stubborn minx. I did not realize how much you meant to me until I nearly lost you—twice—at the warehouse." Everly took a deep breath. "Amanda, do you think you could ever be happy with a crippled old sea dog?"

A wan smile shimmered through her tears. "I have never thought of you so meanly."

Everly frowned. "But my leg—"

Amanda's fingertips brushed the thin scar on his cheek. "It doesn't matter to me. It never has. When I first met you, all I could notice were your incredibly blue eyes." She blushed and would have snatched her hand away, but Everly caught it, pressed it to his lips.

"My dearest Amanda," he murmured. "Marry me. I

want you to be my wife, to be the mother of my children."

Amanda's flush deepened. "Persuade me," she breathed.

Everly's pulse raced. He pulled her to her feet and into his arms, then leaned down until his lips were inches from hers. "I warn you, minx—I can be very, very persuasive, indeed."

Her mouth was as sweet and yielding as he remembered, her skin soft and silky and scented with jasmine. Desire raged through him, and his self-control began to slip. His tongue parted her lips, explored her inner sweetness, holding nothing back. He reveled in the taste of her mouth, the scent of her skin, the feel of her body against his. Amanda gave a little moan. Everly's leg twinged anew, and the pain brought him to his senses; he pulled back, breathing hard, and stared down at Amanda with narrowed eyes.

"Now will you marry me, madam?"

Amanda lifted a hand to her swollen lips and stared at him.

He added, rather sheepishly, "I would go down on one knee and do this properly, but I fear I would not be able to get up again."

More tears threatened her composure. "I almost lost you in the fire, Jack. And when I thought you were going back to sea, it was as though I were losing you a second time."

Everly put a finger to her lips. "Shhh, sweetheart. Marry me, and you will never lose me. Ever."

As she considered this, her expression sobered. "I have two conditions."

Everly straightened, a hard knot gathering beneath his breastbone. "Name them."

"No more intrigue, Jack. No more spies, no more deception. Just a simple life, a home by the sea. And a family. That is all I want."

The captain brushed an errant curl from her forehead. "My career as a spy is over, Amanda, I can assure you that. That whole affair made me feel as out of place as a flounder in top boots." He nuzzled her cheek and placed a small kiss at one corner of her mouth, then the tip of her nose, then the other corner. "All I desire is you. Now—your other condition?"

Her breath caught in her throat. "That you let me pick my own gowns from now on."

Everly kissed the budding dimple in her cheek, and chuckled. "Agreed."

Amanda brushed her lips across his stubbled chin. "I love you, Jack."

His heart soared. "Is that a yes, love?"

"Yes. Yes, I will marry you, Captain Sir Jonathan Everly."

Everly's grin turned wicked. "Good. Now kiss me again."

Amanda laughed, a rough, throaty sound. "Is that an order?"

His lips hovered over hers. "Should I make it one?"

She leaned up into his kiss. "Aye-aye, Captain."

EXPLORE THE WORLD OF
SIGNET REGENCY ROMANCE

Signet Regency Romances

THE MAGNIFICIENT MARQUESS
by Gail Eastwood

Recently returned from India, the new Marquess of Milbourne was the darling of the ton, with half the eligible ladies of the city in vigorous pursuit of his undying devotion. But the handsome young man harbored a dark secret that had made him vow never to love again...

❏ 0-451-19532-9/$4.99

THE BEST INTENTIONS
by Candice Hern

When Miles Prescott's formidable sister, Winifred, descends upon Epping Manor with two eligible women in tow, the widowed earl knows his single days are numbered; but when he ends up being attracted to the sister of the woman everyone expects him to marry, things become a bit more complicated...

❏ 0-451-19573-6/$4.99

LORD DRAGONER'S WIFE
by Lynn Kerstan

When the scandalous Lord Dragoner returns to England, Delilah's hopes of a reconciliation are shattered. The husband who coldly abandoned her has come to seek a divorce. But she is determined to win his heart, even if it means joining him in the dangerous world where no one can be trusted—not even his wife.

❏ 0-451-19861-1/$4.99

To order call: 1-800-788-6262

PENGUIN PUTNAM INC.
Online

Your Internet gateway to a virtual environment with
hundreds of entertaining and enlightening books
from Penguin Putnam Inc.

*While you're there, get the latest buzz on
the best authors and books around—*

Tom Clancy, Patricia Cornwell, W.E.B. Griffin,
Nora Roberts, William Gibson, Robin Cook,
Brian Jacques, Catherine Coulter, Stephen King,
Jacquelyn Mitchard, and many more!

**Penguin Putnam Online is located at
http://www.penguinputnam.com**

PENGUIN PUTNAM NEWS

Every month you'll get an inside look at our upcom-
ing books and new features on our site. This is an
ongoing effort to provide you with the most
up-to-date information about
our books and authors.

**Subscribe to Penguin Putnam News at
http://www.penguinputnam.com/ClubPPI**